Blaize of Glory

Louise Crawford

Hard Shell Word Factory

© 2000, Louise Crawford
Paperback ISBN: 0-7599-0260-7
Published March 2001

Ebook ISBN: 1-58200-607-5
Ebook Published September 2000

Hard Shell Word Factory
PO Box 161
Amherst Jct. WI 54407
books@hardshell.com
http://www.hardshell.com
Cover art © 2000, Mary Z. Wolf

Chapter 1

HIRAM JOHNSON High School in mid-town Sacramento hadn't changed, though I wished it had, wished the school, the memories, the people were all part of a dream. The grounds looked green and well cared for, but the place seemed smaller to me now that I was thirty-one and not an impressionable sixteen-year-old girl.

As I walked down the corridor toward the auditorium, I read signs advertising the musical—opening this weekend—saw Sunny Wright's name. How the hell had I let her talk me into meeting her during the rehearsal? Our friendship had ended on less than cordial terms, but after fifteen years something made her call and beg for help. I wanted to know what.

Yanking open the side door near the orchestra pit, I felt a sense of *déjà vu*, like a lingering whiff of old perfume. I saw Sunny before she saw me. In her bright yellow, long-sleeved leotard and tights, a stick-thin canary surrounded by sparrows, she looked the same as in high school. On stage, she and her dance partner were singing a duet, a chorus line behind them.

An uncomfortable lump formed in my throat, memories coming up that I couldn't swallow back. Abruptly, I realized the music had stopped.

Sunny jumped from the stage and walked toward me, the same slim-hipped, long-legged walk she'd had as a teenager. She took a deep breath, her yellow leotard drenched in sweat, beads of perspiration on her brow. Her hair was shorter now, ear-length, but still black, thick and curly.

"Andy, thanks for coming." She opened her arms, offering a hug, but when I didn't move, hugged herself instead.

I managed a polite smile. "Hello, Sunny. How are you?"

"The same." Her large, dark eyes searched my face.

Still a klepto-nympho? I wanted to ask, but held my tongue. Who was I to judge? I had my own demons.

"Sunny, we're not finished," her dance partner called.

She glared. "Give me ten fucking minutes, Paul! Okay?" Not the sugar-coated Sunny I remembered.

Paul held up his hands in defeat. "Okay!" I noticed his love handles. No spring chicken, but not bad either. Whoever Paul was, Sunny had him wrapped around her little finger.

I wanted out of the auditorium and away from the thick fog of memories. "Like I told you on the phone, I don't do PI work anymore." My tone was impatient.

"Just hear me out. Please. I can pay. But I can't talk here. Come backstage. I'll get my jeans and we'll go for coffee."

The note of desperation in her voice had me grumbling, "All right." I picked up my twenty-pound purse and followed her backstage. The dressing room odor of stale sweat, deodorant, and make-up took me back in time. The lights buzzed softly like a swarm of bees, the hot room filled with bodies in various stages of dress. I wiped sweat from my forehead.

"Excuse me," I said as a fortyish woman jabbed my arm, trying to get into a costume two sizes too small. Good luck.

Sunny pulled on a pair of tight Calvin Klein jeans. Next to her, a teenager took off a pair of long, beaded earrings, set them down, and turned away. Sunny slipped them into her purse with the deftness I remembered so well.

I did an about-face and pushed my way toward the door. Nothing had changed, except they weren't my earrings and I wasn't sixteen anymore.

Sunny caught me out front. "Andy?"

I turned. "It's Blaize," I said. "I don't go by Andy anymore. You want me to hear you out, you call me Blaize, and you give that girl her earrings back."

"Earrings?"

"Save that innocent shit for the guys, Sunny."

She held up her hands. "Okay, okay, An—I'll give them back." She eyed me like we were beauty contestants and I was a point ahead. Did she notice the lines around my eyes, the small worry marks at the bridge of my nose, or did she still see the face I'd worn in high school?

She tucked a lock of hair behind her ear. My hair was the color of molasses taffy, permed, shoulder-length, and to me looked like I'd stuck a finger in a light socket. Hers framed a heart-shaped face and huge dark eyes that went from girlish to vamp in the bat of a man's eye.

For the first time I wondered what childhood woes had made her who she was. We'd never shared much about our personal lives, just stayed together out of need, loneliness and conspiracy. As I looked at her I felt lousy all over again—too tall, too fat, too naive. It took a second to shake off the feelings and grow back into an adult. "Is that why you called? Do you want counseling?"

She looked offended. "No." Silently, she pulled a rumpled envelope out of her purse and pressed it into my hand. I extracted three small notes, read the first, and fumbled the other two, my hand shook so bad. We both dove for them and bumped heads.

"Sorry," I muttered as the words and music of "Mac the Knife" ran through my head. "I kinda hoped he'd fallen off the face of the earth." I wondered if I looked as dough-faced as she did.

Sunny dug in her purse, retrieving a pack of cigarettes. "Shocked the hell out of me." I watched her light up, feeling like a co-conspirator again, hungry for a smoke. She took a drag and smiled, her eyes pleading for help.

I scanned the neatly typed notes before handing them back.

I saw your picture in the paper. I've never forgotten. Mac

See you after the performance. Mac

You and your friend were the best. I've missed you. Mac

The word "friend" made me feel like I'd swallowed a basketball. We'd both been raped by a man we'd known as Mac, and I didn't want to believe he was still around.

"The notes came after my picture appeared in the *Sacramento Bee* with an article about the show."

"That's a closed chapter, Sunny. Don't open it."

She took a deep drag off her cigarette, exhaled slowly. "I didn't. *He* did. I got the last note this morning."

My skin crawled. Unwanted images crowded behind my eyes. "Go to the police," I said softly. "Find someone else to look into it. I've hung out a Ph.D. shingle—I don't do PI work."

A flicker of desperation crossed her face. I shuddered, remembering the glint of Mac's switchblade. I wished I hadn't eaten lunch. " I dug in my purse, found paper and pen and scrawled my ex-boyfriend's name and number on it. "Ross is a PI. He can help you, or recommend someone."

She tossed her cigarette to the ground and clutched the paper.

I backed a step to the manicured lawn, turned and walked away, telling myself not to get involved, that it had nothing to do with me, that it was probably some sick practical joke. The weight of her gaze burned my back. It was April Fool's Day and I felt like one as I hurried to my car. The air smelled crisp and cool, and the sun peeked through the clouds, but it didn't cheer me.

Sunny, yesterday my life was filled with pain... The song ran like a bad echo through my head as I jammed the key into the ignition and revved the engine. She didn't come after me and I didn't regret my decision. Until later.

Right now I wanted to punch something. Not a good start to an evening of counseling that I dreaded. I wanted a smoke, wanted to bury myself in a book, wanted to devour a carton of ice cream— all the above. Most of all, I wanted to forget.

I SAT IN my office, door closed, the *Alcoholics Anonymous Big Book* on my lap—my brain morosely fixated on Mac the Knife and how everything was slamming me at once, when a key turned in the suite's outer door and voices murmured. So much for serenity. I set the book on the small conference table.

My friend Maria, a successful lawyer, and the person I paid rent to, stepped into my office. If she noticed the rearranged furniture—I d tried to burn a little nervous energy—she didn't show it. "Blaize McCue ... this is my niece, Connie Donovan."

I found a genuine smile inside myself for the sixteen-year-old lost waif whose long, dark hair covered nearly half her face. Even though I normally didn't handle rape cases—they hit too close to home—Maria had been persuasive, so here I was. "Nice to meet you, Connie."

She swished her glossy veil of hair revealing a straight nose and a flash of white teeth. "Hello," she said in a voice I strained to catch.

Maria left.

I gestured at the chair across from mine, and realized that

Maria had already explained who I was and what I did, because from beyond the hair, Connie watched me with the eyes of a trapped animal. Had I look that frightened when I was her age?

Shifting in my chair, I glanced around the room, trying to see with a fresh view what she saw. Shelves full of psych books. A small watercolor of a castle rising out of the clouds hung beside the window with my license and college degrees beside it. On a small, two-tiered table in the corner was my latest interest, sand trays, and a scattered array of small figures. What kind of drama would Connie create if I placed the table in front of her, handed her a tray? Hell, with my lack of interpretational training would I even know what it meant?

I pulled my gaze from the miniature people, and focused on Connie again. The silence stretched and I explained I had to report any sexual abuse to the authorities, then shut up.

She hunched forward, her arms crossing tighter, as if to keep her words inside. I hunched forward and crossed my arms, too.

More silence. "Do you like your aunt?" I asked as an ice-breaker.

"Yes." It came out strained. She cleared her throat.

"What about school?"

Her fingers squeezed her sides. "It's okay."

"Sometimes it helps to talk about things. Maria's worried about you."

"I know."

I offered my A-1 empathetic smile while grappling for detachment. "I'd like to help you."

In a ragged whisper I struggled to hear, she said, "Did Maria tell you what—what happened?"

"She gave me a general idea," I said, thinking the word, rape, and hating it.

Silence. She rocked on her chair like a child in need of comfort.

"You went out on a date, didn't you?" I asked.

A nod.

"What happened?"

"This guy—Patrick—he's on the football team—he asked me to a party." For a moment I glimpsed a flicker of rueful excitement—what she must have felt at being asked out by a jock.

I made an encouraging noise, compassion wringing my heart down to the soles of my shoes.

"He was really nice. I mean, I expected him to be pushy." Her face reddened.

A long silence. Her knuckles whitened around the edge of the chair. "He brought me some crackers and dip, and a drink. Maybe thirty minutes later, I felt strange. Dizzy." Her voice cracked.

The room was quiet, yet I had to strain to catch her words.

"He helped me upstairs—to, to lay down." Connie's hair slid across her face. She made no effort to brush it back, her voice now coming from behind the silken mask like a strangled cry, touching the hurt child in my soul. "His face blurred and I heard his voice— like from far off—an echo—asking if I was okay." She brushed her hair back in an angry gesture, her dark eyes avoiding mine. "I think I said yes. Then I blacked out."

Her symptoms suggested Rophynol, a drug responsible for many date-rapes where the victim had short-term amnesia. The cases were almost impossible to prosecute.

"Later, when I tried to stand ... I knew..."

THAT NIGHT, the nightmare came again. This time it was different. This time Connie was there. I stood beside her at the party, a ghost no one could see or hear. When her date slipped the drug into her soda and "helped" her upstairs to lie down, I wanted to tear his fucking head off. I tried to scream, to hurl the telephone at him, but my attempts were futile. I wasn't really there.

Helpless, I watched: Connie on the bed, her dress pushed up to her waist, her tan legs spread, the young man pumping into her unconscious body with gusto.

I retched and turned away, only to find myself staring into a pair of pale blue eyes. I tried to say something, to protest. How could he see me when no one else could? He smiled his fatherly smile. "You can trust me," Mac whispered. I shuddered, my gaze dropping to the knife. He tapped it against his thigh, then lifted my shirt.

Oh, God no! Sunny, where was Sunny? I had to find her and get out. Get away. But Mac's hand gripped my arm, and the knife flashed...

I bolted upright in bed, a scream in my throat, my heart racing. Grabbing my baseball bat, I switched on the light and staggered into the bathroom. Sweat dripped from my forehead. Mac the Knife. Still around? God, he'd be forty-five, fifty, maybe older. He couldn't still be—raping stupid girls like me and Sunny?

Maybe, maybe not, whispered my inner voice.

"Forget it," I told myself, pissed at Sunny for dredging up the past, angry with myself for taking Connie on, angry at whatever karma had decided to dump both at my feet at the same time. I could spell NO, but couldn't easily say it.

I glanced at the radio clock—4:30—and decided against going back to bed. Taking my baseball bat, I propped it in the bathroom corner, then stepped into the shower, determined to wash away the dream and my sixteen-year-old feelings of helplessness.

The phone was ringing when I turned off the water. I let the answering machine pick it up, but I could hear Maria's voice, upset and shaken, the words indistinct. I grabbed a towel and ran to the kitchen. She hung up before I could answer.

I played the message. "Connie's gone, Blaize!" A sob. "I don't know where, I don't know what to do! Help me!"

Hurriedly, I called her home number, then work. What did Connie mean to her? I'd heard the voice of a worried mother before. Amplified, it sounded just like Maria. I stared at the phone as the line rang and rang.

Finally, I hung up, threw on some clothes, and ran a brush through my wet hair. Back to the kitchen, I listened to the message again. Maybe I'd missed something. I hadn't.

For a quiet Sunday morning, this one sucked.

Chapter 2

AN HOUR later, I sat on what I called my front porch, a second-story covered deck of a renovated downtown Victorian. The owner, a fat old geezer named Joe, lived downstairs. Every time he shuffled down to the mailbox I considered the advantages of dying young.

Rain plunked a melancholy tune against the metal overhang as I inhaled menthol—I'd managed to quit smoking for all of two days. As cars zoomed by, I kept an ear cocked for the phone. A train whistle wailed in the distance. Maria's gold Mercedes pulled to the curb. I met her at the front door.

She looked like the world rested on her shoulders alone. "Thank God you're home."

I parked her at my kitchen table, handed her a mug of coffee and sat down next to her. Dressed in a pair of old jeans and flannel shirt, she looked like she'd been up all night. Her rain-dampened hair was as straight and dark as Connie's.

I touched her shoulder, then let my hand fall back to my lap. "Have you called the police?"

She set her coffee on the table. "It hasn't been twenty-four hours." Her tone said she didn't want the police involved.

I raised my eyebrows. "They can still put out an APB."

"Her parents don't want the police involved."

"Her parents or you?" When she didn't answer, I asked, "Has she run away before?"

"Yes." She dropped her gaze, turned her coffee cup like a compass. "After she was—She ran away to her friend's. The parents called the next day and brought her home."

"Did she leave a note the first time?"

"No note either time, no anything. I talked to her friend this morning. Connie's not there."

I remembered Connie's lighter steps as she'd left my office. This didn't fit. "Any idea why?"

A flicker of uneasiness flashed in Maria's eyes. "No."

I leaned forward, annoyed. "I'll need the truth if you want me to help."

She hesitated, then sighed. "Connie's my daughter, but my sister and brother-in-law raised her as their own." Her voice dropped. "Everything was fine—until that boy—"

"Why didn't you tell me?" After everything we'd shared I felt a little pissed. When she remained silent, I stared at the photograph of my mother and brother tacked on the wall and at the one painting I'd produced in college, a wild kaleidoscope that reflected a darkness in my soul I'd tried to blot out with everything from alcohol to food. It reminded me of how far I'd come, and made me thankful—most of the time—for the present.

Maria tapped her fingers against the butcher-block table and fidgeted. Her voice was soft and laced with pain. "I was sixteen when I had Connie. I didn't have a job. I lived at home. When my sister offered to adopt her I was relieved. Teresa, my sister, is eight years older than me. She and Frank couldn't have kids. It seemed like the ideal solution."

"Where's the father?"

Maria shook her head.

"Could Connie have gone to him?"

"No—she doesn't know—" Tears brimmed in her eyes.

I grabbed a box of tissues and passed them over. Just call me Mom. We'd switched roles and it felt strange. She blew her nose. I waited.

Finally she continued in a small voice I'd never heard from her, "When I was fifteen I thought I knew everything, you know?"

I nodded. I wouldn't wish fifteen on anyone.

"I thought there were certain people I could trust. My parents...family...friends..."

My stomach tightened. She said "friends" like she'd just taken a bite of lemon.

"My father was a college professor and it wasn't unusual for students to stop by. This one boy came over often. I liked him a lot.

"Every time he came by and my father wasn't around he gave me attention. I thought he loved me." She shook her head. "Dumb, huh?" A sigh. "I was terrified when I discovered I was pregnant."

She paused, avoiding my eyes. "I was a fool."

I reached for my coffee. No matter how many times I heard this kind of story I wanted to break a truckload of dishes, shoot a few targets full of holes. The taste in my mouth was worse than broken aspirin on my tongue.

"When I told him I was pregnant, he told me he wasn't ready for marriage, a child..." Maria shook her head as though amazed at her own stupidity. "I had to tell my parents. I thought that would be the worst part—then everything would be all right." Her voice dropped, her mouth a ravaged line of pain. "My father called me a whore. Asked me how many boys I'd slept with. He wouldn't believe such a wonderful student would do such a thing. My mother believed me, but wouldn't stand up for me." Her lips curved. "Of course, Connie's father never came around again."

Maria's dark eyes glimmered. I could taste her anguish and it was bitter.

"I told my sister, Teresa. She and my mother worked out a plan. Teresa and her husband, Frank, adopted my baby. I finished high school and worked my way through college and law school." She smiled, bitterness showing in the tired lines of her face. "I was determined to be a lawyer, make a lot of money, prove myself worthy."

I waited for the rest.

"I thought I would hate Connie, but I didn't. When she was a baby, I cared for her on weekends. I loved every minute I spent with her. I thought about taking her back. But Connie's happy where she is. My sister and brother-in-law love her, too. I couldn't take her away."

"So you're her 'aunt'?"

Warmth flooded her eyes. "Yes. We have a wonderful relationship. Maybe better than mother and daughter. She feels free to tell me things, and I keep her confidence."

"Do your sister and brother-in-law know Connie was raped?"

Maria's mouth tightened into a thin line. "Yes. They talked about prosecuting the boy."

I reached over and touched Maria's shoulder. Thought of my own nightmare, my baseball bat, my gun. Would I have those things if I'd sailed through adolescence unscathed? "What happened?" I prompted after a lengthy silence.

She shook her head, a gesture of defeat. "It was Connie's word against his. She'd thrown away her clothes..."

"Did you file a police report?"

"Yes. In case the boy does it again, there's a report." *For what it's worth*, her tone implied. Her hands clenched the mug, and I wondered how much tension it could stand.

"After she ran away the first time we agreed to find Connie a counselor and transfer her to a private school. She's been at St. Mary's for three weeks now and she seems to be doing okay."

"Why'd you bring her to me?"

"She wouldn't talk to her therapist. She went twice and then said everything was fine. When I tried to talk to her about it, get into her feelings, she grew defensive. How could I possibly know what she was going through? I was her perfect aunt..." Maria picked up the tissue and twisted it.

I disliked what I read in her eyes. Sunny's plea for help echoed in my mind along with a blurred vision of Mac's face. "You couldn't tell Connie your secret—so you told her mine? Is that why she agreed to see me?"

Maria nodded.

"Thanks for telling the truth," I squeezed out.

"I'm sorry," Maria said, meeting my gaze. It was more than Sunny had ever said.

I leaned forward. "Could Connie have run to her father?" Slimebag was more like it. He'd seduced a fifteen year-old and gotten away unscathed.

Maria shook her head. "Connie doesn't know about him."

"You'd be amazed at what kids' antennas pick up." I hated this conversation and the pain in Maria's eyes. But something precipitated Connie's running away, and I didn't think it was my counseling; she'd seemed relieved when she'd left. "Did Connie tell you she agreed to see me next Saturday?"

Maria's eyes widened in surprise. "No. I could see she was feeling better. She said she liked you. Said you made her feel good." Hurt showed in Maria's eyes.

I took her hand. "She needs more than family right now."

Maria brushed her hair back from her face, the gesture

reminding me of Connie. Her gaze drifted around the room, then returned to me. "I just hope she's okay. I worry where she spent the night. If she's alone. If she's not alone."

I held Maria's gaze. "Who is Connie's father?" And where was this conversation leading? It was more than a need to talk.

She pulled her hand away and shifted on the chair. "He's married now, two children—the model of perfection—Gordon Whitman."

I gaped at the state legislator's name. "What in the hell do you do when you run into him?" As a lobbyist, Maria spent a lot of time at the Capitol, buttering up lawmakers to earn her salary.

"Turn around and walk away, or look through him as if he isn't there." Her jaw looked ready to snap. "He doesn't remember me." The simple statement made her cry.

When she'd dried her eyes, I leaned forward and asked, "What do you want from me, Maria?"

Her face flushed. She leaned forward, her tone persuasive. "You know the ropes. And I can't involve the police. They didn't believe her before. They'll only make things worse."

I waited, silent. I'd earned my keep in college by doing private investigative work with my boyfriend. Seven years ago.

Her pitch rose, desperate, "If the cops pick her up, haul her downtown, Connie will never forgive me. You know how kids are at her age."

I slowly shook my head.

"I talked her into telling the cops about the rape, and it didn't do any good. She'll be humiliated all over again answering questions. I can't put her through that!"

"I'm a psychologist, not a PI. I just did that to get through school."

"You worked with Ross—"

My jaw clenched. My ex-flame. I had worked with him for five years. Also shot off my mouth to Maria a couple of times about liking it. Damn, damn, damn.

"Please, Blaize."

I couldn't turn away. I thought of the pain I'd heard in Connie's voice, seen in her light green eyes, eyes almost the color of mine. A therapist had kept me from killing myself fifteen years ago. Connie needed someone. So did Maria. "I'll see what I can find out."

Maria gave me a grateful smile, relief in her dark eyes.

"Just for forty-eight hours," I added. "Then you have to go to the police."

Why did I feel like I'd stuck my head in a noose?

I ARRANGED to meet Maria's sister and her husband at their home, a ticky-tacky three-bedroom, two bath, single-car-garage-style house in south Sacramento. More *déjà vu*. I'd spent my childhood in a neighborhood like this.

I walked up the cement path past the overgrown lawn, Maria's five-hundred dollar check burning a hole in my wallet. "For expenses." The money bugged me—made me feel too committed. I knocked loudly on the door.

Maria was small, compact and dark, but her sister was tall, too thin, with mousy brown hair that trailed to her shoulders. Despite the cool, rainy weather, she wore a faded cotton housedress and sandals. Her red-rimmed hazel eyes made her look closer to fifty than forty.

"Teresa Donovan?"

She nodded.

I offered my hand. "I'm Maria's friend, Blaize McCue."

She nodded again and gestured me inside. The narrow entry area felt like a shrine with pictures of Jesus and Mary on every wall. The odor of stale cigarettes lingered. I reminded myself I'd had enough smokes for the week.

We sat in the clean, comfortable living room, and I glanced around. "Is your husband here? I'd like to talk to you both."

Teresa hesitated. "He was called to work."

If she was going to lie, I was wasting my time. "Maybe he doesn't want to talk to me..."

She twisted the fabric of her housecoat in her hands. When she looked at me there were tears in her eyes and I felt like a heel. "Frank said to tell you whatever you need to know, but it just makes him crazy—what that boy did to Connie." Tears splashed down her cheeks. "She won't talk, just goes in her room and closes the door. Now she runs off..."

I murmured something I hoped sounded comforting and then after an appropriate pause, asked, "Can you give me a list of Connie's friends? Anyone you can think of—"

"We've called everyone," Teresa said. "No one's seen her since she changed schools."

"I'd still like to talk to her friends," I insisted. After a brief disappearance into the kitchen, she returned with a handwritten list. Names and phone numbers had been scrawled down one side of the paper.

I tucked it into my purse and moved to the fireplace. A recent photograph of Connie sat on the mantel between a baby picture and another of her as a gawky young girl. She'd grown into the high forehead, strong nose and full lips. I picked up the latest photograph. "Could I make a copy of this?"

Teresa came over, took the picture from the frame and gave it to me. "Did you need anything else?" she asked.

"Could I see her room?"

With a tired sigh that said she just wanted me gone, wanted to be alone with her fears, she led me to the back of the house and paused in a bedroom doorway.

Under Teresa's watchful eyes, I went through the white French provincial desk and matching dresser, then moved to the closet. Other than schoolbooks and homework assignments, I saw nothing personal. On the top closet shelf, next to a shoebox, was a book of restaurant matches. *Frank Fat's*. A souvenir from dinner with Maria? Maybe. But the legislators hung out there too. I replaced the matches, checked the clothes: a couple of Catholic school uniforms, sweater, jacket, a party dress, a couple of shirts. The uniforms hadn't changed much in twenty years.

After a few more questions that lead nowhere, I retreated to the front door and handed her my business card, the one that read: Blaize McCue, Ph.D., Substance Abuse, Emphasis on 12-Step Recovery. Beneath it, in my wallet, I still had an old private investigator card with Ross' phone number, my name. I'd actually used it a couple of times. Now I kept it as a reminder of what I didn't want in a man. I scribbled my home phone on the back of the Ph.D. card and handed it to her. "If Connie comes back tonight, please let me know right away. If she doesn't, you'll need to file a missing person's report in the morning. In the meantime, I'll check with Connie's school, and friends."

Teresa nodded.

"Oh, who was the therapist she saw before me? Maria mentioned a woman, but not her name."

From the kitchen she retrieved a bent card with a thumbtack hole in the upper center. I read the name with silent misgiving: *Darla Pike, Ph.D.* I'd encountered her in professional circles, had seen a couple of her former clients and decided she didn't rate a two on a scale of one to ten. I doubted Connie had said more than one word to Darla, if that.

"Any idea why Connie chose last night to run away?"

Teresa glanced at her feet. "No."

I thought she was holding back, but I'd done enough pressuring for one day. "If you think of anything, give me a call. Leave a message if I'm out."

"Thank you," she said as I stepped past Jesus' crucified form and out the door. How could they stand all that suffering on a daily basis?

I drove out to McClatchy High School. The McClatchy family owned the *Sacramento Bee*; the newspaper was as close as I ever got to them. As a teenager I'd thought the high school beautiful, like a southern plantation mansion. Now it looked a little worn around the edges. When I saw the empty parking lot, I could have kicked myself. Sunday! Way to go, Blaize.

Things didn't improve on the way home. A sudden downpour drenched me as I ran upstairs. I dropped my purse on the table, turned the heat on under the kettle, shrugged out of my wet sweater and pants, grabbed a towel and dried off while I checked the answering machine. One message.

"Andy, uh, Blaize. This is Sunny. I've tried to reach the PI, Ross Johnson, but he hasn't returned my calls." She sounded strange. Drugged? Scared? I couldn't tell. After a pause she continued, "I'd like to hire a bodyguard. I can pay. Can you recommend someone?"

Attila the Hun? I wrapped the towel around my hair. How had light-fingered Sunny come by so much lucre? She hadn't worn a wedding ring—which didn't mean diddley—but the Sunny I knew

would have worn a five-carat rock if she'd had one to show—
although maybe not while performing. The other question on my
mind made my hands tremble in a way they hadn't for years. I'd
thought I'd buried the past, thought I was safe. Why did Mac the
Knife send Sunny those letters? Had he been in hibernation? Hung
around Sacramento all these years waiting for Sunny to come back?
Had we just never crossed paths? Hard to believe. Hell, this entire
quagmire I'd suddenly stepped in was hard to believe.

I picked up the phone and dialed, feeling rigor mortis attack
my jaw. "No, no, no, no," I practiced.

Sunny answered on the first ring. "Paul, you bastard!" she
screamed into my ear. "If you don't stop seeing her..." Her words
were slurred and I realized she was either blitzed or well on her
way.

I felt a moment of guilty pleasure at the thought of Paul
screwing around, and waited until Sunny slowed down.

"Paul?" Silence. Her voice grew scared. "Who is this?"

"It's Blaize. Returning your call. Ross knows the right people.
If he hasn't called back it means he's tied up on a case, but he will
call. Just give him a couple of days—"

"I need someone now!" She wailed.

Oh hell. "If he doesn't call you by tonight, call me back and
I'll see what I can do—"

I hung up first. Damn the past and Sunny Wright for bringing
it all back.

I went into the bedroom, a bright array of purples, pinks, and
blues that intersected somewhere between stylish clutter and
slobsville. As I pushed away thoughts of Mac, I wondered about
Connie Donovan. Did she know about Whitman? If so, how and
when did she find out?

Maybe one of Connie's friends had the answer. I called the list
of names Teresa Donovan had given me. Whoever said PI work was
exciting had an overactive imagination. After the third answering
machine, I decided to try my luck Monday afternoon. I had two
clients scheduled for that morning. Maybe by then my fears about
Mac would be buried in my subconscious and I could concentrate
on Connie's case. Or maybe I'd talk myself out of playing PI and
hand the case over to someone who knew what the hell they were

doing.

I PHONED MARIA that evening and asked about Frank Fat's. Had she ever taken Connie there?

"Not that I recall," Maria replied thoughtfully. I knew her next question before she asked, "Why?"

"I found a matchbook in her room. Thought maybe you'd taken her there. You like the place."

"So does Whitman. I avoid it now."

Had Connie gone there out of curiosity, hoping to see her natural father? My mind spun scenarios. None fit the facts.

Maria's voice rose. "I bet that boy who raped Connie is the same way—has already forgotten what he did."

My hand tightened around the receiver. Maria was sitting on a powder keg of anger that made mine seem like a firecracker. "Sorry, Maria." I wanted to suggest counseling. I bit my lip. She wasn't asking for advice.

"Blaize?" Her voice brought me out of my reverie. I'm like Pavlov's dog when I hear "rape." All my humanitarian instincts go out the window and I want to shoot the bastard's balls off with my .32. Maybe I was sitting on a matching powder keg.

We talked a few minutes about nothing before hanging up. This call, on the heels of Sunny's, brought up more emotional baggage than I could stand. It would take the gym, ice cream, or cigarettes to get me through the evening. Or all three? No. I didn't want to pump iron, didn't want to leave my comfy velour couch.

Which was better: a wrinkled face and the probability of lung cancer, or dimpled thighs? Ice cream.

Hell, the only person I slept with these days was Jay Leno...and my baseball bat. I thought of Mac and shivered.

Chapter 3

MONDAY MORNING both counseling sessions ended on a
positive note—a nice change from the weekend. Feeling better, I
drove to McClatchy, the high school Connie attended before she'd
been raped. First on my list was Connie's bleary-eyed counselor.
Within fifteen seconds I knew I'd hit a dead end and beat a retreat,
spent the rest of my day trying to catch Connie's friends between
classes, asking questions before the next bell. Late in the day, a lie
flickered in Belinda Bowers' eyes. I waited for her at the front steps
after the last class.

She came out alone, several texts clutched to her chest, a
fanny-pack slung over her shoulder. Her hair was short, the color
red most kids hate. I wondered how she and Connie had linked up.
Connie, like my old friend Sunny at that age, looked older and had
curves, Belinda, like me at sixteen, looked
twelve—but rapists seldom care.

"Belinda?"

She veered away, then stopped. "I don't know anything."

"I didn't say you did. Do you have a bus to catch?"

"I walk."

"I'm just trying to help Connie. Let me drive you home."

She didn't say anything, but followed along to my dark red
Saturn. My pride and joy. When I opened the door, she eyed the
creamy leather bucket seat appreciatively before sliding in. Just
don't drool on it, I thought as I turned the key. "How about a soda
or something?"

She shrugged.

I took it to mean yes. "Connie could be in danger," I said.

A thoughtful look replaced indifference.

"You live far?"

She shook her head. "Naw. Just off Thirty-fourth."

"Near Connie," I thought aloud. She didn't react.

I parked next to the Tower Theater, a Sacramento landmark, and led the way to a small coffee shop next door. Belinda might enjoy their sodas and desserts more than the French roast my taste buds were screaming for.

As she sipped hot cocoa and nibbled a chocolate chip cookie, she started to talk. "Connie and I weren't real close, but we talked and ate lunch together. Mostly we talked about boys, or what we planned to do after high school. She called me Saturday night."

"This last Saturday? Before or after she ran away from home?"

"Before." Belinda wore a hangdog expression. "She was upset about her dad. She was crying."

Which dad? Frank Donovan? Or Gordon Whitman? Was either one worth crying over?

Belinda took a long swallow of her hot chocolate. "I'd never heard her cry before. She sounded really torn up but wouldn't tell me anything more."

"Did she say where she was going?"

Belinda pushed her cup away. "She hung up."

I digested the information, wondered if Connie had found out she was adopted, and that her real father lived in Sacramento. Or that Maria was her mother. But how? In one night, within a two or three hour period?

I drove Belinda home, gave her my business card and standard spiel. "Call me if you think of anything helpful."

It was nearly five o'clock. So far I was batting zero, no idea why or where Connie ran. But if something happened between nine and midnight, when she was home, then Teresa and Frank probably knew what it was. I decided to tackle Frank, surprise him on his doorstep.

I hung out in front of their empty house until seven p.m., then gave up. My stomach growled, thoroughly unhappy, and I roared off to the nearest Taco Bell. I inhaled two chicken burritos and a diet coke. Almost better than a smoke, I thought as I drove home.

Feeling gritty and limp, I pushed open my door. The blinking red button on my answering machine welcomed me home. News of Connie? I pressed 'playback.' Sunny's voice cooed from the speaker. God, batting a thousand.

"Uh, Blaize. I just called to say thank you." A throaty chuckle.

Jeez, Louise.

"Ross is wonderful...makes me feel soooo safe."

Gag me with a spoon.

A pause. "Oh, I wanted to invite you to the show Friday night. At eight. I'll leave a couple of tickets at the door for second row, center."

Sunny was the most self-serving person I knew. Why would she do that? Forget her. First thing in the morning I'd tackle Frank Donovan and wring whatever information I could out of him. The longer Connie remained missing, the greater the odds she was never coming home. My gut was getting tighter by the hour.

TUESDAY MORNING I climbed the steps of Frank Donovan's workplace. Although he wasn't employed by one of the Big 8 accounting firms, it appeared from the immaculate lawn and fresh paint, light gray on the walls, dark red trim that DeCinzo, Wells, and Donovan were thriving.

What would they charge to do my taxes? Too much, I thought, as I eyed the large waiting area, beautifully appointed with rich cocoa carpet, and wood and brass furnishings. Complete with a lacquered secretary behind a dark wood desk. She had the phone plastered to one ear as she hammered on a computer keyboard. I flashed my shrink card. "Frank Donovan?"

She waved me toward the stairs. "First door."

Dick Tracy, eat your heart out.

Frank's door was closed. I heard voices, opened it quietly. His back to me, he had the speakerphone on, a coffee mug in one hand, audit reports spread over the desk. He turned, saw me and slopped coffee over the top of the speaker as he tried to turn it off, like a kid caught in the cookies. Teresa yelled from the box, "She must have heard us!" An angry sob. "It's been two days!"

She as in Connie? Heard what?

Frank grabbed a napkin and wiped up the spill, threw the napkin away, then said to the phone, "Calm down. She'll come back." He frowned. "I gotta go, Terr. I'll talk to you tonight." He cut the connection, his eyes doing a slow crawl up and down my body as he lit a cigarette.

A handsome man, aging well, he had dark brown hair streaked

with gray, piercing hazel eyes that looked sharp enough to nail me to the wall, and a lazy smile that insinuated he would like to do just that—despite his wife and daughter.

"You must be Blaize?" He stood up and offered his hand. It was warm and dry. Close to my height, he looked me in the eyes, gave me smile I didn't like. It reminded me of my brother's pet boa constrictor.

"Teresa said you couldn't see me because of your work schedule," I smiled, "so I thought I'd help you out." I knew it was a lie, and his eyes said he knew it too.

"Teresa overreacts." He sat down.

I remained standing, and tightened the belt on my trenchcoat. "You don't think her disappearance is serious then?"

"Connie's been unpredictable ever since that boy—" he broke off, savagely mashed out his cigarette and looked up at me with another smile. This one said "life sucks" instead of "let's fuck."

Feeling a glimmer of compassion, I said, "Connie called a girlfriend Saturday night, before she ran away."

Frank cocked an eyebrow.

"She said she'd found out about her father."

"You think she found out she was adopted?" He shook his head. "I wanted Connie to know. Shit! But Teresa was afraid if we told her it would only lead to more questions. Like who were her natural parents." He leaned over his desk, found the pack of cigarettes and lit another.

I sniffed at the smoke. Quitting smoking was hell. "So you argued about it? Did she hear who her real parents were?"

A shrug. "She could have. We were drinking and angry. We said a lot of things that night we should never have said. I don't know how much she heard." He scowled. "We fight about it a lot. She could have heard it ages ago."

"Without saying anything?"

Frank glared. "Connie's always been a quiet kid. Sometimes I'd see questions in her eyes one minute and the next she'd be smiling and I'd think I'd imagined it. But ever since she started high school she's been withdrawn."

"Most teenagers go through that stage."

"This seemed different to me. Like she was suddenly angry

with us but afraid to express it." He sucked on his smoke. "What good is this doing?"

"Do you have any idea where she might be?"

His eyes flashed. "You're the Ph.D. You tell me."

"And you're her father." Asshole. "You're holding something back. Maybe your fight with Teresa went beyond yelling? Maybe you threw a few punches?"

His face flushed, but I wasn't sure if I'd hit the jackpot or just pissed him off.

The forty-eight hours I'd promised Maria were almost up. "Maybe you'd rather tell the police." I picked up my umbrella, slung my purse over my shoulder.

"Get the hell out of here."

I didn't move. "Have you filed a missing person report?"

His phone rang. He glared at me. "This morning. Teresa insisted." Another shrill ring. For a second I saw a hint of worry that was quickly masked. "She's just punishing us," he said as I set my card on his desk. Trying to convince himself?

I left, drove down I Street, past the Hall of Justice—a building that could have created the budget deficit all by itself—and nabbed a parking space in front of the city jail. After feeding the meter, I headed around the corner to the old four-story, granite Police Department where Missing Persons and Homicide lodged.

Pat, my college dorm buddy, worked the missing person's desk on the third floor. Phone propped against her ear, she popped gum between her teeth and doodled on a note pad. Square and compact, she looked very solid and dependable. She gave me a wave and after she hung up, I explained about Connie.

She rolled her blue eyes and her dark curly hair bounced around her shoulders. "Geez, Blaize, I just took the report an hour ago! What do you think this is? The runaway sign-in bureau?"

I smiled, held up my hands. "I know it's early."

She scowled. Then the lines of exasperation turned to curiosity. "You know her?"

"She's a client of mine and I'm worried."

"And I'm an overworked civil servant." She flipped open a two-inch thick log book. "See all these entries? There's eight to a page." She slammed it shut. There's three of these books for this year—so far. And one of me."

I clucked sympathetically. "Need a vacation?" I jingled my car keys and her expression turned hungry. She'd been with me when I bought my Saturn and was still socking away pennies to replace her antique pile of junk. "Get me all the dope you can on Connie by tonight and you can have my car this weekend."

Pat's eyes lit up and she grabbed the phone. "I'll see what I can do."

I TALKED TO Maria on the phone as I drove out to the yuppie suburb of Fair Oaks where Connie had attended St. Mary's.

"She's dead..."came out a strangled whisper of anguish.

"Maria—you don't know that. She might just be acting out, teenagers do that sometimes." I could almost see the tears in her eyes. I said more reassuring words I didn't quite believe, then said goodbye.

The staff at St. Mary's had nothing of value to tell me. With every blank look and I'm sorry, I didn't know her," or "I didn't talk to her," my frustration mounted. The girl had transferred here after being raped and no one wanted to talk about it.

I stormed back to my car, drove home in a state of recklessness, and stomped up the stairs into the house. Slinging my purse onto the couch, I jammed a stick of bubblegum in my mouth and chewed.

By the time I calmed down, my jaw ached. When I checked my calendar, I balked. I had a dinner date and was in no mood for anyone's company. If Pat called I wanted to be here—for Maria, too.

I flopped on the couch and punched in Lon's number. He was a wild guy, great-looking, and an outrageous dresser—and gay. Also the best male friend I had.

I told him I felt lousy, which was true, and he told me about his new "flame." At the end of the conversation, he asked, "Standing me up for anyone special, Blaize, girl?"

I thought about Sunny, and Mac, and almost laughed. "Nope, just beat." Damn the lump in my throat. Relationships were a pain in the butt, but right now I wished I had a chest to snuggle against.

"Sweet dreams, Sugar," Lon said.

"Yeah, right, Lover." I hung up, crawled between the covers of my too-big bed and wrapped myself around a pillow. Lon might be having sweet dreams but I had another night of Jay Leno to put me under. I dozed off with the TV on, and the baseball bat beside me.

Pat's call woke me Wednesday morning. The sun was out, the sky a brilliant blue. Her voice trampled my brief flush of optimism like hiking boots over fresh green grass. "Blaize, Connie Donovan's at the morgue."

I fought for air. "An accident?"

"Murder." She cleared her throat. "Stabbed. She was found near the river. Nude. No ID. That's all I know. I'm on my way out to the morgue now."

Murdered. "Meet you there," I murmured and hung up, then stumbled into the kitchen. Jesus. Swallowing back tears, I steadied myself with the counter while scrounging through a kitchen drawer for the half-crumpled pack of cigarettes I'd hidden in the back. For just-in-case. Like now. I lit a bent smoke, brushed a tear from one eye. Damn. Not my fault. But the news shook me bad. Why did I have the sick suspicion that Connie's murder was only the beginning?

Chapter 4

THE MORGUE resembled a two-story architectural dinosaur. I liked to avoid this part of town. The refrigerated basement had a funereal pallor, smelled like rotten eggs, and made me queasy.

"The ID's already been made—sorry," Pat said.

"Who made it?" I asked, glad I didn't have to look.

"Her parents...and the woman you rent your office space from."

"Maria Quintera?"

Pat nodded.

Poor Maria. I'd hoped to spare her this. "How bad was it?" *It* being the body.

"Her face was okay. The rest—pretty bad." Pat's expression reminded me of our college days, before a big test. The I'd-rather-be-anywhere-but-here look. Bad.

"When will the coroner's report be released?"

She shrugged. "Talk to Detective Zoloski."

"Zoloski?"

"Homicide, twelve years now. He's good."

At what? I wondered, seeing the catbird grin on her face as she handed me a card with his number.

I shoved it in my purse, thanked her, and left to go to the office, where I'd promised to meet Maria. I didn't need a fortuneteller to know that she wanted me to find her daughter's killer. "Leave it to the police, that's their job," I planned to tell her. But her face haunted me. Fifteen years ago both our lives changed. I'd become a shrink. She'd made the big time as a lawyer/lobbyist. She had a lot to lose once the cops and press ran amok through her past. Her career meant a lot to half the women in town, and to me— as her friend, and Connie's therapist. The cops weren't gonna like me on their turf.

Too bad for them.

MARIA WAS SEATED behind her desk, a half-empty bottle of Southern Comfort in her hand. An empty glass in the other. Only once, when she'd lost a big case, had I seen her drink something other than wine. Now I doubted the whole bottle would be enough. She motioned me toward a chair. "Want one?" Her hand shook as she filled a tumbler with whiskey and spilled it all over the desk.

"Sure." I grabbed some paper towels. I preferred a gallon of ice cream, but a commiserating drink was the least I could do.

After a couple of gulps, Maria put down her glass, and pulled a file from the bottom desk drawer, tossing it across the polished surface. I reached for it, then hesitated. The file tab read Gordon Whitman. "I want you to find out if he had anything to do with Connie's death," Maria hissed.

Kill his own daughter? Whether or not he knew who she was, this would shake up the Capitol. But it seemed one hell of a leap from paternity to homicide.

Maria lifted her glass again, "Then catch him with enough evidence to convict him. I don't care how it gets there."

Her sad, lop-sided smile tugged at my resistance. Still, I shook my head. "I'm a shrink, not a PI," I reminded her. "If, and it's a *big* if, Whitman's involved, catching him won't be easy. He has a lot of pull."

"Are you afraid?" Her dark eyes challenged me, and I felt like I was back at summer camp, playing "truth or dare" around a campfire. Truth-sayers got crucified.

"Yeah." I swallowed. "But that's not why I think you should go to someone else." I was willing to look for Connie's killer—but I had limits. "I don't have much savvy around the Capitol. Some PI's do."

"Like your ex-boyfriend, Ross?" she sneered.

"Yes, for one."

She slammed her fist on the desk. I flinched. "I wouldn't trust him or any other man. A man raped Connie, stabbed her to death and left her lying by the river like garbage!"

Had someone breached police security? I didn't know yet if the murderer had raped Connie, didn't know if the cops had found anything to indicate the killer's gender.

"Please, Blaize. I'll feel better if I know someone... She's just another case to the cops, but you knew her."

No. It was on the tip of my tongue to tell her this was a big mistake. "All right," I said, "I'll give it a shot." Panic prickled on my neck. What was I saying? I was sticking my head on a guillotine. When the alcohol wore off, maybe I could plead temporary insanity and bow out.

Her mouth pressed into a thin, vengeful line. Maria had a place picked out in hell for her daughter's killer.

What about me? I suddenly realized I wanted to know the truth, wanted the murderer behind bars. Maybe atone for the fact I'd let Mac run free fifteen years ago. I'd tried never to look back. Did everything I could to forget him. Now, I couldn't turn my back on Connie's ghost or Maria's anguish. I refilled both glasses. "Want to talk?"

Her voice came out little-girl-like. Her lips trembled. "I saw her...at the morgue. Like a slab of butchered meat. My baby wasn't there at all." A tear spilled down her cheek, splashed onto the desk. Then another. She took a breath and reached for a tissue. "I need to be alone, Blaize."

I stood, uncertain whether she was okay alone.

She laughed grimly. "Don't worry. I'm not going to kill myself." She held up the bottle. "This is all I'm going to kill."

"You know where to find me." I left her door open and retreated into my bleak office. I was too keyed up to sit down, so I walked to the sand tray and played with the figures. No good. The silence was suffocating. I dug out Detective Zoloski's number and dialed.

He answered on the first ring. "Detective Stephanos Zoloski," he growled between crunches. Potato chips? I disliked him immediately.

I offered my name. "I'm a psychologist. I worked with Connie. I thought it might be a good idea to meet."

His breath quickened and I knew I'd caught his interest. "If you know something—"

"I'd rather talk face-to-face. You free for dinner tomorrow night?" I figured by then he'd have more information to spill, provided I found the right tactics to open him up.

I MET ZOLOSKI Thursday evening at Mace's. The classy place fit
my budget once a year—on my birthday. However, Maria was
footing the bill and wouldn't balk—unless he guzzled alcohol like
some cops I knew. I half-hoped he would, it would improve my
chances of getting information. I waited at the bar. I'd forgotten to
ask what he looked like and had told him only that I'd wear a blue
shirt and black jeans. My shirt was actually turquoise silk and my
jeans—well, I look good in denim. Maybe the outfit would help me
fish out more information from the man.

With a name like Zoloski, I expected a big, Polish blonde.
What actually walked in and sized me up in about ten seconds flat
was something else.

His thick, black hair brushed his shoulders. A late thirty-
something face, slightly sunburned across the forehead. Dark
eyebrows framed dark green eyes that complimented a nose which
looked as if it had been broken at least once. It made him more
attractive. His square jaw suggesting arrogance might be a problem.
He smiled and my blood ran hot. God, the women in the force
probably swooned when he passed by. How in the hell had he
remained single? Or did he leave his wedding ring at home?

"Blaize?" His voice could have melted marshmallows.

Damn, why couldn't he have been blond? I've never been
attracted to blondes. "The only one I know," I murmured. I offered
my hand. "Detective Zoloski?"

"That's me," he said. His hand was warm and dry and his eyes
made me tingle in all the right places. The maitre'd arrived to say
our table was ready and led us to a corner booth. Zoloski set a
manila envelope beside his plate.

Connie's file? Case notes? He'd want something in exchange
for a peek. What? In the old days, my virginity. Nowadays?

The waiter directed his expectant gaze at me. "Virgin
Margarita." Maria's Southern Comfort had burned a hole in my
stomach.

Zoloski echoed my order.

I must have looked surprised.

"Not all cops drink beer," he said with a mischievous smile.
"Besides, I've gotta work tonight."

"Does that mean you're only an alcoholic on weekends?" I shot back. The cops I knew drank like they needed A.A.

Zoloski's gaze met mine, warming me over once again. "I'm not much of a drinker and I'm usually occupied with other things on the weekends." *Women*, the husky note in his voice implied.

I sipped my water, then set it down. "So, do I call you Zoloski or Stephanos or what?"

Most people call me Steve." From the slight tightening in his expression I could tell he wasn't fond of Steve.

"Maybe I'll stick to Zoloski." I had a feeling being on a first-name basis with someone as good-looking as him could be trouble.

He leaned forward slightly. "Is Blaize your real name?"

"Nickname—a la Pat. I'll let her fill you in." I wasn't about to explain that in college Pat had accused me of running from relationships in a blaze of glory and Blaize—with an "i" for individuality—stuck.

He appeared to digest my answer along with my tone, which said "treading on personal territory here, back off." Next he would ask my *real* first name. Surprise. He didn't.

I eyed the envelope, wondering how desperate he might be for information and figuring I'd find out by the end of the evening. We bantered until the waiter brought our drinks. Zoloski gave me a speculative look. "You come here a lot?"

I shrugged. "Once in a while."

"Why don't you order then?"

This was not in the cop mold. "Sure you want to chance it?"

He grinned. "I like to live dangerously." He took a sip of his drink. "Besides, you're paying."

Too true. I chose grilled halibut, my favorite, and watched a slight frown slide across his face. Uh, oh, he didn't like fish.

After a moment, his eyes narrowed slightly and his nicely sculptured lips straightened into a firm line. The repartee was over. "I talked to Frank and Teresa Donovan this morning. They said they'd hired you to find Connie."

Were they covering for Maria? Had they mentioned my PI license? Something in way he looked at me said they did. "Then you know I used to do PI work?"

"Used to?"

"I'm a psychologist, not a PI."

His eyebrows nudged up. "But your PI license is current. I checked.

I was going to find out how desperate he was for information a lot sooner than planned. "I haven't done PI work since I hung up my Ph.D. shingle," I said, my gaze straying toward the envelope. "Is that Connie's file? The autopsy report?"

He nodded. "Copies of everything we've got—which isn't much." And which you aren't about to see, his tone implied. But he had brought it for a reason and he hadn't left.

Great, my mind quipped. I had really hoped for a hot lead. Of course, if he had a hot lead he wouldn't have showed. The guy must be desperate. I held up my drink. "To truth, justice, and the American way."

"Don't forget profit." We touched glasses and suddenly the atmosphere became intimate. I set my glass down and lowered my gaze until the heat surge cooled.

When I looked up, his face reflected business again. "Connie's parents weren't very forthcoming with information. Why did they call you?"

Teresa and Frank obviously hadn't mentioned Connie was adopted. I covered my surprise by sipping my drink. "The lawyer I work for is Teresa's sister. She recommended me when Connie needed counseling."

"Because of the rape?" He didn't say "alleged rape," which made me like him more. "Did you talk to the girl?"

"Once. Last Saturday."

"Before she ran away?" He was watching me carefully.

I nodded. Murky waters ahead. How much did Maria want me to say? How much could I hold back? This was a murder investigation. I had doctor-patient privilege to fall back on. I was under no obligation to offer information. Yet.

Zoloski pushed on. "Her father seemed to think this is all the fault of the boy who raped her. You talk to him?"

"No."

His eyes questioned my investigative abilities. "Why not?"

Gut feeling. I hesitated. "I didn't think it was connected."

He leaned forward, looking more like a cop and less like a

hunk. "Connie was a recovering rape victim. I assume she talked to you about it. You did counsel her right?"

Was he one of those cops who didn't like shrinks any better than PI's? I didn't like his tone, but held onto my cool. Connie was dead. I didn't have to keep mum about our conversation, but I was reluctant to go into it. "I saw her once. And yes, she did tell me about the rape," I answered evenly.

"She must have said something to make you think this guy wasn't important." When I didn't answer, his tone grew condescending. "I mean, she talks to you, then runs away and turns up dead."

I felt like I'd been hit in the stomach. Any attraction I'd felt disintegrated. The question was, how bad did I want a peek at Connie's file? Not bad enough. I found myself standing up. "Listen, Zoloski. I'll say this once, if you don't like it, then you can *shove this dinner where the sun don't shine*." I gripped the edge of the table. "Connie talked to me about the date-rape because she knew I'd understand." Why did I say that? I plunged ahead. "When she left she was feeling better. Maria noticed it too. Whatever set her off, made her run away from home, happened sometime between eight-thirty Saturday night when she left my office, and midnight, when Teresa realized Connie was gone. Frank and Teresa had a big fight that night. Maybe something they said set Connie off. But it was *not* the date-rape and it sure as hell wasn't me."

Now I felt as deflated as a helium balloon stuck on a nail. The lines of Zoloski's face rearranged themselves into a more compassionate design and I wondered what kind of inference he was making about my words. His contemplative green eyes made me uncomfortable.

"Pat warned me you had an Irish temper. I deserved it. Please, sit down. This hasn't been the best of days and I took it out on you."

An apology! Damn, what next? I didn't want to sit, but didn't want to leave either.

He picked up the manila envelope and held it out like a peace treaty. "You tell me everything you know and I'll give you a look."

I sat and recounted the counseling session with Connie, and my impressions of Frank and Theresa. "You said they had a fight before Connie ran away? They tell you what it was about?"

How did I answer without giving away Maria's secret? I reached for the envelope.

He covered my hand. "What was the fight about?" he repeated.

"Frank said he and Teresa were drunk, arguing. Connie got upset and bolted." I eased my hand and the envelope from his grasp.

He looked like he wanted to snatch it back. "If you can tell me who you've talked with since Sunday
and what they said, it will save me some time."

Our grilled halibut arrived, giving me the opportunity to ignore his request. I took a bite. "Ummm."

He threw me a wry smile that said I hadn't escaped yet, then cut off a healthy chunk of fish. "This is great," he said a moment later. "How come when I barbecue fish it either comes out dry and tasteless, or mushy?"

"If you're asking for cooking advice, don't. I hate to cook." I sipped my water. "I'd rather eat out, eat junk, or not eat, in that order."

"It must be the right formula." His green eyes flashed approval.

I took another bite of fish, my gaze stuck to the plate, my head reeling. I'd rather have him for dessert than cheesecake. I squelched the thought. No entanglements. I looked up, could tell from his sexy smile that I'd caught him picturing me in a supine position. It wouldn't hurt to loosen him up, I thought. "I work out three times a week, unless I'm over-booked with clients." My words were running together but I couldn't slow them down. "If I'm under a lot of stress I go to the club five times a week and veg-out on the weekends."

"What do you do for fun?"

Sex, drugs and rock'n roll, my brain quipped. Again, I caught that quirky grin and mischievous glimmer in his eyes that said we were on a similar wavelength—both of us after information and playing a game to get it. But I had a feeling this could go beyond that. Was I ready for another intimate relationship? Most of the time I was too damned angry at the male species or too angry with myself for picking the wrong guy. Detective Zoloski looked the type to have a black book two inches thick, not to mention oil and water mixed together better than a cop and a shrink/PI. Then again, with a cop's hours and a cop's pay...and a cop's curiosity... "I like to play racquetball," I blurted.

"An indoor sport..."

I took another bite of fish, then almost spit it out when I laughed.

He leaned closer. I could smell his aftershave, light and citrusy. Definitely appealing. "What do you like to do outdoors?" he asked.

"Fish, hunt, and drink beer," I rattled off, working to remember this was about Connie's file and getting information. "You?"

"Read poetry, go on picnics, make love under the stars."

Was he serious, or what? I closed my mouth. This was getting *way* too dangerous. I felt scared. I felt hyper. Energized.

"Are you attached, hitched, and/or living with someone?" he asked.

"None of the above. You?"

"None of the above."

The next thing I knew I was asking him to accompany me to the Festival of Favorites, the play starring light-fingered Sunny at Hiram Johnson's theater the next night. I had to put Sunny's tickets to good use, didn't I? But when he said yes, I wondered how much of his interest involved Connie, and how much was for me?

I DROVE HOME, ground some fresh coffee, sat at the kitchen table and opened the manila envelope. Evidently Pat had told Zoloski I was trustworthy. He loaned me the file, but wanted everything returned the next evening. I didn't want to look at photos. I turned on Clapton's *Unplugged*, listened to the blues for a moment, then slid the envelope's contents onto the table.

I stared at the grainy photocopies of the photographs of Connie's corpse, feeling sick. Butchered meat, Maria had said. She was right.

Connie's body had been discovered beside the pier near Old Sacramento, just off the American River bike trail. A curious dog had dragged an early morning jogger into the bushes, and after the guy lost his breakfast, he'd run for help. Whatever tracks might have existed had been wasted by the dog, the jogger, and regurgitated granola.

Connie had died from multiple stab wounds to the upper torso. Shallow thoracic cuts forming a vaguely circular pattern were present. I wondered what Zoloski made of that. It nagged at my brain but nothing surfaced. I continued reading. Connie had been dead for four to six hours. Early rigor mortis was present. Skin cool. No maggots had hatched. She was found nude, her arms crossed over her chest. One cut on her right hand. Trying to defend herself? Where were her clothes? Had her killer hoped she would remain unidentified? The police had searched both banks of the river, questioned boat owners and other joggers. *Nada*. Except for the boy Connie had accused of date rape, Zoloski had no suspects. The father had refused to let Zoloski talk to the boy alone. Maybe I should try. It was that or the Capitol and Gordon Whitman.

I studied the pictures of Connie's body, her arms folded across her chest, reminding me of Disney's Sleeping Beauty holding a rose—a horror version. Roses made me think of Mac the Knife, and I wasn't sure why. Something he'd said way back when? The harder I tried to remember, the further away the familiar feeling sank. Finally, I shrugged my uneasiness off, poured some brandy in my coffee and took it into bed. I'd see Connie's date-rapist, and then legislator Whitman tomorrow. That would make my day. I turned on the TV and slipped between the sheets with Koppel, who wasn't much comfort.

Chapter 5

FRIDAY MORNING I went to my office, counseled two clients, one six months sober in A.A., one eleven months sober in D.A., Debtor's Anonymous, with ten years of sobriety in O.A., Overeaters Anonymous—my alma mater. Strange how the disease of addiction threaded its way into everything.

Now I worked, or worked out to stuff my feelings. Better than jumping from a size eight to a twenty-four like a yo-yo? Maybe. Good therapy? No. Sometimes it was the best I could do.

Mid-morning, I returned to McClatchy and bee lined to the library. After a quick peek at the yearbook, I knew Connie's rapist, Patrick Chapman was a good-looking teen, and the varsity quarterback. The librarian proudly told me they'd had six wins, one loss, and directed me toward the PE building.

Beyond it, the coach's shrill whistle drew me. He blasted irregular warnings as I watched the seventeen and eighteen-year-olds jog around the track. Before I could zero in on Patrick Chapman, the track coach came up. "Who are you and what do you want?" His eyebrows bristled.

I smiled brightly, irritated by his macho stance, sure he was one of those Neanderthals who thought shrinks were only for craaazy people. "I'm a stringer for the *Orangevale News*," I lied, then smiled. "You're having a great season. My editor thought it would make a good story. Mind if I talk to your quarterback?"

His chest expanded a good six inches. "Writer, huh?" Turning, he yelled, "Hey, Patrick, come here!"

Patrick walked up, not even breathing hard after his laps. His forehead glimmered with dampness. "Yeah, Coach?" He eyeballed me and I eyeballed him. Ted Bundy? Given time, who knew?

"This lady wants to talk to you." The coach yelled, "Move it!" at another kid but showed no inclination to leave.

I flashed him a provocative smile. "Go head, Coach, I'd like to see you in action. We'll talk *later*." The man actually winked and moved down the track.

"What's this about?" Patrick asked with a uncertain glance toward his coach. The guy was reaming out one of the kids for being a "lazy ass."

I smelled Patrick's sweat, met his too-old dark eyes with my mature hardball look and said bluntly, "It's about the charge Connie made against you several months ago."

His jaw dropped. Whatever he expected, this wasn't it.

"Where were you Saturday night and Sunday morning?"

He grew younger by the second. And scared. Guilty? I couldn't tell. "You cops don't give up."

I didn't enlighten him.

"My dad's going to be pissed off." The prospect seemed to please him. "Look, maybe what happened with Connie was—" He couldn't seem to find a word. "That was four months ago!"

Maybe?

He shrugged like an innocent victim. "Look, she's been at a different school for three months." He whined, "I haven't seen her."

"Saturday night, Sunday morning," I said impatiently. The coach was winding down.

"Saturday night we had a football game. I was here until after ten, then at Matt's house until one. His dad drove me home. I went to bed." He paused. "Sunday I watched football with my dad."

"Matt who?"

The coach was on his way across the track, heading toward us.

"Matt Meadows." He pointed toward a smaller kid in black sweats.

Time to retreat.

AT HOME, I made two sets of notes of my conversation with Patrick, re-read Connie's file and slipped one set into the envelope. I stretched, thinking of my next move. Gordon Whitman's name kept popping into my mind. I could use my consulting work as a smoke screen. Say I was doing a multivariate study on jerks in the legislature.

The phone rang. Zoloski's baritone voice caught me off guard. "How about dinner at my place before the play?"

His place? This guy moved fast! That or the case was still stalled and desperation had overruled any cop qualms about my PI license. Butterflies fluttered through my stomach. "You cook?" I said it as politely as I could muster, but he laughed anyway.

"Most single guys do. That or they eat out a lot, like you."

I was not a guy, but I figured he knew that, or would try to find out. "What's on the menu?" *Not me*, that's for damn sure I told myself.

"I was just gonna throw a couple steaks on the grill." He paused. "Pat told me you're driving her car, I better pick you up."

I thought of Pat's "last legs" Plymouth and gave him directions.

AFTER A QUICK rain dance in the shower, I dried my hair and slapped on some make-up. Not bad. My favorite outfit, an expensive turquoise skirt and top, improved the picture. Not bad at all. I headed back to the kitchen and the phone.

No one at Maria's house. But she answered the office phone, surprising me.

"What makes you think Gordon Whitman did it?" I asked.

"Blaize?" She sounded sleepy. Or hung-over? Both, maybe.

"Yeah." I waited.

"Gordon messes around with hookers, gets mean once in a while, the type of stuff the good-ol'-boys' network sweeps under the table."

"How do you mean?"

"I don't know." She said it quietly.

I thought of Zoloski. If I told him Connie's connection to Whitman he might trade information. I wasn't sure I wanted to do that. Pat had access to police records. But she had my car for the weekend, what more could I offer?

I called Matt Meadows, the quarterback's friend, and confirmed with his father that the boys had been together. Great— my gut feeling proved right—I made notes of the conversation and reviewed what little I knew.

A KNOCK ON my apartment door sent my blood pressure into overdrive. I shoved the new notes into Zoloski's envelope, grabbed my purse, slipped on my turquoise heels and opened the door.

Zoloski smiled, his eyes warm, and gave a low whistle.

Jane Fonda, eat your heart out! Heat crawled up my neck despite the cool April weather. Walking to the car I took in his pressed Indian cotton shirt, soft and comfortable, yet dressy. Black levis and black snakeskin cowboy boots filled out the picture. My kind of clothes. All he needed was a six-gun. I smiled and handed him the packet. "Thanks."

He responded with an infectious grin. "I'd rather hold your hand," but he took the envelope first. I didn't tell him about the interview notes I'd stuck inside. He might appreciate a surprise. I enjoyed the feel of his hand and the fact he was taller in spite of my two-inch heels.

His vintage car turned out to be a handsomely restored 1973, 240Z. Burgundy leather, black dash, polished chrome wheels and the metallic red paint job must have cost a few grand extra. Did he know I liked red?

He lived about twenty minutes from downtown, just off Antelope in a new development. I eyed his house as I got out and wondered if I should bite the bullet and check in for the night—a month—a year?

Whoa girl, slow them doggies down! I reminded myself of mowing lawns, pulling weeds, and all the general maintenance stuff I hated. Most of all, I reminded myself that Ross had looked good—at first. And that Zoloski was a cop, and he was after information. Just like me.

The living room had a high, vaulted ceiling and a lot of inside light shone through a wall of windows. The air conditioning bill had to be outrageous.

The sectional couch was covered in muted colors, like the decorator had swallowed a beige paint pot. The glass coffee table, oak wall unit, framed jungle prints and huge umbrella plant all made me think: *You Tarzan, me Jane.* But I smiled gamely and followed him into the kitchen.

He opened the sliding glass door and ushered me onto the well-lit patio. The sun was going down in a riot of pink and orange over a landscape consisting of pure lawn, a patio table, chairs, and barbecue.

"I like your house."

He smiled. "Keeps me busy, but I enjoy it." He lit the charcoal, disappeared inside, and returned with a bottle of white wine and two tulip glasses.

"Okay?" He held up the bottle.

"Sure." I didn't warn him that alcohol went straight to my head and made me giggly.

"May dinner taste as good as—" His gaze met mine and I almost filled in the blank with "sex."

"As good as you look," he finished. What a detective! The guy could read minds. He pulled his chair close to mine and sipped his wine. A bird chirped, then another. I closed my eyes enjoying the moment.

I heard him leave and return. He set a plate of raw vegetables and dip on the table. "It's dill weed."

I took a carrot, dabbed it into the bowl and crunched. "I'm impressed." I finished it, took another, feeling as fluttery as a girl on her first date and finding it difficult to remember cops didn't like PI's. But once I found Connie's killer, my PI work would be behind me.

He said, "You're awfully quiet."

Was he looking for serious conversation? Women talked serious, men talked work, sports, and sex. My taste in men had been lousy, I admit. Maybe Pat had done me a favor giving me Zoloski's number and I should be grateful, but I felt nervous.

The phone rang. He went inside, talked for a minute, then returned wearing a scowl.

"The IRS?" I joked.

"My ex-wife," Zoloski tossed back. "She wanted to borrow my sailboat for the weekend. I said yes."

"How long were you married?" Nosey me.

"Three years." An expression of pain clouded his eyes. "We've been divorced two, but she still calls."

"Kids?" If kids were involved, I wanted to know.

"No, thank God. *That* would have been a nightmare." His tone was vehement. I must have looked surprised; he added, "Too many of my friends are divorced—with kids. I swore I'd never have kids until I was sure as I could be about the future."

"You want kids, then?"

He shrugged. "Maybe. If I find the right pastimes. My job's hell on relationships."

I felt my lips curl. "Tell me about it." We laughed together and the warmth reappeared in his eyes. Without preamble, he leaned over and kissed me lightly on the lips. I inhaled the scent of soap and citrus.

He pulled back and his gaze held mine.

We'd just moved beyond the "let's trade information" stage into unmarked territory. I gulped my wine.

He turned to the barbecue.

I kicked off my heels and walked across the lawn to the fence, my feet sinking into the freshly mowed grass. Like a caged animal, I paced the perimeter. Warning bells rang in my thoughts. I wiggled my toes, feeling insecure. He wasn't pushy, a new type of guy for me. A part of me wanted to cut and run. Worst, I expected the roof to fall in, expected divorce to follow marriage, expected disrespect and abuse in a relationship.

I heard his soft footfalls on the lawn behind me, felt his nearness. "Dinner's ready." He hugged me casually, and walked me back to the patio. Two fresh glasses, half-filled with red wine sparkled on the table. He lifted his glass.

God, I felt so horribly sad at my own expectations of relationships. Either too little, or too much. What happened to the giggles?

"What's wrong?"

I shook my head. "It's not you. Sometimes my past hits me over the head when I least expect it." I smiled, pushing the emotions down.

He smiled, then gave me a sober look. "You scared?"

"Are you?" I shot back.

With speculation and perhaps a hint of uncertainty in his emerald eyes, he leaned over and kissed me again. This time his hand slid to the back of my head, his fingers stroked my hair. I melted and he broke away. But his eyes stayed with me. "Yeah, Blaize, I'm scared."

I smelled "burn," and his gaze shot to the barbecue. "Holy Toledo!" He rescued two steaks from the inferno. "I hope you like it black and bloody."

I laughed, my mood starting to lift. "I hear charcoal's good for you."

He served the steak with baked potatoes and a green salad on white china with stainless steel utensils and crystal water glasses. My kind of guy. We batted small talk back and forth between bites, finding out we had more than weight-lifting and racquetball in common. He boggled my mind when he mentioned he'd been seeing a counselor for the last year and a half, working out leftover baggage from his marriage. His expression registered happy surprise when I admitted to a love of target-shooting, fast cars and a lead foot.

In between conversation, I ate a mountain of salad, and stoked up on complex carbs. He looked somewhat in awe when I finished every bite of potato. "Just don't bring out dessert," I said as I dabbed my mouth with a napkin.

"Didn't make any," he admitted with a slow smile that said he could think of at least one substitute.

My heart skidded to an abrupt stop, then remembered to beat again. "We ought to get going. The show starts at eight."

"Relax," he said with a laugh, his eyes crinkled in enjoyment. "We can spare ten minutes. I'd like you to see my pride and joy."

What? A waterbed? I followed him through the house and to the garage door.

He flipped on the light, illuminating an E-type Jag, sanded and ready for paint. We moved around the long, sleek hood and I opened the door. The interior was dark brown. Yellow streaks of paint still remained around the edges of the doors and I knew it would be beautiful when finished.

"You'll repaint it yellow?"

He nodded. "You bet."

"You remind me of my brother."

He groaned. "That's not what I want to hear, Sweetheart."

I laughed. "I meant about cars. He's in the auto repair and paint business. Whoever covered the seats did a great job." I ran my hand over the supple, cool leather.

"Thanks." Zoloski acknowledged his workmanship with a gesture. Damn, he kept breaking my "cop" stereotype.

I eyed the beautiful hood. "Does it handle like the Z?"

"Better." He pulled a set of keys from his pocket and tossed them over the car. "You drive."

I slid behind the wheel, not needing a second invitation. As he climbed into the passenger seat, I found the ignition and the car roared to life. It felt vibrant. So did I. In my imagination the svelte bonnet glistened mellow yellow. Slowly I let out the clutch and the car moved down the driveway and into the street. I glanced at Zoloski to see if he'd closed his eyes in terror. Their green depths sparkled. Brave man.

The car purred around the neighborhood ignoring the speed limit despite my best effort to "hold it down." Zoloski threatened to write me up for reckless driving. I couldn't stop laughing. I felt wonderful.

I parked and we switched to the Z. Bummer days. He drove. We made it into our seats as the curtain went up.

Much as I hated to admit, Sunny was good. So were the others. I waltzed down memory lane right with them.

As the lights came up, I led Zoloski toward the stage. "I'll introduce you to Sunny." We made our way threw a milling crowd to the back door. I pushed it open and stopped. Sunny and Ross were locked in a clench. I backed into Zoloski. The shock must have shown on my face, because he lifted me off my feet, swung me back through the door and down the stage stairs to the aisle.

Why was I upset? Why did I care who Ross or Sunny made it with? Yet it brought up feelings of betrayal. He'd lived with me, but screwed anything in a skirt. And all through school Sunny had stolen every guy I'd shown an interest in. They deserved each other. Yet I was calling them both all kinds of names inside my head while I practically race-walked to the car. I was angry at myself for letting something so petty get to me now. They were adults. Free to do what they wanted.

Zoloski leaned against the car and pulled me against his chest. "Want to talk?"

"Not really," I murmured, while his concerned expression encouraged me to continue. "I was surprised Sunny was...well, whatever."

"You know her?"

I shivered. "Sunny and I went to high school together." I thought of Mac and rubbed the goosebumps on my arms.

Zoloski opened the door. "Want to come back to my place for a glass of wine?"

My stomach tightened. I thought of my cluttered flat, my empty, queen-sized bed. Don't sleep with a man on a first date, I told myself. Technically, it's a second date, my mind whispered. But I wanted comfort, not sex. And I wasn't sure of his motives. He hadn't brought up Connie—yet.

"I think you need someone to hold onto tonight."

Did this guy read minds or what? "Yes." I felt awkward, out of my element in asking for what I wanted. It was easier to encourage my clients to more adult behaviors than practice them myself. As I climbed in the car, I wondered: Would he push for sex?

He didn't and I fell asleep wrapped in his arms. Feeling safe and secure, I was rudely awakened by the phone.

"Zoloski," he muttered into the receiver as he sat up. The bed squeaked. I sat up too, straightening my clothes. "What?" his tone sounded off-key, his eyebrows lifted and he glanced at me. I went to the bathroom, still listening, but the other person did the talking. When I returned, he'd switched on the bedroom light and was pulling on his boots.

Good thing we weren't in the middle of a groan and moan session. "Work?"

He looked unhappy. "A homicide," but his tone said it was more than that.

A tremor ran down my spine as I slipped on my shoes and finger-combed my hair. "And?"

"It's your friend."

My mind shrieked, Pat? Lon? Maria? Oh God.

"Sunny Wright."

"Sunny?" I repeated. Then I thought of Mac the Knife and my blood ran cold.

Chapter 6

I'LL DROP YOU off on the way," Zoloski said as he grabbed his shoulder holster and gun.

I followed him to the Z. "I want to come with you."

He shook his head. "You ever see a homicide?"

Yeah, I almost said, my father after a car ran him down. "I might be able to help."

He threw me a hard look. "If you know something Blaize, tell me. This is murder, for Christ's sake!"

I crossed my arms and rubbed, still felt cold. "What happened?" The clock on the dash glowed three-twenty a.m.

"She was stabbed. A lot."

He took the first turn fast, the tires squealing, and I wished I were driving. I loved to drive fast, especially when overwhelmed with emotions, like now. Sunny. The old 70's tune ran through my mind, *Sunny, yesterday my life was filled with rain...* I grabbed Zoloski's arm and nearly made him jump lanes across Antelope.

He swore as he swerved.

"She'd hired a bodyguard."

He threw me an inquisitive look. "Why'd she need a bodyguard?"

My jaw froze at the thought of telling Zoloski about Mac the Knife. "She'd received some threatening mail."

"How well did you two know each other?"

"I told you," my voice cracked. "High school friends. Why? Am I a suspect?" My humor fell flat.

"Well, I get the feeling you didn't like her."

Very perceptive.

Zoloski rubbed his chin as though deep in thought. "You were wrapped in my arms all night. Maybe I should report that, give you an alibi. But then my boss might shoot me for sleeping with a PI."

"I'm a psychologist, and all we did was sleep."

"You think he's gonna believe that?" His expression said he found it hard to believe and I wondered if he regretted last night. Then I thought of Sunny and forgot my relationship worries.

It didn't take long to get downtown that time of morning. The address Zoloski had was in Old Sacramento, a ritzy first-floor condo near the water, shaded by oaks and sycamores. Police were all over the place, holding curious neighbors at bay as well as questioning them. Zoloski whisked me to front door of the complex. "Stay here."

"I'm going with you!" Somehow I thought if I could see Sunny, I'd know if Mac killed her.

He tossed me a look of pure exasperation. "That wasn't a request. I need to do my job and you'll only be in the way."

I nodded unhappily. The officer at the door gave me the evil eye. Freud might have said he had vagina-envy, if we lived in a matriarchal society. I didn't subscribe to Freud. Turning, I scanned the crowd, searching for a familiar face, something to take my mind off my fears. Mac might come for me next. He had before.

A big guy who looked like a bar bouncer was arguing with a policeman, gesturing toward the apartment. Curious, I inched away from the front steps and down toward them.

"I'm her bodyguard, damn it! I have a right to go in!" The big guy yelled at the cop

"Not now, Mr. Anderson. But I'd like to know where you've been."

Anderson ran his hand through his thick brown hair, his expression tired. "She was upset, drunk, yelling. I couldn't calm her down. I called my boss, Ross Johnson, and we decided she'd be okay alone for a half hour. She had two dead bolts, barred windows, and a panic button by her bed. All she had to do was press it. I drove to the store, bought her a bottle and some smokes. When I got back..." he gestured at the gawking crowd. Lots of somber, yet curious faces. "I wasn't gone more than forty minutes. What happened?"

The cop shrugged. "Stick around. Detective Zoloski will want to talk with you."

Anderson's mouth tightened as the cop retreated inside.

Around me people murmured, cops questioned neighbors. A

woman said she'd heard screams and called the cops. A man echoed her. Another man, an older, skinny guy whose profile seemed familiar, said he'd seen her door ajar and gone inside. He sounded like shock had set in. "There was so much blood I knew she was dead. I got out fast."

Good, maybe he hadn't trampled the evidence. Was he a suspect too?

I touched Anderson's arm to get his attention. "Sunny was stabbed," I said quietly, questions lining up in my head. Did he know about Mac? How much had Sunny told this guy? "I was a friend of hers. Did she say why she hired you?"

He sized me up for a moment and after I offered my name, said, "Some joker's been sending her threatening notes."

My stomach clenched.

I heard my name and turned. Zoloski sidled up alongside, slipped his arm around my waist. He nodded at the bodyguard, flashed him a I'll-talk-to-you-in-a-minute look, and escorted me a few paces away. "I'm going to be here awhile. I'll have one of my men take you home."

I wanted to say no, but the look in Zoloski's eyes said "no compromises." I nodded.

"I'll call." He squeezed my fingers, then handed me off to a uniformed cop and turned to Anderson. Did I look like a football?

MY FLAT FELT stuffy, but I wasn't about to open any windows—even on the second floor. I didn't consider Old Joe, my landlord, to be much protection. From what I'd seen over the last five years, he slept in front of the television all day.

I put on a pot of coffee and reshuffled my notes. My insides were shaky and every little creak snapped my gaze up from the kitchen table. Nothing I reviewed held an answer to the question sizzling like white lightning in my brain. Had Mac murdered Sunny? Or was it a coincidence—a robbery or something?

Not a big believer in coincidence, I retrieved my baseball bat, took it with me to the couch, turned on a late-night flick, and promptly fell asleep. The phone rang at a quarter after six, nearly throwing me into heart arrest.

"Blaize?" Zoloski sounded like his adrenalin had run out.

I tried to focus my eyes as well as my thoughts. "Hi, Z-man. You caught me napping."

"Z-man? How about Stephanos?"

I envisioned a tired smile on his face. "'Fraid you're stuck with Zoloski or Z-man, for now."

A pause. "I need to come over."

Cop talk for Q and A. While I waited, I pulled out some hazelnut coffee beans from the freezer and filled the grinder. As it whirled, so did my thoughts. I felt queasy, my senses on overload. What the hell was I going to say about Sunny and the past? Wing-it?

Fifteen minutes later Zoloski rapped on my door, the sunrise an angry splash of red and orange behind him. He looked fried as he sagged onto my blue couch and closed his eyes. I went to get coffee and when I returned he was asleep. I let him doze alongside my baseball bat as I redistributed the clutter in my apartment.

My shoulders slowly relaxed as the minutes passed and I put things away. Every now and then I glanced at Zoloski. He looked quite loveable stretched out on the couch. I shook off that thought and strayed into the kitchen. Breakfast-time passed, but for once in my life the thought of food was nauseating. I started in on the Tupperware clutter hidden in the cupboards.

He caught me at it. "Thanks for letting me catch a few z's. You okay?"

Just startled out of my skin. "A-okay." I shoved the rest of the plastic behind the door, thinking how much I'd love a cigarette. I nuked coffee instead and joined him at the table. We sipped in silence. When I reached the bottom of the cup, Zoloski straightened, and I saw questions coming. I straightened, too.

"I talked to Anderson, Sunny's bodyguard. Did Sunny drink a lot?"

I shrugged. "We weren't bosom buddies, Zoloski. I hadn't seen or talked to her for—" my mind estimated, "twelve years, at least. She called last week, said she wanted to see me." I closed my eyes. I'd walked away.

"About what?" Zoloski's tone was gentle. Coaxing.

"She showed me some threatening letters she'd received since coming back to Sacramento. She was frightened. I told her to go to the police. She didn't want to. Wanted me to recommend a bodyguard. I gave her a number of someone who could help."

"Your old boyfriend, Ross Johnson?"

"Yes. You talked to him?"

A nod that made me uneasy. Before I could ask what Ross told him, he said, "What did the notes say?"

I shuddered. "Did you find them?"

Zoloski didn't answer. "What did they say?"

"They said he hadn't forgotten her." My voice sounded small. Damn, I hated that. "That he would see her after the performance." My stomach knotted. I clutched my coffee cup like a life preserver.

"Did she say who he is?" Zoloski pressed.

I would have given anything to avoid this conversation, but something in me refused to run. "*We* called him Mac. Wasn't his real name."

He blinked in surprise. "You knew him, too?"

"You could say that."

He jotted something in his note pad.

I sighed when he looked up, face expectant. "We ran into him when we were in high school. He must have been thirty, thirty-five. Old to me back then." Memories trapped the air in my lungs.

"Where'd you meet him?"

I felt like I was in a speeding car and going over a cliff. "At a show we were rehearsing. He was part of the production crew. Somebody you say hi to, but don't really notice."

"A show?"

"Sunny and I danced in high school. We performed at local schools, universities. We belonged to a jazz dance troupe. This show was for charity. We rehearsed on weekends for a couple of months, then performed it downtown."

"Did he live downtown?"

"Somewhere around D Street, I think."

His silence prodded me. I took a deep breath, words rushing from my gut. "After the last performance, there was a cast party. At the producer's home. Sunny and I weren't sure of the address. Mac offered to direct us in exchange for a lift from his place. We picked him up at his apartment. He shared it with somebody, his girlfriend, I think. She wasn't around."

As if he knew what was coming, Zoloski said, "I'm sorry I have to put you through this, Blaize."

Yeah, nothing like the wringer to douse a potential romance. I shrugged like it didn't matter. "We went to the party. Both of us got plastered. Liquor wasn't something I had around my house, Sunny's either. She threw up and the producer kicked us out. Mac needed a ride home, so he drove us back to his place in Sunny's parents' car. She threw up again all over the back seat."

My own nightmare unfolded with each word and I wanted to disappear just as I'd wanted to fifteen years ago. "Mac gave me paper towels, soapy water and offered to make a pot of coffee while I cleaned up Sunny's car. All I could think about was how pissed her parents were going to be. I scrubbed the seats until all I could smell was disinfectant.

"When I went back inside it was dark, except for the kitchen light. I saw the untouched pot of coffee, and Sunny's filthy shirt on the kitchen counter. I called her name. Then I heard noises in the bedroom. Sort of a muffled scream. God, I was so scared! My head hurt and I wanted to vomit. But I just stood there, in the living room, frozen. Mac came out of the bedroom. Naked. A knife in his hand. I was terrified, but if I ran I'd leave Sunny."

I paused for breath, wanting to stop. I couldn't look at Zoloski's face. "He was smooth, told me how much he liked me, how much he'd wanted me from the first moment he'd seen me dance. All the while, he kept patting the knife on his thigh, the threat there. He dragged me to the floor and yanked down my jeans."

Zoloski touched my hand and I flinched. He gripped harder as if to reassure me.

I stared at the table, my mouth frozen shut, struck by an Antarctic blizzard. I felt empty as the tin man, my jaw in need of oil. I licked my lips, cleared my throat. I had to finish. "I was a virgin, Zoloski. Sixteen."

Zoloski's hand warmed mine, an encouragement.

"When it was over, Mac hauled me toward the kitchen, where he had some rope. I was so damned scared I couldn't move—even when I realized he wasn't finished." I closed my eyes trying to blot out the memory of that paralyzing fear. Fear I could still taste like iron on my tongue.

"What happened next?"

"Heels on the stairs." My ears strained all over again for the loud clicks, and the rustle of a grocery or shopping bag, then the jingle of keys.

I shuddered with remembered relief. "He shoved the rope and knife in a drawer, then threw my clothes at me, grabbed Sunny and threw us out the back door. Sunny was still drunk, semi-conscious, blood on her legs. That was when I realized he'd raped her, too." I paused, feeling queasy. My shoulders and neck had never felt so tight. I had the inane thought that if I were a guitar my strings would snap.

Zoloski gently released my hand, wrote in his notebook, and sipped his coffee, his professional calm helpful.

"We made it to the car. I drove home. I was terrified, could hardly believe what had happened. I called Sunny's parents in the morning and told them she had spent the night. They didn't question me. She often spent the night at my house after a late rehearsal.

"The next day I could barely walk. Sunny, too. We never told anyone what happened. I quit performing after that. But we saw each other at school. Mac the Knife became a sick joke between us. A bond I couldn't break, despite the fact she continually lied about me to guys I liked, stole from me and treated me like dirt. When I went to college, I heard she'd moved down south to LA."

Zoloski was writing again, his dark hair shadowing his forehead before he unconsciously brushed it back.

I felt hung out to dry and so alone. Wounded. The rawness seemed more than I could bear. I imagined myself a stoic piece of granite, impervious to pain. I needed a cigarette.

Zoloski looked up. "So, since you graduated, you hadn't seen her until last week?"

"You got it, doc. The full skinny."

An awkward pause followed. "And you never reported what happened?"

The quiet words made me sick again. I shook my head. I'd gone into psychology to work through all this—then done my best to forget Mac. Because of my food issues, I'd focused on counseling recovering addicts. I'd thought Mac was buried forever.

"Did he ever say what he intended to do with the rope, or the knife?"

I shook my head again.

"Did you ever tell anyone?"

"In therapy while working on my Ph.D." I shrugged. "I told Maria I'd been raped, but not the circumstances."

His hand rested briefly on mine. "Could you identify him?"

"All I remember are eyes like pale blue marbles," I said softly. "I'd never really looked at him, you know? And that night—I was trying *not* to look."

"I know this is tough for you, Blaize."

His tone wasn't patronizing, yet it angered me. How could he know what rape was like? He was male, just like Mac.

"Chances are this guy's done time during the last fifteen years. I'd like you to look at the mug books."

I didn't tell him I thought it a waste of time. I just nodded wearily. I felt numb, so tired that I wanted to sink into the floor.

"You need to sleep." Zoloski had me up and in his arms before I could protest it was only the afternoon. He put me into bed fully dressed, pulled the blankets over my shoulders, and turned out the light. "I'll be back later."

Darkness seeped into my consciousness as my head sank against the pillow. The floodgates opened and memories I'd banished for fifteen years filled my mind. I dozed in a land of nightmares, shame, and quicksand.

Chapter 7

I AWOKE TO the smell of bacon and eggs. Rolled over, sat up, and stared at my antique footboard. I grabbed my baseball bat. "Zoloski?" I rasped, my mouth like dry toast. I glanced out the bedroom door, could see Zoloski sitting at the kitchen table with a cup of coffee and newspaper. I set down the bat.

He looked up, smiled, then said, "Needed your key to lock the door when I left. Brought it back. Hope you don't mind scrambled eggs for dinner."

Well, my tale of Mac hadn't scared him away. I felt a strange mix of relief and disappointment. "I'll be out in a second." I stripped, took a three-minute shower, ran a brush through my hair, slapped on some mascara and threw on a subdued gray tunic and leggings.

Zoloski gave me an eye-tour as I entered the room. "How come when I sleep in my clothes, I wake up looking like a dirty old man."

I smiled, thinking he looked handsome, trustworthy, comfortable in his own skin—all appealing traits.

He touched my hand briefly, then moved to the stove. "Coffee?"

"Yes," I said with sudden enthusiasm. He looked damned good standing in my kitchen. A flutter of nervousness broke out in my stomach. Too good to be true? I pushed the thought down.

After a fantastic meal that would take me a month to work off, his tone became personal. "I'd like to spend some time with you, but right now it's kinda hit and miss. Can I stop by tomorrow?"

I hesitated, wondering if he had any sneaky expectations lined up behind the request. So far he'd done nothing to earn my distrust—still... "I thought cops never took time off until they caught their man."

His expression was watchful, but kind, the look of a very

patient man. "That's why it's hit and miss." His gaze warmed. "I'll call first."

"What about the case? Your boss?"

His mouth tightened. "Let's just take this one day at a time, okay?"

"Okay," I said, certain his boss didn't know and wondering how long he expected to hide our relationship. I started to ask.

He leaned over and kissed me lightly. "You need to check out the mug-books."

"Can't wait."

THE POLICE STATION was only five minutes from my place. I hadn't studied mug shots since I'd surprised a burglar in my flat two years before. Looking for Mac's watery blue eyes made this experience ten times worse.

Hours after staring at unappealing faces, I closed the final book with a thud of fatigue and failure. As I sat back, I began to feel guilty; I hadn't thought about Connie Donovan in twenty-four hours. I had planned to see Gordon Whitman. Eyeing Zoloski, I wondered if he knew about the state legislator's connection to Connie. Should I ask? Not yet.

Zoloski extended a cup of freshly brewed, black as night, machine vendor coffee. The first sip gagged me, the second burned a path of destruction all the way to my stomach.

"No luck?" he asked.

I shook my head and regretted it immediately as a headache stabbed between my eyes. My brain expanded to the edges of my skull, threatening to explode.

Zoloski took me home, gave me a neck-rub that turned into some light touchy-feely. He left before we progressed to heavy panting. I fell asleep on the couch.

The shrill ring of the phone jerked me back to consciousness. I rolled off the couch, banged my knee and elbow and sat up, cursing as sharp pain shot up my arm. Whoever nicknamed the elbow "funny bone" had a sick sense of humor. I reached for the sound, the apartment pitch black. My eyes found the VCR clock. Seven a.m. My answering machine picked up before I could find the receiver.

Maria's confused voice echoed from the kitchen. "Blaize? I heard about your friend. I'm sorry." A pause. "Have you found out anything about Connie's killer?" Another pause. Tears. A sob. "I'll be at the office all day." She sniffed. "You've got a stack of mail. Some of it looks personal."

Her voice wrenched my heart. Wonderful. This was Sunday, I told myself. Day of rest and all that stuff. I felt like an emotional basket case, caught in a manic-depressive cycle of Zoloski-highs and Maria-lows, hardly equipped to talk to her.

I got in the shower, heard the phone ring again and swore. Curiosity won over inconvenience. Dripping at a fast run into the kitchen, I fumbled the receiver like a football, finally got it to my ear. It was Zoloski.

"Do you realize what time it is?" I asked, not quite masking my irritation. A puddle of water was spreading at my feet.

"Yeah, but I figured after so much sleep you'd be up." He seemed unaffected by my tone. "Besides, I wanted to catch you before you left. Thought I'd swing by for lunch. Sound okay?"

"Lunch?" Although a part of me tingled at the idea of spending time with him, another part spewed second thoughts like a volcano. Along with the lava flowed guilt: I should forget lunch and work, I should find Connie's killer, see clients, make money, pay bills. *Shoulds* ran deep in my veins and kept me in the company of safe men like Ted Koppel, Jay Leno—all sealed behind a picture tube. The biggest risk in life was not to risk at all—how many times had I told a client that?

Oh, hell. "What time?" I avoided using his name. Zoloski sounded impersonal, yet I wasn't sure how my mouth would handle Stephanos.

"Eleven-thirty."

I told him I'd be at home. I slipped into a pair of slacks, tugged a green short-sleeve blouse over my head and brushed on some mascara. While looking at my clear skin, I had the happy realization I hadn't smoked in days. Wow!

Ready for lunch three hours early, I picked up the phone, called Ross, said as little as possible and managed to get Anderson's phone number. Unfortunately, he had nothing more to add to what I already knew. Let Zoloski handle Sunny's murder investigation, a part of me whispered as I hung up. Another part worried I'd be dead if I waited too long. I made a few more calls, paid some bills, and debated with myself until the Z-man knocked on my door and called my name. Then Sunny vanished from my mind in a flurry of hormones. Dressed in a light tweed jacket and twill slacks, Zoloski looked ready for anything. Was I?

The first thing he did was thank me for the Q and A notes of my interview with the quarterback. His thanks ended inside the door with a deep kiss that turned my insides to quivering hot mush. He swept me into the kitchen, plunked down two huge hamburgers from the mom and pop place on Twelfth and handed me mine. "Got everything on the side for you so you can build your own."

The air sizzled between us. I concentrated on creating my perfect hamburger, tangy catsup, fresh tomato and lettuce. My taste buds sang.

This guy's too perfect, I thought. Too gorgeous. Too everything. I swallowed the last of my burger and mumbled something about the cool weather, about my landlord, about running errands.

"You nervous?"

I hesitated and he read my face.

"I know what I want, Blaize," he said softly. "But I'm in no hurry. It's just lunch." He winked. "I have to get back to work."

Those words drew me to him even more.

At the door, Zoloski grinned, the skin around his eyes crinkling with warmth. "Come over for a late dinner?" he asked.

"What time?" I asked, suddenly sober, wondering where this relationship would end.

He tilted my chin up with his fingers, saying, "Nine-ish," before brushing his lips across mine. "I'd like you to stay—for dessert."

His arms wrapped around me, but that flutter of panic hit again. It had taken me two therapists and twice as many years to work through enough emotional baggage so that I wasn't plagued by nightmares. Then I'd met Ross. He'd been a good lover—taken me and sex into a new threshold. He'd been wonderful—as long as there were no strings, no expectations, and an abundance of female attention—like a woman every night of the week. I shut off my negative thoughts and focused on Zoloski. He kept breaking the mold I wanted him in. I said in a half-teasing tone, "What did you have in mind?"

He kissed me softly. "Whatever you're ready for."

That night, it turned out I could handle holding and touching. He snuggled like a pro.

WE MANAGED to avoid talk of work and murder until morning. How I hated Mondays!

Relaxed, feeling a glow of happiness I had rarely experienced, I showered, dressed, passed by coffee perking, and found Zoloski on the patio. The Z-man's gaze was riveted to the gloom and doom section of the newspaper. Wordlessly he handed it over.

Sunny's picture looked pretty good. The brief story described her death as the probable result of a burglary gone wrong. The bodyguard wasn't mentioned. Detective Zoloski was, with the habitual "no comment at this time." The article didn't reveal anything new, except who Sunny had been married to, and divorced from. A Hollywood producer. Was that where her money had come from?

I set the article down, studying Zoloski. Although my heart called him Stephanos, my tongue was slow to change. Labels stick with me. "You keeping Mac the Knife's threats a secret?"

He hesitated, then gave me a nod.

I crossed my legs, tried for nonchalance. "What do you think happened?"

"I'd rather not speculate." His tone said back off.

I held up my hands. "Hey, I'm just brainstorming here."

His gaze was wary.

"Look, if Mac killed Sunny I have a vested interest!"

He frowned. "Stick to counseling and let us handle this."

Power struggle time. "I'm not quitting until Maria fires me."

His eyes narrowed and I realized I hadn't told him about Maria and Gordon Whitman. Damn! I extracted my foot and explained, watching uncomfortably as his lips compressed more and more.

His eyes remained unfathomable green pools. With a slight edge in his tone, he thanked me for the information.

I wondered if he was going to throw obstructing justice or

some other threat at me to shut me down. When he didn't, I said, "Do you know anything about Whitman?"

Zoloski shrugged, but seemed to follow my drift. "You really think he'd do that to his own kid?"

The remark surprised me coming from a cop. "Shit, Zoloski. You know people do sick stuff to their kids all the time. He might not even know he's her father."

He didn't argue, but his expression said he wasn't buying.

"Can't you at least check him out?" I asked.

"If you promise to stay out of it."

"I'm not asking you to not do your job," I said.

"And I'm asking you to stick to your Ph.D."

"Let's just leave each other's jobs out of the equation."

He didn't look happy with my solution, and surprised me by asking, "So what about tonight?"

"Are you asking for another date?"

"Only if I escape from work at a decent hour. Dinner?"

Heat crawled up my neck. "You don't have to bribe me." I smiled. "But since I hate to cook..."

"Whatever happened to: the way to a man's heart?"

I leaned over and brushed my lips across his. He pulled me onto his lap and I slid my arms around his neck. "I've been told there are other methods," I said.

"Yeah?" The word came out husky. "Tonight?" His hands rubbed my back while he nibbled my ear, kissed my neck.

"I don't know if I can wait that long," I breathed, loving the scent of him.

A smug look on his face, he stood, bringing me to my feet. "Patience makes the heart grow fonder, or so I've been told."

"Or forgetful."

He ran a thumb down from my ear to the hollow in my neck and grinned at whatever he saw in my face.

My legs felt like rubber.

"See you tonight, Sweetheart."

Chapter 8

I DID A quick switch with Pat, got my car back—in one piece and full of gas, thank you very much—and headed downtown. The yellow brick road to the Capitol was not just crowded, but corked. The Spotted Owl Protest had struck. Massive logging trucks clogged the lanes around the Capitol and had the entire police force directing traffic. I lost an hour getting to the nearby Ellis building, then had to flex my biceps to get a parking spot.

Thank God the steps to the Capitol were clear.

Whitman's secretary sat like a good guard dog outside his office door. Speaking on the phone, her eyes gave me the once over, then dismissed me as nobody. Before she could move, I opened Whitman's door and walked in. He too was on the phone, his face registering irritation and surprise. The guard dog followed me in, whispering furiously that I could not just walk into the assemblyman's office.

I plopped into an open chair. "Why not? I pay my taxes."

Whitman dropped the phone into its cradle.

"Should I call security?" the dog barked.

I eyed Whitman. A man in his late forties, he had perfectly styled silver-blond hair, smooth, pampered skin, and flawless teeth. His gray suit, blue silk shirt and dark blue tie spelled power. "No, I'll handle this, Joan." His easy response spoke of ego and overconfidence. I disliked him, and figured my Ph.D. wouldn't cut any mustard with this guy. He waited until the door closed to say, "I like to make appointments with my constituents."

I crossed my legs, glad to be wearing pants, as his gaze flickered where I didn't like. "I'm not a constituent, Mr. Whitman." I deliberately left off his title.

He frowned.

"I'm a private investigator," I said. Smiling, I enjoyed the shock in his eyes. Manufactured? Maybe.

"What's this about?" He drawled just a little too much.

"Connie Donovan. The girl murdered on the bike trail near here."

His eyes narrowed. "You've got five seconds to tell me what that has to do with me."

Curious, I counted to five as he glanced at his watch.

"Joan, call security," he said into his intercom.

"Sixteen years ago you seduced Professor Harold Quintera's fifteen-year-old daughter."

The pencil in Whitman's fingers snapped. His eyebrows came together in a frown, his lips a thin, angry line.

"Maria," I continued, "had a daughter which she gave up for adoption. Connie Donovan. *Your* daughter."

If he knew anything, I had to hand it to him, he didn't flinch, his eyes cold, unreadable steel marbles. But the toe of his shoe, peeking out the side of his desk, flexed, straightened, then flexed again. According to Gestalt, the man was nervous and/or upset. If he were a client I'd ask what his foot was trying to say.

Our eyes locked in a battle of unanswered questions. Who would blink first?

Eyes steady, he hit the intercom, hard. "Joan, cancel security. Everything's under control." He fixed me with a cool gaze. "If one word of this hits the papers, I'll sue your ass for everything you own!"

"Paternity can be proved, *Mr.* Whitman," I said it with a sweet smile that I hoped he found emasculating.

He leaned forward, his face suffused with blood, a vein above his right temple throbbing to a beat all its own. "What is it you want, Ms.—?"

"McCue."

"McCue," he repeated, the inflection sounding more like "bitch."

I leaned forward, eyeball to eyeball, and hammered him machine gun style. "Did you know Connie Donovan was your daughter? Did she contact you before she died? Where were you Saturday evening through Sunday morning?"

Whitman jumped to his feet and for a moment I thought he might take a swing at me. "Get out of here, Ms. McCue, and take your filthy innuendoes with you!"

Radiating a calm I didn't feel, I shrugged and left the room, not bothering to close the door. In the elevator I gripped the railing with sweaty palms. I wasn't sure what Whitman would do, but I knew he'd do something. What career politician wouldn't? I ran to my car, slid behind the wheel, pulled onto L Street, and double-parked in front of the bus depot. Several panhandlers hit me up for "spare" change and a taxi driver gave me the finger for taking his spot. Tough luck.

Ten minutes later, Whitman's car pulled out of the L Street garage and headed toward Old Sacramento. If he was late for a dental appointment I was going to be pissed. I pulled into traffic, forgetting the old CYA adage: *Cover Your Ass*.

My car suddenly jolted and swerved right as someone rammed me from behind. Son-of-a-bitch! I slammed the brakes and barely missed the car on my right.

Another jolt sent me skidding toward the intersection. With a gut-wrenching squeal, my car sideswiped a signal pole and jerked to a halt.

With shaky fingers, I unfastened my seat belt and tried to open the door. Stuck. I put my feet against it and pushed. As it popped open, I slid off the seat and onto the street. A teenager helped me up.

"You okay?" He looked as shaken as I felt.

I glanced at my car, saw the damage, and nodded. "Sure, no sweat." I felt sick. "What happened?"

"Some guy slammed into you!"

"Did you get a license number? See the driver?"

The kid shook his head. "I was too surprised. I mean, he did it on purpose. He was driving some beat up old clunker. I was behind him. At first I thought maybe his foot had slipped and he meant to hit the brake because of the light. But after he hit you, he swerved, sped up and hit you again!"

I glanced around. Rubberneckers stared back as they crept passed. I wrote down everything the young man remembered, took his name and address, then waited for the police. After giving my statement, I rode in the tow truck to my brother's repair garage, out in the boonies of Rancho Cordova.

My brother had thick, blond-streaked red hair and a cool exterior that always kept me guessing. We wore our walls differently, but they were there. Despite that, his light green eyes said he cared as he hugged me. Standing back, he shook his head, then wise-cracked, "Think you need a Sherman tank, Sis."

I had the feeling he might be right.

AT THE SENATOR Hotel office complex, I stepped into the elevator with several lawyers and politician Willie Brown. Though shorter than I expected, what he lacked in height, he made up for in charisma. He chatted with the lawyers and threw a smile my way, his white teeth flashing from the darkness of his ebony skin. I found myself smiling back. Dressed in a fantastic light blue silk suit that would have paid my monthly rent several times over, he looked sharp. He and his friends got off on the eighth floor and I continued on, feeling as though I'd moved up a notch in society.

The feeling wore off as I passed Maria's office and heard her despondent voice on the phone. Was she pretending to work? I shut the door to my office and eyed the mountain of mail on my desk. I attacked it, my thoughts still chugging uphill on Connie's case: reviewing my talks with Whitman; Connie Donovan's adopted parents, Teresa and Frank; her friend Belinda; and the high school rapist, Patrick. Where did it all lead? I wanted to narrow my suspect list down to Whitman—he'd raised my hackles. But I remembered the bad vibes Frank Donovan gave off, the thought that he was lying about the Saturday night Connie ran away. I needed to talk with him again.

After opening a phone ad for better rates, a real estate ad for better office space, and a clothing store offering better prices, I came to a blank, white envelope. *Andrea McCue* was printed above the office address in backhanded block letters. A lefty? No one came to mind. I slit open the envelope, and unfolded the letter-sized piece of stationery.

Dear Andy,
Roses are red, violets are blue,
I haven't forgotten you.
You and Sunny were special.
Thinking of you,

Mac

My heart froze, my mind refusing to accept the reality of the words. I read them again. Then again. A Kodak moment of the worst kind. The note read like one Sunny had received. Now she was dead.

With deliberate calm I knew would give way to shakiness later, I found an unused sandwich bag in my desk, shoved the note and envelope inside, and called Zoloski. He wasn't in. Never a cop when you need one! I left a message and slowly replaced the phone.

"What's wrong?"

I whirled in my chair, startled by Maria's voice behind me. She knew nothing of Sunny, or Mac, and I wanted to keep it that way. She had enough to cope with. I forced a calm note into my voice and told her I'd been in a fender bender, I was still a bit shaken from the close call. I covered Mac's note with a file. "How're you coping?"

She shrugged. "Okay." She had bags under her eyes and her olive skin looked nearly as white as mine. Her expensive, usually well-fitted clothes looked thrown on as if she'd grabbed the first available garments.

I filled her in on the investigation, trying to blot out Mac's message that kept flashing through my mind.

"What next?"

At the moment I wanted a cigarette and to be alone, to absorb the shock of Mac's note. I thought of my upcoming rematch with Frank Donovan. Thought of Whitman. "It might be better if you don't know."

She nodded slowly, as if lacking the energy to argue. "I've got a referral for you—someone from WEAVE. She said she'd call to make an appointment." The way she said it implied she didn't give a damn whether the woman called me or not. Not a good sign. She dropped a pink phone slip on my desk.

Why did I always feel like I wasn't doing enough, or hadn't done enough? I watched her go back to her office.

Stop thinking about Mac. My foot tapped a rhythm all its own as I lifted the file and stared at the note. Like a fortuneteller's crystal ball it predicted a future—instead of romance and flowers—roses and blood. Mine.

My thoughts jumbled. I'd thought of calling Connie's previous counselor, hadn't I? The woman whose professional ethics revolved around the dollar sign. She'd be thrilled to hear from a peachy keen associate like me. I got her answering machine. Hot damn. Another confrontation to look forward to.

I finished my mail, nothing else remotely threatening, except to my pocketbook, then took out Mac's letter and read it again. The stark black ink against the snow white paper seemed unreal. I could almost hear Mac's whisper, "Roses are red, violets are blue, I've never forgotten you," in the same foreboding voice he'd used fifteen years ago. Was this how Sunny felt? Had it taken two more letters to prod her into action?

How would Zoloski react if I butted into his second murder investigation? He'd been desperate for leads or he'd never have accepted my help with Connie Donovan, but Sunny too? I thought about the curious onlookers the morning of Sunny's murder, the soft murmur of voices. Zoloski had a list of neighbors. Had he talked to them? Had anybody noticed anyone suspicious?

Sure, like a guy with pale blue eyes and a butcher knife?

I had a gun, but depending on my .32 was a risk. I glanced at the letter again, thought of Sunny's death, the bodyguard's failure, and Zoloski's words, "she was stabbed a lot." I'd never had to shoot someone and I didn't want to now, but then again, if it was Mac... I stuffed the pistol into my already over-full leather bag. A concealed weapon can be trouble, my mind nagged. So could Mac.

The phone rang. I half-expected to hear Mac's voice following up on his love letter. Zoloski caught me off guard. He was doing that a lot. "Blaize. You called. The message says urgent." His tone was worried.

"I'm at my office, at the Senator Hotel." Suddenly my inner shakiness wobbled into my voice. "I got a death threat from Mac."

Dead silence.

"It's a letter, like Sunny's."

"Jesus, Blaize. You all right?"

No, I was scared. "Never been better," came out instead.

"Oh, yeah?" He paused, and I heard him talking to someone in the background. He came back on, "Bag the letter. I'll be right over. Ten minutes." More talk sounded in the background. "You've had one hell of a day and it's not even dinner time," he teased.

Despite everything, I smiled.

"Hang in there."

"Thanks." I told him I'd meet him in the lobby and the phone clicked in my ear. After dumping all the junk mail into the round file, I told Maria I was going to the bank, and left. In less than five minutes Zoloski screeched to a double-parked stop just beyond the glass doors.

In six long strides he had me wrapped in his arms. I felt safe, wished I could stay there forever, but pulled away.

"Come on." He guided me out the door. "Let's talk in the car."

I got in his Z and handed over the letter. I rolled down my window while he read. In Capital Park across the street, the cement paths were filled with walkers, joggers and government types escaping their responsibilities among the massive oaks and sycamores. My gaze lingered on the rose gardens off in the distance. The park was one of the most beautiful in the state. It all looked so green and peaceful.... Zoloski was talking and I tried to refocus. "What?"

"...a couple of days to analyze the letter, check for prints, and analyze the paper and ink..." His voice dropped off.

My expression must have read scared because he pulled me closer. "It'll be all right, Blaize. You're not alone."

For once I had no breezy comeback. The circle of his right arm was enough.

His lips brushed my hair. "I've still got to work Connie Donovan's case." His tone was firm, yet gentle.

I sat up straight.

"I need to talk to Maria Quintera again," he continued. When I didn't answer, he added, "She was uncooperative before. If you could get her to open up..."

"She doesn't put much faith in cops," I said. "But I'll try."

"Thanks."

"She doesn't know my car smash wasn't an accident and she doesn't know about Mac."

Zoloski scowled. "I thought you said some jerk didn't see the light and hit you from behind."

Uh-oh, I should have told him. "I'm sorry. I didn't want you to worry."

He touched my face gently, but was obviously pissed. "Don't lie to me, Blaize. For whatever reason. If I can't trust you then our relationship doesn't mean shit."

Relationship? I wasn't sure I wanted one. "I'm sorry," I repeated. "It wasn't that big a deal. I'm fine."

"What *is* a big deal with you?" he shot back.

I swallowed. "Mac. You."

He hugged me, but I could feel his head shake as he stroked my hair. "Damn it, Blaize, you scare me."

I sat up and we eyed each other. "I'll talk to Maria, tell her not to hold back." I gave him my A-number-one-shrink-knows-all warning look. "Be gentle."

"Hey, she's the one with nails." His tone said: I know what I'm doing, don't tell me how to do my job.

I'd probably react the same way if he told me how to counsel addicts in recovery, but I had to work to make it go down. We were on touchy ground emotionally, and I wondered if I shouldn't back off.

We rode up the elevator in silence and he followed me into the suite. Maria frowned as I led Zoloski into her office. "I told Detective Zoloski you were Connie's natural mother," I said, feeling a flush of embarrassment. "He needs your help, Maria." She started to protest and I cut her off, "The police are on your side, here. They have more resources than I do. You can trust him." I shut my mouth and backed out. Zoloski closed the door behind me. Thanks a lot.

The temptation to listen made my attention stray from the consultant files I needed to review and update. Boring. But Zoloski kept his voice low and Maria's was naturally soft, so all I could hear were indistinct murmurs. I read over the file in front of me, jotted a few notes about the final report I needed to send out, yawned, then heard the door open.

Zoloski came out, his expression calm. I glimpsed Maria at her desk. She looked fine. Dying of curiosity, I accompanied Zoloski to the lobby, but he said she hadn't told him anything I didn't already know. "It's nearly five o'clock. I've got a couple more hours to put in." His dark eyes asked if I had something that would keep me safe and out of trouble.

Phone calls, I thought. A counseling session. Quarterly taxes.
Filing. Double yawn.

"You want me to pick you up here around seven?"

"I need to rent a car. Would you mind if we stopped at a place
on Fulton before dinner?"

He gave me a sideways grin. "You never stop, do you?"

"Do you?" I countered.

"I'm a patient guy. Good things take time." His bedroom eyes
sparkled mischievously.

"Sometimes perseverance isn't enough," I said. But this time it
was. I wanted more than holding and touching as I looked at him.
The molecules between us zapped with sexual tension.

His gaze held mine. "Is that why you're so ready to rush into
things?"

I thought about the past week. I'd gone from Zoloski on the
phone to Stephanos in bed, but nothing was being rushed in *that*
department. "Some things," I said, imitating his crooked grin.

"Including your interview with Whitman?" he asked seriously.

"How did you know?"

"Whitman complained of harassment to a friend and I got
whiff of it."

"So why aren't you browbeating me?"

"You're a psychologist, used to reading people. I figured you
might have got something out of him."

I felt a flurry of childish pleasure at the compliment. "I got him
angry, and he denied fathering Connie, but about lost it when I
mentioned paternity could be proven. Other than the fact I didn't
like him, I didn't get much."

He raised an eyebrow as though he didn't agree. His
expression softened.

"What are you thinking, Zoloski?"

He winked.

I grinned. Here I was standing in the lobby of the Senator
Hotel, the place where lobbying first began, thinking wild sexual
thoughts and liking it.

"I was thinking about you. In my bed..." He touched my
shoulders. "I'd like you there again tonight." His green, green eyes

questioned, promised, hoped.

"Skin-to-skin?"

He leaned over and whispered, "I want to make love to you." He kissed my neck, sending shivers down my spine. "If you're ready."

"Zoloski?"

He nibbled my ear. "If you call me Zoloski one more time, I'm going to drive you straight to my place and give you a little more practice with Stephanos."

God, how could I be doing this after my car had been wrecked and my life threatened? "Stephanos!" I squeaked. I pushed him toward the front entrance, grinning wickedly.

I watched him swagger across the lobby, drooled a little at the tight muscles I knew lay underneath his "detective" outfit, then regrouped. I had work to do.

Whitman had obviously wanted to make a point—if he was responsible for my collision. But I didn't think he wanted to kill me. Maybe after my next visit—but next time I'd have my trusty .32.

And Frank Donovan? If I jerked his chain a little, what would rattle out?

And then there was Darla Pike, aka Madame Medusa, Connie's counselor. She might be coerced into telling me something useful.

Lastly, there were the people at Sunny's apartment complex. That was where Zoloski was focusing his time. Did he know something I didn't?

I couldn't believe how optimistic I felt. Zoloski was as good an influence on me as Lon, and the Z-man wasn't gay. Wonders never cease.

In that frame of mind, I counseled a recovering addict I'd been seeing for six months, and nudged him with the idea he might be ready to quit therapy. Then I worked on my tax forms until Zoloski rescued me. When he told me he wanted to assign an officer to follow me around, I said no—persuaded him to wait a few days. The idea of being watched by anyone did not appeal. When I told him I wanted to pursue a few leads after dinner, he surprised me by agreeing. I couldn't tell if he meant it. His dark green eyes regarded me with the same intensity as always and his after-dinner kiss in the parking lot was hot, exciting, and made me want to reconsider. Yet he didn't invite me again, or push. Just gave me a slow smile that made my insides melt. Then he drove off into the sunset. Too late, I realized he'd avoided my questions about Sunny's neighbors, and her autopsy. Damn, he was better at sidestepping than me!

WITH MY ADRENALIN up and a set of wheels under my butt, I hit Frank Donovan's house. Teresa was staying with her mother, he said, and we had the house to ourselves. Oh joy. I followed him into the smoke-filled living room, the TV blaring baseball. He switched it off. I inhaled deeply.

Before the fumes could knock me down, I attacked. "You lied to me about why Connie ran away."

He ran his fingers through his dark hair, his face tight. "I don't know what you're talking about." His eyes said otherwise.

"Look, if you want to find your daughter's killer, then give it to me straight. Or I'm off the case."

He hiked an eyebrow. "You wouldn't do that to Maria."

"Oh yeah?" I challenged.

"Shit." The fight left him. His shoulders sagged. "Most of what I told you was true. Teresa and I were drunk and fighting. But it wasn't over Connie's adoption. It was over an affair I'd been having."

"So, Connie heard it and left the house?"

He fidgeted like he had ants in his pants. "Not right away. She came into our bedroom. Teresa was crying, throwing things in a suitcase, calling me a liar," he shrugged, "among other things. I tried to tell her to shut up, this wasn't something Connie needed to hear, but she wouldn't stop yelling. Suddenly Connie was screaming."

Frank looked sad. "I don't know who was more surprised, Teresa or me. Connie never yelled. God, ever since that boy—she'd been so quiet. I could see she was furious, thought it was because of what I'd done. But when Teresa called me a liar again, Connie interrupted. I'll never forget the way she looked, as if she'd been waiting a lifetime to throw her knowledge in our faces. And this was it. 'Quit calling him a liar!' she yelled. 'You've both lied to me all my life!'"

Frank paced around the living room, then stopped to light another cigarette. "She ran out." He sagged into the easy chair. "That's the last time I saw her. My God..." his eyes teared up, but none fell. Instead he sucked harder on his cigarette, regained control, then glanced at me.

My mouth watered for nicotine. "So, she knew about her adoption. Did she give any indication about how long she'd known?"

He shook his head.

I thanked him, left him sitting there, alone in his empty house. Did Connie know Maria was her natural mother, Gordon Whitman her father? The fact she hadn't asked indicated she did. How had she found out?

I found a pay phone and called Belinda Bowers. She didn't sound thrilled to hear my voice. "You said Connie called you the night she ran away. That she wanted a place to stay."

"Yes." A quiver sounded in her answer.

"She told you she'd been adopted, didn't she?"

"Yes," she whispered.

I sensed relief.

"I swore to Connie I would never tell."

"Did she know who her parents were?" I waited with a sick gnawing deep in my gut. Had Maria told Connie? Or had Connie found out the truth elsewhere? Either way, Whitman was looking more suspicious. I thought of the matchbook from Frank Fat's I'd found in Connie's closet.

Finally, Belinda answered, "Yes. She told me."

"Damn it, Belinda. Connie's been murdered!" I let my harsh tone sink in, then added, "Did she say who they were?"

"Yes."

I was getting tired of one-word replies. "Who?"

"Her aunt, Maria. And some councilman. I don't remember his name."

"Did she say where she was going that night?"

"Someplace near the river. To look for her father. That's what she said."

My pulse quickened. I thought of Connie's clothes, which had never been found. Where were they? Was that where Whitman was headed when I'd been rammed? "Did Connie give you any clue as to where that place was? Could it have been a boat?"

"No." She coughed. "I don't know. Maybe." A pause. "I wrote everything down I could remember about that night and mailed it to you yesterday." I heard the unshed tears.

"Thanks for your help, Belinda." I hung up and checked my watch. Ten o'clock.

I felt torn between Zoloski and taking another crack at Whitman. I rolled the dice in my head and opted for Zoloski, still not quite Stephanos in my mind. Knowing I should go home and not doing it felt wonderfully wicked.

The grin he gave me at his door was wonderfully wicked as well.

Skin-to-skin, making love had never felt so good.

Chapter 9

ZOLOSKI AND I started off Tuesday morning like the weather: overcast and gloomy. Dressed for work, we sat across from each other at his kitchen table while the coffee bubbled and hissed its way into the pot. "I want you to stick to counseling," he said after I told him about my interview with Frank Donovan.

Did he think great sex meant he could tell me what to do?

At my mutinous silence his voice rose. " This isn't a long lost love you're looking for, or a divorce case for an angry spouse looking to prove infidelity. You're out of your league, Blaize.

"Maria hired me. I'm not quitting."

"The guy's a killer."

"I can take care of myself."

"Damn it! I'm telling you to drop it!"

I didn't like his tone or the way his palm slapped the table. In a huff of mixed emotions, I headed for the door and drove off in my rental wreck. He didn't come after me. I made it several miles before my left brain kicked in. Being vulnerable and making love sets off a chain reaction of fear and withdrawal in me that takes a while to overcome. I shouldn't have left. Obviously he had his own fears or we wouldn't have yelled at each other. Funny how sex— even great sex—didn't replace communication. Why did I need a kick in the butt to remind me? I pulled over and used my cellular.

Zoloski had it on the first ring. "Yeah?"

"Stephanos?" I said, hoping he wouldn't hang up.

"Blaize? Damn it, why'd you run out?"

I dug for an honest answer. "I was afraid you'd talk me out of what I'm doing."

"Damn it," he sounded really frustrated. I could almost see his frown. "Would you come back so we can talk this out? I'm sorry I blew up. The more you said, the more worried I got. You're looking for a murderer."

"So are you!" My voice jumped to a medium yell.

I could hear his breathing. "Please come back." The pain in his voice caught me off guard, wrenched my heart.

"Five minutes." I hung up.

He was standing outside the front door, his tie askew, his shirt sleeves rolled up. Rain drizzled off his front porch, smelling sweet. We hugged and he drew me inside. The next thing I knew we were kissing. Breathless, I stopped the progression.

"You've got to trust me," I said. "With this case, and in our relationship. I'm not your ex-wife."

His eyes flashed pain. The great motivator. He had been divorced two years, gone to counseling, and had made great strides from the man he told me he had once been. But his wife had betrayed him, and I could see it would be an issue between us. I worked odd hours according to my clients needs, wasn't used to reporting to anyone, and wasn't about to have my whereabouts questioned.

He poured coffee.

"Aren't you late for work?" I took a sip. Chocolate mint, the way to my heart.

"I told them I'd be late." He took my hand, his touch gentle. "I'm not perfect, Blaize. I know that. Or Gina wouldn't have left for someone else." The words cost and I knew it.

"Let's just take it one day at a time, okay, Zoloski?"

He brought my hand to his lips. "What was that?"

"Stephanos!" I squealed, and a moment later we were on the floor, laughing our heads off. Lying on top, I yanked playfully in his tie, then pushed myself up. "I have to go."

He glanced at the wall clock. "Me too. When can I see you again?"

"How about when you get Sunny's autopsy report?" I immediately regretted my flippant tone.

Scowling, he held my shoulders. "Is that what this is all about? Getting information?"

Where was the pill for foot-in-mouth disease? I shook my head. "No." I swallowed. "Maybe it started that way, but not now."

Better not be, his eyes warned, but his tone was teasing, "First Connie Donovan's report, now Sunny. I knew I should have turned and run the minute I saw you." He kissed me lightly.

"Why didn't you?"

He grinned. "Maybe I like a little trouble. Maybe I wanted to know what *you'd* found out. Save some overtime."

I punched his arm, and after a few more lines of comic relief, I promised I would call that night, then ran to my wreck. As I cruised down Antelope's triple lane speed trap, I had the sudden, scalp tingling sensation of being watched. I slowed. Cars passed. No car behind remained consistently there. Still, the name Mac the Knife kept popping into my head like a jack-in-the-box. Did he know where I lived? Did he know about Zoloski?

I stepped on the accelerator and the big boat lurched forward. The light was green, the lane clear. In seconds I was on the freeway. I got off at Madison Avenue, still watching my rearview mirror and seeing nothing out of the ordinary. The blue and white line of the Sierra Nevada loomed in the distance. I shrugged off my apprehension and headed toward Fair Oaks, a quaint village beneath ancient oaks, now sucked into the burbs of Sacramento, and infused with new money. Driving past Bridge Street and the river made me remember crazy childhood days of swimming in the rapids, walking across the mud flats, jumping off the bridge. Playing with fire. Was I still playing? I shrugged off the question and parked.

Darla Pike's counseling office could have come from the set of Hansel and Gretel. The waiting area was empty. The receptionist's smile melted into a scowl when I said who I was and what I wanted.

"She's with a client," she explained. "I'm not supposed to interrupt."

I glanced at my watch. Quarter to nine. At the standard fifty-minute hour she'd be finished in five minutes. I smiled and took a seat. "I'll wait."

Darla and her client emerged ten minutes later. I ignored the client and studied Madame Medusa. Her bottle red hair was neatly arranged in chignon. She wore an expensive off-white suit with an emerald silk blouse, and long fake nails of lacquered pearl. A radiant confidence shone from her eyes until her patient left, then she turned on me, the light blue turning frigid as ice. "You've got nerve coming here."

"It's about the murder of one of your former clients," I

snapped back. "Connie Donovan."

Her expression turned wary. She opened the door to her office and gestured me inside. The last time I'd visited was to accuse her of unethical conduct. Unfortunately, I hadn't enough proof to do anything. But I knew she was guilty and so did she. She was a con artist, her clients the marks. It made me sick.

I looked ahead at the large, polished oak desk. Before it were three chairs, nicely upholstered and worth a fortune. Small tables with tissues sat beside each one. The office glared "success" and if I didn't know her, I might have liked it.

She crossed the room and sat behind her desk, left me standing. "So why are you here?"

"I'm working with the police on the Connie Donovan case," I said, hoping Zoloski wouldn't kill me for the lie.

"You have proof of that?" she sneered. "I wouldn't want to turn you in for abuse of professional ethics."

I smiled. "I still have those letters your client wrote, about your sexual advances. They may not hold up in court, but sure would sound good in the *Bee*."

Her face paled slightly. "I'll sue your ass off," she said softly.

Beside Mac's death threat it didn't sound like much. And she'd have to get in line behind Whitman. "Go ahead." I held her gaze.

She swiveled around. "Get to the point! What do you want?"

"Everything you know about Connie Donovan."

Darla opened the cabinet beside her desk, thumbed through a mass of files and removed one. She flipped it open and scanned her notes intently.

Trying to read upside down is a bitch.

After a moment, she glanced up, her lips tight, then handed me the file.

I sat down, trying to decipher her notes. Three months ago, Connie ("C") had come to see Darla about an alleged rape. Alleged! I felt like allegedly punching Darla in the nose, but read on instead. More notes on her mother ("M") who'd accompanied her, than on Connie. Her mother had talked, Connie had not. I skimmed the next page, then glanced up. "You saw her three times?"

"I believe so."

"And her mother came too?" Therapy usually consisted of the therapist and the client, not the client's mother.

Darla shrugged. "The daughter was uncommunicative, the mother was not. In fact, on the final visit, the daughter refused to come in. She stayed in the waiting room."

"What did Mrs. Donovan tell you?" I wasn't sure how much more I could squeeze out of her. Her eyebrows lifted. "Donovan?"

I felt like someone hit me with a two-by-four. "Who came in with Connie?"

"Connie never introduced the woman as her mother. Her name was different, but I figured she'd divorced."

"Her name?"

Darla took back the file and flipped to the back of the last page. Even upside down I could read, Mother: Maria Quintera.

I closed my gaping mouth. What the hell was Maria trying to pull?

"And Maria's still seeing you." I guessed.

"A live patient is a confidential matter," Darla answered with a sweet "piss-off" smile.

I didn't bother to thank her and she didn't bother to see me out.

Chapter 10

MARIA, MARIA, Maria, the song from "West Side Story" played
over and over in my brain as I drove. She wasn't at home or the
office. I walked down L Street to the Capitol and entered the
hallowed halls for the second time in as many days. Gordon
Whitman was out. His guard dog secretary said he was on vacation
with his family for a week. Her tone said she remembered me, so I
didn't try to charm her out of any information. I shrugged, headed
down the marble stairs and Frank Fat's. My mouth was watering for
the chicken salad and my brain was hoping Wing Fat would be
there. The astute watcher of Sacramento intrigue would know
Gordon Whitman and might connect him with Connie Donovan.

THE COOL, DIM atmosphere of Sacramento's most famous
watering hole always conjured dollar signs in my brain. But though
the chicken salad was excellent, it didn't dent my pocketbook too
much. My waiter, possibly a great grandson of the original Chinese
immigrant, was happy to study Connie's picture and show it to the
other staff. They collected at the sweeping, lacquered bar while I
admired the golden Buddha and spied the governor in the back
room.

A young Chinese teen remembered her. "She looked kind of
lost. That's why I noticed her." The rest of the staff moved off.

"Did she meet anyone here?"

He studied the picture some more. "There was a woman,
sitting near the door. This girl spoke to her, then sat at her own
table—alone." The boy handed back Connie's picture. "I have to
get back to work."

"One more question. Did you notice her talking with anyone
else? A man?"

His expression became thoughtful. He shook his head. "No,
but she did ask me if the legislators ate here often." He paused.

"She asked about Assemblyman Whitman."

Pay dirt! Didn't even need Wing. "Anything else?"

"I told her he usually comes in for lunch on Wednesdays."

I thanked him and left. Any other questions regarding Whitman would have been answered only if I flashed a badge. The legislators were Frank Fat's bread and butter.

My thoughts veered to Maria. She'd withheld a lot of information and I wanted to know why. Guessing was making me crazy.

I FOUND MARIA at home, her two cats peering up at me with curiosity from behind her legs. "Blaize, what are you doing here?" She sounded worried.

"Mind if I come in?" I stepped inside before she could reply. "I couldn't reach you at the office." I eyed her Aztec decor, struck by its simple beauty as I followed her into the living room. It had an open starkness with touches of color from Indian pots and weavings, and several large, framed prints. Signed, no less. Always made me want to inhale the unobtrusive perfection. A panoramic view of Folsom Lake lay beyond the windows. How much did a house like this cost? Half a million? More?

I'd worked with Maria for five years and never questioned her lifestyle. She was a lawyer. Some lawyers made lots of money, lobbyists too.

"I talked to Darla Pike."

Maria's expression tightened, her warm olive coloring fading to pearl. "She told you I was Connie's mother." She said it matter-of-fact, gesturing for me to sit.

I paced around the room, working to stay calm. "I thought it was a big secret. Frank Donovan said Connie knew she was adopted, though neither he or Teresa had told her. You did, didn't you?"

I felt a momentary pang of guilt as tears spilled over Maria's cheeks. But she'd talked me into finding the killer, then lied to me. She nodded and brushed her black hair back from her face, exposing lines of fatigue. "I told her. But not because I wanted to."

I waited—wanting to yell, "Spill it!" like the Grand High Inquisitor.

"Connie often came over, when she wanted to escape her parents. They have problems." Maria's gaze flickered toward the hall. "Last month she went through my desk, said she was looking for a pen." She threw out her arms in a hopeless gesture. "It doesn't matter now. Whatever the reason, she found some personal letters I'd written. They told her enough to figure it out." She wrung her hands.

"Can I see the letters?" I wondered if I knew her at all.

She twisted the ring on her finger. "Gordon was giving me money to keep quiet about Connie."

"*Giving* you money?"

"Okay, so I was blackmailing the son-of-a-bitch!"

I shook my head. "You lied to me, damn it! God only knows why you wanted me to investigate. I sure as hell don't!"

She yelled back, "I hired you to find Connie's killer! The blackmail is irrelevant." She swallowed. "Connie's life was worth more than I stood to lose." A strange smile crossed her lips then dissolved into nervous laughter I recognized as exhaustion. "It's so funny," she said between gasps. "Because of Gordon I had Connie, and because of Connie I had the means to squeeze him good. He couldn't risk calling my bluff." Her eyes clouded, a depressed mask descending over her face.

I suspected I was seeing the real Maria and felt sorry for her. I didn't want to be her judge or jury. We'd both been hurt sixteen years ago. "Do you think the blackmail drove Whitman to hurt his own daughter?" But why, if he'd been paying for years? Unless Maria had upped the ante.

Maria scowled. "He was capable of deserting a fifteen-year-old virgin when she became pregnant. You tell me!"

I raised my eyebrows, then mused out loud, "It would have been easier to murder you."

"Connie knew he was her father and she knew about the blackmail."

"Christ, how did you explain that?"

Indignation flared in Maria's eyes. "I asked her if she were given the chance to make that boy who raped her pay, would she take it?" Maria's eyes shone with righteous anger. "I thought you of all people would understand. I needed to *do* something. I had to get back at that bastard somehow! When he took office, I knew I had him." Her voice dropped and she twisted the fabric of her knit top between her fingers. "It wasn't the seduction I couldn't get over, Blaize. It was the fact I did nothing but wait for the baby to come. Then I gave it away as though it was nothing. For years that's how I've felt—like nothing!"

I understood more than I'd have liked. I unclenched my teeth and took a deep breath, hating bastards like Gordon Whitman and Mac the Knife. But blackmail! No wonder she didn't want the police involved. She had more than her career at stake. Where was justice? I didn't see prison as an answer or a cure. I didn't want to think about it anymore. "I'll write up a report about everything I've found out concerning Connie's murder. You can give it to the police or a PI. I'm off the case. What you do about Whitman is up to you."

Maria nodded, her mouth a line of regret, her voice tight. "Thanks, Blaize." She and her cats followed me to the door.

"You might want to find a better therapist than Darla Pike," I said in parting.

HALF A MILE down Fair Oaks Boulevard, my rental wreck started jerking like a shotgun. Bad vibes?

Zoloski wasn't at work or home, but I caught Pat at her desk. When I told her that I needed a ride home, she sighed. "I shouldn't tell you this, but I will. Zoloski got the autopsy report on Sunny Wright. It rattled him—bad. I have a feeling he's either having a drink with the guys, or sitting on your doorstep."

Chapter 11

I STRAPPED myself into Pat's banged-up Ford and waited for her to talk. Once we hit the highway 50, she looked at me sideways. "Zoloski's falling for you big time, no?"

My face felt hot. "What?"

She grinned. "He asked me about your name. I told him you were a fast runner so he better treat you right."

I kept a blank face. "You said he was upset."

Her expression clouded. "I ran into him on the stairs. He looked like he'd gotten a good kick in the balls. He'd just got the ME's report."

"What could the medical examiner have found?" I pondered aloud.

"That would make Zoloski sick?" She shook her head. "I can't imagine! You wouldn't believe some of the gross pranks he and my brother played in high school."

I held up my hands. "Don't tell me. You'll ruin his perfect image."

"Hah! You think all men are egotistical, self-centered peabrains." She laughed as we got off the freeway. "I can hardly ruin that!"

She didn't know I had the Z-man practically on a pedestal. "Is that what you told Zoloski—after you told him I run fast?"

She chuckled as she pulled in front of my place and cut the engine. "Of course not. I told him you'd be a challenge, but worth it. And you had a lot in common, if you could both get past your poor opinions of the opposite sex."

I smiled, relieved.

"Was I right?"

"Don't let it go to your head." I got out of the car and slammed the door. "Thanks, Pat. I owe you lunch."

Pat waved and wheeled her old Ford into the street. As her

taillights disappeared, someone touched my shoulder. I jumped a mile.

"It's after six, Sweetheart." Zoloski nuzzled my neck. "And I'm hungry."

"Jesus!" I exhaled, angry and relieved. "Don't sneak up on me."

He gave me a sheepish look. "Sorry."

My anger wilted. "Where have you been all my life?" My Ingrid Bergman imitation came off sounding more like Marilyn Monroe. Didn't matter. I led the Z-man upstairs. Through the window I saw Old Joe parked in front of the tube.

The dust was growing like mold inside my flat, and I needed to do something soon. Like tomorrow. I checked my answering machine, while Zoloski studied my one attempt at painting that I'd boldly hung on the dining room wall. Had he ever heard of Sylvia Plath? Did it matter?

My mother had called. She sounded depressed. What else was new? I'd call her back when I could muster up some compassion.

Zoloski turned from the painting. "So, where've you been?" In his too casual tone lay a tightness I recalled from that morning.

"I'm a grown woman, Zolos—Stephanos. I know how to use a gun. I'm well-versed in self-defense and have enough anger inside to kill any bastard that dares step through my door uninvited."

He held up his hands in a placating gesture. "I know. It's just that—"

"Did you get the autopsy report on Sunny?" I asked as if guessing.

He saw right through me. "Pat told you, huh?"

I nodded and moved to the stove, put a filter in the coffee maker. "What'd it say?" I started counting scoops of coffee.

He hesitated.

"Hey, I have a right to know. Mac's after me, too, remember?"

His words came reluctantly. "Sunny Wright was killed with a knife similar or identical to the one used on Connie Donovan."

I lost track of what number I was on and turned to look at him. From his drawn expression I knew there was more.

"In both cases there's a similar wound pattern on the chest, traces of semen, and foreign skin found under the victims nails.

They matched."

Blood roared in my ears as I turned back to the sink, in need of something to do. I filled the coffee maker and turned it on. I'd told Maria I was off the case. My gut now said no way. If Mac murdered Sunny then he murdered Connie too. A tremor caught me by surprise and I clutched the sink as the horrible thought stabbed me: could Connie be dead because of her connection to me? I didn't want to believe it.

I reached for two coffee mugs and dropped one.

Zoloski knelt and helped with the mess. "It's not your fault," he said as he dumped the pieces in the garbage.

Tears burned my eyes. I buried my head in his shoulder, feeling weak and at a loss to cope. He held me for several long moments.

I had to get to work. Take action. I shored myself with several deep inhalations, then retrieved another mug. I considered Connie's father, Gordon Whitman. I'd had no inkling, no *déjà vu* in his office. Nothing about Whitman had sparked a reaction. Although I couldn't remember Mac's face, didn't know his real name, I found it hard to believe I wouldn't have reacted to him, physically, emotionally—in some fashion—if he was Whitman. Still, I wasn't ready to abandon my prime suspect for Connie's murder. "Maybe Whitman knew Sunny. You said her door wasn't forced, right?"

"Right, but why sign the letters *Mac*?" Zoloski played devil's advocate. "Why send them?"

I sank into a chair as water sizzled in the coffeemaker. "So where does that leave us?"

Zoloski frowned at the *us*. "It leaves *me* with a big fat zero in suspects until I unearth something new."

I uncrossed my legs, then recrossed them, my brain spinning. "What did Sunny's neighbors say? What about the guy that found her body?"

Zoloski shrugged. "His name's Matthew Caldwell. An unlucky bastard, probably, but I'll talk to him and a couple of others again." He brushed his hair from his forehead. "Just to be thorough."

I got up, poured two cups of cafe mocha and sat down. "I'd like to go with you."

Zoloski inhaled the aroma and took a sip, then shook his head.

I pleaded and cajoled.

He held firm.

I gave up for the moment, took a sip of coffee and updated him on Maria. "I still think Whitman's capable of murder," I finished. I really despised that guy.

Zoloski set down his cup. "Forget it. I called his office, talked to his secretary and reviewed his schedule for the week. The night of Sunny's murder he was on his way to Los Angeles for a two-hundred-fifty-dollar-a-plate fundraiser. A thousand people can testify to his presence. He did leave early and fly directly back here, but that puts him at the extreme end of the death time frame. Whitman would've had to hit no traffic from the airport to Sunny's just to get there prior to the discovery of her body. He's a public figure. If he'd been there someone would have seen him. No one saw anyone unusual that night, except the bodyguard."

"Shit." I plowed on. "Does he have an alibi for the time Connie was murdered too?"

Zoloski shrugged. "He was at home with his family, watching TV."

"Forensics is sure the two crimes were committed by the same person?"

He nodded.

"Then if we list every person, every contact Sunny and Connie had over the last, say, three to six months, we should find a common denominator." Whitman was still on my list.

"Besides you?" Zoloski said softly.

I swallowed painfully, knowing he was doing his job, not out to hurt me. "Yes. Maybe Connie and Sunny knew each other."

Zoloski shook his head. "We'll have to look on our own time. The note Mac sent you doesn't *exactly* threaten you." His hand tightened around his coffee cup. "My boss is blowing steam about my associating with you at all. And I've got two more homicides on my desk." His gaze skidded around the room.

I shifted uncomfortably. I was next on Mac's list. "Can we go back through your old files of unsolved murders? Look for similarities? Maybe this guy has killed before."

Zoloski frowned. "I've faxed for info from other agencies. No one's responded yet." His expression said, *I hope this isn't the beginning of a roll.*

I was thinking of the knife Mac had frightened me with years ago, of the rope he'd never used, of the blessed interruption, heels clicking on the stairs.

Zoloski took a last swig of his coffee, and grabbed his coat off the back of the chair, his face reflecting determination. "You like Taco Bell?"

"Love it," I said as I slung my purse. It grazed his shoulder.

He let out a howl. "What's in that thing? A cannonball?"

I smiled. "A .32, an extra clip, some mace, pepper spray, a box of wad cutters for target practice, my wallet, tennis shoes, make-up..." Too late I realized I'd just admitted to carrying a concealed weapon.

Zoloski whistled, but a glimmer of warning lay in the back of his eyes. "Damn plane overhead drowned out your voice. You said, mace and pepper spray?"

I nodded.

He gave me a tight smile. "Just don't lose it."

I squeezed his hand. "I won't."

We took the stairs two at a time.

As I started to climb into the passenger seat of his car, I nearly sat on a white, letter-sized envelope, my name printed in block letters across the front. Zoloski saw it at the same time, had his gun out and was already searching the empty parking lot with his gaze.

I felt like I'd swallowed a baseball as I carefully lifted the envelope. The Z had been locked. I'd watched Zoloski put in the key, heard the lock pop. We'd been inside ten, maybe twenty minutes. The thought that Mac had watched me arrive home sent shivers down my spine.

"Go inside and lock the door, Blaize. Call the station, tell them what happened, that I'm here, and we need the lab techs to go over the car."

"What are you going to do?"

He smiled. "Old-fashioned police work. Knock on doors. See if anyone noticed anything suspicious."

I gave him a doubtful look, but he ignored it, gave me a hug and led me back upstairs. "We'll catch this guy, Blaize."

Although his words were meant to reassure me, they didn't. I kept thinking about Sunny.

I picked up the phone and dialed the police, relayed Zoloski's message, then rummaged through my kitchen for a pack of cigarettes. My half a month of abstinence was over.

Chapter 12

WHEN ZOLOSKI finally came in it was after nine. He sat down, kicked off his shoes and sighed. I rubbed his feet while he gave me the run-down on what he'd found.

"A guy next door saw someone near my car. Some old fart looking for a handout, he thought." Zoloski jerked as I rubbed his toes a little too hard.

"Sorry."

He put his feet down. "The guy didn't remember much. Just that whoever it was wore some kind of tan rain slicker. His hair was maybe gray or blond, and he wore a cap."

Whitman? Somebody I had yet to meet? The coffee in my stomach churned like radiator fluid. "Did he see the man's face?"

Zoloski shook his head.

"Big guy or small?"

"Couldn't say."

"Fingerprints?"

"Gloves."

I rubbed my eyes, they were gritty and the nicotine in my cleaned-out system was making me jumpy. "What now?"

"We'll examine the note. Check it with the other one. See if there's a lead."

I reached for the pack of cigarettes, saw Zoloski's disapproval and realized he didn't know I smoked. I frowned back defiantly. "I quit two weeks ago," I said, extracting one. But I didn't light it.

"He's not going to get you," Zoloski said firmly.

Could I have that in writing? My expression must have said I didn't stock much faith in the law, because he pulled me onto his lap and hugged me.

"I know you're scared."

I held onto him like a life preserver. "He's out there," I whispered, "watching..."

Zoloski pulled back, looked into my eyes. "You could stay...at my place."

I studied his face, read only concern in his expression. How long had he been thinking about me living with him? The entire two weeks we'd known each other? I shook my head. "No way! I'm not running like a terrified rabbit!"

The concern tightened into angry lines. "I just want you safe!"

"I can't stay with you forever, and you can't baby-sit me twenty-four hours a day. All he has to do is wait until you and your watchdogs are gone."

Zoloski's eyebrows drew together. "Can he wait that long?"

"For all we know, he waited fifteen years—until Sunny returned."

Zoloski's mouth became a frustrated line. "What's your plan?"

"Find him before he finds me." I plopped back in my chair, gulped down a swallow of lukewarm coffee, yuck, and waited for my brain to buzz with brilliant mystical intuition, what Zoloski called "one of his famous hat tricks." It took a few minutes. "Can I go through Sunny's things? Has someone claimed them?"

Zoloski sighed. "Yeah. Her brother ID'd her body yesterday. We gave him the okay to pack up her stuff. There wasn't much. Her condo looked like a hotel room."

I wondered why, but asked about the brother. "Does he live in town?"

"Close enough. Nevada City. He's raising chickens and selling real estate."

The little gold-rush town, white-washed Victorians, flashed in my memory. Try as I might I couldn't remember much about the brother. Just that he'd been older, kind of quiet, moody. A wimp. "What's his name?"

Zoloski seemed to be making up his mind whether to tell me. Finally, he shrugged. "Nathan Wright."

I smiled my thank you. "Did Sunny have much cash, assets?"

He nodded. "Yeah. Half a million liquid in the bank."

Half a mil! In the back of my mind I'd expected light-fingered Sunny to be broke or living off someone. I wondered if she might own real estate in Los Angeles where her ex lived. "And you went through all her stuff?"

"My partner did." A note of disappointment crept into his voice. "Said it was neat and tidy. Found zilch."

"Who inherits?" I asked, rolling the unlit cigarette between my fingers and wishing I was outside so I could smoke it.

"Charities."

My cigarette rolled across the table and into Zoloski's lap.

He pitched it back.

"Sunny wasn't the type to give her money to charity."

"So you say. So her brother says. He was shocked as hell."

"He was?" I got up and topped off my coffee.

"Yeah, he was."

I took a sip. My vague image of the wimp didn't conform to my killer image—especially if he didn't profit from her death—and hell, he certainly wasn't Mac.

"He claims the charities bit was a shock. But that she'd told him he wouldn't inherit anything."

I waited, knowing there was more. I resisted tweaking Zoloski's nose to speed him up.

He sipped from his cup, then said, "Sunny told him that if anything happened to her she was leaving everything to one of her lovers. She never said who."

Would that include her co-star? How far would that Paul guy go for money? "If that's true, it kind of lets her brother off the hook."

"Yup." Zoloski glanced at his watch, then slipped on his shoes. Neither of us had slept much the night before. Right now he looked bleary-eyed as a bloodhound.

"You still want to look through our unsolved cases, see if you can find—m?" He stopped, got a thoughtful expression. Picked up the phone.

"Jack, Zoloski here. You remember the two guys that visited the department last month?" A pause. "They were going through our old files." A longer pause. "Yeah." He grabbed the pad of paper and pen on the counter and jotted names. "No, I'll send a fax. Thanks." He hung up, leaned back in his chair and grinned.

"What's up, Sherlock?"

"I think I remember another case. Four years ago. Sutter County. Body arranged in the same way."

"So he hasn't been waiting," I muttered, feeling sick.

"You still want to check our unsolveds?"

I gave him a cheesy grin, the kind I used for family pictures. "Hey, us workaholics never quit."

Zoloski didn't react.

"When are you going to talk again to the guy who discovered Sunny's body?"

He picked up his jacket, then gave me a sidelong look that teased and measured me at the same time. "My counselor said I have to make adjustments in relationships. Compromise. If this is it, I'm in for trouble."

I picked up my purse. "With a capital T." I thought I saw the hint of a grin on his lips as he followed me out.

FILES, FILES everywhere—files, files always there. The stupid rhyme wouldn't quit as I resolutely shut away the horror in the file I was holding. "What time is it?" I grumbled.

"Five," Zoloski grumbled back. "I start work at eight."

I eyed my stack of remaining files, then eyed his. His were nearly gone. My competitive spirit rankled. He looked at my red-rimmed eyes and pushed back his chair. "Why don't we save these for tomorrow? I mean tonight. We'll finish up...then go to dinner."

"All right."

His eyebrows rose, my easy agreement an obvious surprise. Fatigue took the tiger out of my tank.

We trudged downstairs, replaced all the files we'd gone over and put the remaining ones in a box with Zoloski's name. It was a pleasure to leave the old jail, and go outside and breathe a little free air. I managed not to worry about Mac the Knife until Zoloski painstakingly searched my apartment and checked the windows. "You want to take a catnap here?" I offered.

He smiled and gave me a hug. "You sleep."

He'd missed the hint—I *wanted* a bodyguard. The thought of Ross flashed through my mind and I discarded it. I could take care of myself.

"The place is staked out, Blaize. You'll be okay. Sleep." His lips brushed my forehead. "I'll catch a nap over lunch."

I didn't argue. I had my .32 and my bat, and a feeling he was going back to the files. "If you find anything new, you'll tell me?"

He nodded but didn't speak, gave me a light kiss that turned into a deep one, then paused at the door.

"I know," I said, beating him to the punch. "Lock the door and be careful."

"For a beautiful broad you're damn smart." His offhand grin made me melt. I locked the door and crawled into bed. Tomorrow, no, later today, I amended sleepily, I'd drive up to Nevada City for Sunny's funeral and talk to Nathan Wright. As the fog drifted into my mind, I thought of Zoloski. He wouldn't like my pursuing the case. He wanted to lock me up in a safe place with bodyguards while he chased Mac. Damn, relationships were tough.

THE MAZE-LIKE streets of Nevada City, laid down by men apparently interested only in their next drink, brought back memories. I'd spent several weekends here during my college years. And gotten lost. The idea of looking for Nathan Wright's house didn't thrill me.

I checked my watch. After one. The rental car bounced up and down like a horse at fast trot. I hoped it would hold together long enough to make it back to Sacramento. I was supposed to pick Zoloski up at five.

It was nearly two when I somehow miraculously found Nathan Wright's house. It would take another miracle to get me back to Broad Street and the freeway.

I pulled in alongside a flashy black Porsche. A line of cars were parked under a row of massive oaks beside a rustic timber house. A few chickens surrounded the car, squawked as I got out. Looking for a handout? As I walked to the door, I wondered if the inside of the house resembled the Porsche or the chickens. The air was soft and cold and I pulled my jacket closed. Somber New Age music drifted through the open windows. Steeling myself for funereal faces, I knocked loudly on the door.

Nathan Wright answered my first knock and stared at me, a puzzled expression in his overlarge blue eyes. They went with his Romanesque nose. The expensive suit and cowboy boots didn't fit my memory of him in paisley and bell-bottoms, secluded in his bedroom with a magazine. His eyes widened as recognition hit.

"Andrea? I got the message on my machine, but I wasn't sure..."

"It's me. I go by Blaize now, not Andrea."

He grinned at me as if we were long lost friends. "Blaize?"

"Sorry I missed the funeral," I said before he could as about my nickname.

"It's okay. Come in." His animated expression reminded me of Woody Allen, incredulous, yet pleased as punch to see me. I could hardly remember talking to the guy.

A gold ring with a dark blue piece of turquoise glinted on his right hand, along with a gold wrist chain. "The lawyer told you about the boxes Sunny left you, huh? They're in the spare bedroom."

Boxes?

He led me into a combination entry/living room, the ceiling wide-beamed with plate glass windows across the back, overlooking a green canyon. The room smelled of cigarette smoke and pot. Beneath the cloudy haze, twenty or thirty people milled about, eating, talking. I wondered who they all were. Trying to curb my curiosity and impatience, I asked, "Was it a nice service?"

Nathan shrugged and led me through the crowd to a sparsely furnished bedroom, moving boxes stacked in the middle of the floor. He didn't seem disturbed about Sunny's death, about the funeral ...yet his surprise at seeing me showed he was capable of emotion.

"Were you and Sunny close?" I asked in the doorway.

He paused, turned away from the bed, the light shining straight down on his receding hairline. He seemed to be deciding on how much he wanted to say, and finally settled on, "Sunny was a mystery, Andrea. I don't think she was close to anyone."

He sank down on the edge of the bed. I leaned against the doorjamb. "After her divorce, she drank enough booze and took enough sleeping pills to kill herself. I found her. Called 911. That was the only time we talked with any sincerity. She said she always wanted what other people had, just had to have it, but when she got it, it didn't matter anymore. After that I kept in touch, but we just chit-chatted, like strangers."

I thought of Sunny's kleptomania. At one time in my life, I'd tried to fill the empty hole inside with food, cigarettes, and sex.

None of it worked. Through recovery I had finally come to terms with that. Someday, when I slowed down, I'd think about it again. Right now, I wondered about Sunny. "When did she tell you about her will?"

"Last month. Out of the blue—just brought it up. I hadn't seen her since the hospital incident. She asked me to come to her place. We talked. She seemed anxious—smoked the whole time—but wouldn't tell me why."

Mac's first letter? The timing was right.

"She said you were a psychologist now, that she might talk to you."

"We talked briefly." I glanced toward the two boxes.

He took my hint and hefted the top dusty carton, sealed with brown tape, on the bed. I crossed to it, my eyes on the box.

Nathan looked curious too.

I opened my purse, extracted a pocketknife and cut the tape. Dust tickled my nose as I pulled the box open. A tiny spider jumped from the edge. I let it go, my gaze riveted on the contents. Photographs. Tons of them. I pulled one out, didn't recognize anyone, turned it over and read: Barry M. "Who's Barry M?"

"Barry Michelson, her ex-husband." Nathan glanced over my shoulder at the picture. "That was before they married."

I pulled out a dozen more photographs, her ex in many of them, read the scribbled handwriting on the back, and still recognized no one. "Are you sure this is for me?"

He shrugged, a flicker of doubt in his eyes. "She left instructions..." He smoothed his hair back.

"Can I look in the other one?"

In answer, he hauled the next one over to the bed.

I cut the tape. "Did the police search these?" I would have expected the boxes to be left open, in a heap.

"Yes. I resealed and stacked them after they left."

I read the felt-pen writing scrawled on the side. "Musicals." I looked at Nathan. "Did you go through all of them?"

His reply was stiff. "I glanced in as I sealed them."

"Remove anything?"

He looked offended. "Of course not," he said with as much dignity as royalty.

All right, so my remark was offensive, but I was starting to feel edgy. Memories of Sunny and Mac the Knife hovered too damn close for comfort.

My eyes slid over the cardboard. Musicals. Sunny and I had danced together in a musical. I pulled open the box. More photographs.

Nathan peered over my shoulder as I picked out a picture.

I recognized a dancer from our dance troupe, the first to accuse Sunny of thievery. Should I sing the blues? I pushed the memories down. Not the time or the place. "These must be mine." I tossed the picture back and closed the box. A box of bad memories. My hands on the tape, I paused. Mac had known us then. Had she taken a picture of him?

I had the sudden urge to talk to Zoloski, tell him I might have something. But there were still people to talk to, including her co-star, Paul.

"Help me carry them to my car?"

He picked up the first box.

I hefted the "Musicals" box and followed.

"You aren't leaving already, are you?" he asked as he shoved the box into the back of my rental.

There was something pathetic about Nathan, an inner sadness I hadn't seen until now: his eyes questioning, his shoulders bent just enough to hint at how he might look in ten to twenty years. For a second I saw a glimmer of Sunny in his facial expression. Disconcerted, I used a gentle voice I saved for stray animals. "No. I'd like to talk to Sunny's friends, stay for awhile."

Back inside, I asked, "Is Sunny's ex here?"

"Barry?" Nathan pointed out Sunny's ex, Barry Michelson, as he shoved a stuffed mushroom into his mouth. A good-looking guy: fortyish, short, but lean, dark hair, tanned skin, and a beige suit that reeked of money. The petite blonde on his arm that couldn't have been more than twenty-five. In the photographs he appeared older and chunkier—and no blonde on his arm.

I nudged Nathan. "Introduce me to everyone. Leave Barry for last."

Nathan's eyebrows rose, getting the picture that I wasn't here just to pay respects. Most of the people turned out to be part of the cast in Sunny's play, including her co-star Paul. Dressed in a black pin-striped suit, white shirt and red tie, he looked worse than he had on Hiram Johnson's stage. His hand felt like a glob of wet noodles. I restrained my desire to wipe my palm on my pants, then observed his glazed eyes, and did it anyway. He wouldn't notice.

"Nathan," I smiled sweetly, "could I have something non-alcoholic to drink?" While he was gone, I studied Paul. Was he sweating so much because he was drunk, or was I making him nervous? "I knew Sunny in high school," I said. "How did you meet her?"

Paul shrugged. "A show in LA." His words slurred. He gulped down the last of his drink and looked desperate for another. "I knew someone had threatened her."

"But she didn't tell you who?"

He shook his head. "I still can't believe she's dead."

The buzz of conversation around me sounded more like networking than a funeral party. I had a feeling Paul was the only one present who mourned Sunny's death.

Nathan showed up with my drink, diet cola over ice, and resumed introductions.

Paul moved off toward the bar.

"Where are your parents?" I asked Nathan between conversations with a dancer who looked disappointed I wasn't someone more prestigious, and a director who looked in worse shape than Paul.

Nathan glanced around the room. I saw a glimmer of sorrow. "They were kinda broke up. Didn't stay."

I held back my next question as he introduced me to another dancer, the one whose earrings Sunny had ripped off in the dressing room at Hiram Johnson. Now they dangled from her ears. Sunny had returned them!

A quick succession of people that hardly knew Sunny followed. Finally, we reached her ex.

"An, uh, Blaize, this is Barry Michelson."

Michelson's gaze ran up and down my black pantsuit as though considering me for his casting couch. But there was a twinkle in his dark eyes that made me like him in spite of the look. He shook off the blond appendage and extended his hand. "Nice to meet you." His teeth gleamed when he smiled, and his eyeteeth reminded me of Dracula.

I had always rooted for the vampire. Something to do with my own dysfunctional childhood, no doubt.

"Blaize is the psychologist. She and Sunny were friends in high school," Nathan said.

I wasn't sure whether to kick him or hug him.

When Michelson's smile stayed in place, I realized he wasn't intimidated. He said, "A psychologist, huh? Have any famous patients?" His tone was wry.

"Are you volunteering?"

He pursed his lips. "Me?" He paused, as if considering the thought. "There's better ways to use a couch." He winked, radiating charm.

I didn't point out that my clients sat in chairs, lying down was outdated. "I doubt my ex-boyfriend would come to my funeral," I said, wondering why he was here.

Michelson asked, "No ex-husband in the wings?"

A natural flirt. "One ex-boyfriend is enough," I responded. "So, why are you here?"

"I called him," Nathan interjected.

I gave Nathan a tight smile. Butt out.

Michelson read my expression and asked Nathan to look after the blonde while we went outside.

Stomach growling, I grabbed a mushroom on the way. "You and Nathan know each other—besides through Sunny?"

Clouds had rolled in above the trees, fluffy white cotton balls against darkening blue. Any other time it would have been lovely.

Barry's face was shadowed. "Sunny was the reason we kept in touch after the divorce. When she tried to kill herself I asked Nathan to keep an eye on her."

I digested the information as we walked a lit path alongside the house. After the stuffy inside air, I appreciated the pine smell and cool breeze. We zig-zagged down the hill. "How close an eye?"

Michelson spoke as we walked through the trees. "He called her every morning, nights too if she sounded depressed—just kept in touch."

Nanny Nathan? I held back a smile. "So he called and told you about her death, the funeral?"

Michelson brushed back a low branch and held it until I'd passed. "Yeah. He called and told me she'd been murdered, to expect the cops. I wasn't much help." He paused, studied my face, then glanced over my shoulder, his eyes clouding over. "You want to know why I came?" He shook his head. "I loved her. I'd have given her the moon. But once we were married—" he snapped his fingers. "Game over. The challenge was gone." His voice rang with regret. "Such a waste. She could have been a star. But she couldn't stop drinking and had to sleep with every guy that came along."

"And you were faithful?" I tried for noncommittal.

"At first, yes." He sounded pissed.

I ducked beneath a low pine tree branch and produced a more sympathetic voice. "How long were you married?" Off in the distance a large pond shimmered, the area lit by the late afternoon sun. I headed for the boulders rimming the water.

Barry's footsteps crunched behind me. "Fourteen months."

"She left some pictures. I don't know a lot of the people in them. I'd like you to take a look."

He strove for casual, but his neck muscles looked tense. "You think she knew the person who killed her?"

"Most murder victims do." I eased toward the pond, stepped up onto the nearest boulder and looked out over the water. Suddenly I wished Zoloski were here, arm around my shoulders, enjoying the quiet beauty. I felt Barry's watchful gaze. Stepping down, I gestured toward the house. "The pictures are in my car. Would you take a look?"

He started back up the path without answering.

Was that a yes? Abruptly, another question popped into my mind from left field. "Barry, do you know Gordon Whitman?"

He stopped, turned around. "I've gone to several fundraisers, know him enough to say hello. Why?"

"What about Sunny? Did she know him?"

"I introduced them once."

Confirmation!

Barry shook his head and frowned. "She didn't like him. Said he gave her the creeps." He paused. "Funny."

A prickly chill ran down my arms. "What?" I waited, uneasy,

impatient.

"She said he reminded her of someone."

I took his arm and picked up the pace. "Who?" Was I trembling from excitement or fear?

"She never gave a name. Only that, 'he reminds me of someone' in this strange voice. She was drunk at the time." We stopped near the front porch while Barry's face reflected thought. "Said it in a little girl voice." He looked at me. "Like she was scared." Does it mean anything? his gaze asked.

Like maybe he reminded her of Mac? I swallowed. "Sure she wasn't just drunk?"

He conceded that might have been it.

I motioned toward the gravel drive, led the way to my car, unlocked the trunk and hefted the first box.

His look questioned my sanity. "I thought you meant a *few* pictures. Not a truck full."

"It's not as bad as it looks. I only want you to go through this box. Come on." I plopped down on a porch bench, the cold air made my taste buds long for a hot cup of coffee.

"Look, I'd like to help," Barry said, "but I've got a plane to catch." He checked his Rolex.

"Just give me ten minutes." I shoved a picture in his face. "Who is this?"

He stared at the color photo of Sunny and a guy I didn't know, then scowled. "That's the guy she was living with before she moved in with me." He glanced again at his watch, then several more pictures, impatiently uttering names as I scribbled on the back of each photo. After exactly ten minutes, he stood up. "Can't miss that plane. If you want to fly to LA I'll look at the rest in the air."

I thought of Zoloski, our dinner date, and the fact that I hadn't called him all day.

"You can make up your mind while I get my associate, Melody."

Some associate, I thought briefly, considering the other box Sunny had given me. Pictures from a past we'd shared. No reason for Barry to take a look at them. I'd leave it in the trunk until I got back. Having it made me feel like Pandora. Unpleasant adolescent recollections lay buried in that box. It should have said "Broadway

Blues." I wanted to open it inside my apartment, alone, with a pack of cigarettes and a carton of ice cream. The box held our performance memories, captured by her camera. My pulse raced. Had she captured Mac's face? I was afraid I wouldn't know if she had.

I lugged the box of photos I wanted Barry to identify back to the trunk of my car, shoved it in beside the other box, and slammed the lid. Was I spinning my wheels with Barry? He'd already told me Sunny and Whitman knew each other—given me a connection. It's not enough, my mind whispered. I pulled my cellular from the depths of my purse and jabbed in Zoloski's number. Nothing. No juice. I ran in the house, but Paul had the phone in a death grip and Barry, Melody, and Nathan were leaving. Shit! I caught up with them on the porch. Barry looked irritated. Melody glared at him.

Lover's spat? Passing Nathan at the front door, I caught up to Barry and Melody as she yanked open his car door. "I'll follow you to the airport."

All the way down Highway 49 and the Interstate I hoped for an available seat on the plane. Hoped my credit card wouldn't bounce. And *prayed* Zoloski would understand.

Chapter 13

MELODY WAS clearly unimpressed with Sacramento's "quaint itty-bitty cow-town" airport. I was sick of her mouth before the plane took off, physically tired from the long day I'd already put in, and worried about the cost of flying first class. I wished again I'd had time to call Zoloski. He'd be pissed I hadn't picked him up.

"Sit in Blaize's seat," Barry said to Melody as I was about to sit across from them.

"Barry—"

"Don't argue. Just do it."

Her gaze narrowed murderously, but she complied.

I squeezed the box of photos between my legs and opened the lid. Pulling out a handful of snapshots, I pushed one under Barry's nose.

Melody leaned over. "What're you lookin' at?"

Barry frowned. "Go to sleep, Melody."

She glared at me, like it was my fault, then turned to the window. The plane rolled forward. I ignored the female flight attendant who checked our seat belts. Barry didn't. I nudged him to regain his attention.

He tore his gaze from her backside. "Work, work, work. You've got a one-track mind."

"So do you," I shot back, remembering the once-over he'd given me. I handed him another photo.

He studied it, frowned, then his eyes lit with recognition. "That horny old goat," he murmured. An old man with a very young woman. Behind the 'goat' were the blurred faces of another couple. *Déjà vu* struck as I stared at the scenery, the blurry man and woman, but it didn't stick. Damn! I tried to reel in where and when I'd seen them or the location. Failed.

Barry pointed at the old man. "That's Derek Jones." He moved his finger a half inch. "And that's Amanda Stretman." I recognized the name of the B-film star. He moved his finger to the blurred female face behind Stretman. "And that—" he narrowed his eyes, "looks like an actress named Harper and her brother." His tone said he wasn't sure about the "brother" part or the name Harper. It rang no bells.

"Where was it taken?"

Barry shrugged. "Derek's back yard? Some place in Beverly Hills."

I took the picture, stared at what looked like a big estate or convincing movie set. Still no luck. I wrote the names on the back. At this rate I'd need a room for the night and some way of luring Barry that wouldn't soil my virtue. I took a minute to call Zoloski. Flying deluxe had its good points. His voicemail picked up and I left a quick apology and "be home late" message.

Barry nudged my arm, his expression impatient. I took the next snapshot from him and wrote the names he dictated.

We made it through three-quarters of the box before the seat belt lights flashed. I grabbed the last two handfuls of photos and stuck one in his lap with a pen. "You do those. I'll do these. Left to right."

He flashed a *You owe me* look and picked up the pen.

I offered a friendly smile. Dream on. Interrupting his writing with several pictures from my stack, I turned them over and jotted the names he gave me.

The captain's voice echoed through the cabin: "Thank you for flying United..."

Barry triumphantly tossed his last photo in one of three yellow barf bags I'd marked with my name. All three were filled to the brim. I stuffed the bags into the box. I thought of the one picture that had triggered something, hoped my brain would kick in before my funeral. The airline peanuts burned in my stomach.

Melody yawned and squirmed in her seat just as Barry identified the people in my last two pictures. "You're a slave driver," he said, a gleam in his eyes. "I ought to hire you to direct my next picture. Save me half a mil."

My mind flashed to the money in Sunny's bank account. "Barry, how much money did Sunny get from the divorce?"

He stood and pulled on his jacket. "Why don't we talk over a drink? You can ask whatever you like. We can get to know each other." He winked and stepped into the aisle.

"Sounds good," I lied. By the time he figured out he wasn't getting anything but a "thank you," I planned to be on a plane north.

Melody shot a glance at Barry that held daggers. "I want to go home."

Barry's expression went cold. "Go ahead." He led the way off the plane. I let Melody pass, hefted the box against my chest and followed slowly, hoping they'd work things out before I caught up.

LAX, short for Los Angeles International Airport, could have stood for laxative: crowded, noisy, moving. Conveyer belts continually purged themselves. If this place didn't cure me of crowds, nothing would. If you have lots of luggage and are changing planes, LAX is synonymous with hell. This time, I had nothing but the photographs, and I wasn't going anywhere but back home. Home. Where was that these days?

Behind a reservation desk, a poster of Waikiki Beach caught my eye. Jostled by the endless crush that flowed around me, the silver sand, azure water, and lush green foliage looked enticing—especially when I put Zoloski in the picture. Thoughts of Zoloski led to his job, my unofficial job, the investigation: Mac the Knife... Where in hell was Barry?

A hand came down on my shoulder and I jumped, then turned into him. "Sorry," I murmured, removing my foot from his instep. He'd lost the blonde.

Barry flashed another vampire smile and gestured toward a small, darkened bar. "I have a table." At least he hadn't suggested his place. I suspected Melody was already ensconced there.

With my feet resting on the box, my elbows irreverently askew on the table, my chin balanced on my palms, I nodded as Barry ordered himself a scotch and me an Irish Coffee. I needed the caffeine and hoped the whipped cream would calm my stomach. What would the booze do?

"How'd you get a name like Blaize?" Barry asked.

My gaze drifted to the far-off reservation desk which flashed amidst the sea of bodies like a beacon on a stormy night as I thought of Pat, the nickname "Blaize of Glory" and circumstances I'd rather forget. I shrugged. "It's a mystery to me."

"A nickname?"

Give it up, I'm not talking. "How much did Sunny walk away with after the divorce?"

"A couple of mil."

"Nice take for fourteen months of marriage."

He smiled, his tone philosophic. "Better than hanging out your dirty linen in a courtroom."

I thought of the fifty-fifty property laws. "How much could she have gotten?"

"You mean how much am I worth?" He smiled. "Fifteen, twenty." Give or take a few million, his expression said.

Our drinks came. Mine went down like hot velvet. I leaned back and sighed.

"You know, I've got some pictures of my own," Barry said after a swallow that emptied half his glass. He gave me the once over again.

"As in etchings?" I shook my head. "I've got a boyfriend who's ready to kill me as it is."

"All the more reason to live it up. You can only die once."

A cold chill coursed down my spine. "Yeah," I murmured, a part of me wanting to stay in LA away from Mac. Zoloski's face loomed behind my eyes. "Be right back." I made a beeline for the reservation desk before fatigue beat me into submission and I grabbed a hotel room.

My stand-by flight had left. How come I hadn't heard its departure announced? Damn it all! The next flight home was in two hours. I got the reservation and trudged back to the bar.

Another Irish Coffee waited. Another scotch rested next to Barry's hand.

I resumed my seat and spooned whipped cream into my mouth. It made me think of pumpkin pie, Thanksgiving, still seven months away, and my thirty-second birthday. Would I live that long? "Tell me about Sunny."

Barry hiked an eyebrow. "I'd rather impress you with my quick wit."

Did my face convey how impressed I wasn't? I hoped not. "Tell me about Sunny," I repeated.

"All work and no play makes for a dull woman." His gaze

dropped to my chest.

"In this day and age, a safe woman."

His smile smoldered. "A damned stubborn one, too," he murmured. He finished his drink, handed me a business card and stood. "Change your mind, give me a call."

"I had some more questions about Sunny."

"I'm not into talking." He eyed me like rare steak. "Goodbye, Blaize." He bowed. "May we meet again."

I smiled. No way, *José*. He didn't seem to expect a response. I sank back against the chair and closed my eyes.

"WHAT DO YOU mean you're in LA and you'll be home around midnight!" Zoloski yelled via Ma Bell.

I held the receiver a foot from my ear and counted to ten.

"Blaize!"

"I left a message on your work phone," I hollered back. "Just listen a minute!"

I pictured him brushing his dark hair back from his face with impatience. "Look, it's ten-twenty," he said. "I get up at six. I've slept a total of eight hours in the last three days."

I had an image of him pacing the kitchen.

"I'm sorry, Stephanos. But this is important." I lowered my voice. "I miss you."

"Yeah?" His voice lowered, too, got that soft edge that melted my kneecaps. "So—what's so important down there?" he asked.

"Sunny left me two boxes of photographs."

"She did?"

"Yes. I went through one box with her ex. He identified almost every person—mostly LA movie types."

"Anything pop?"

"Her ex said he introduced Sunny to Whitman; she didn't like him."

"An introduction is a start," he acknowledged. "Anything else?"

I thought of the blurred faces in the one photograph, and the rolling hills behind. "Not really."

"Wake me when you get here. We'll talk then."

"I'll get there as quick as I can." I leaned against the phone booth, my mouth dry, my head light, my stomach in need of antacid. Mostly, I needed to be in Zoloski's arms. I glanced at the box of photographs at my feet and wondered if it had been a wild goose chase. But that one photograph nagged at my memory. Zoloski called his hunches "hat tricks." Would this turn into one? I retrieved the snapshot, studied it. Nothing—but frustration.

"Flight Two-forty-two is now boarding."

That was my number. I shoved the picture back in the bag, closed the flaps, and hurried toward my gate. I marched onto the plane as I imagined Super Woman might, shoulders square, back straight, eyes sweeping over the empty seats as though they contained my royal subjects.

Super Woman left me half-asleep in my seat before the plane cleared the runway.

Chapter 14

ZOLOSKI DIDN'T answer as I banged my knuckles on the front door. Muttering a string of expletives, I went around to the gate. My handy-dandy penlight didn't feel like much protection as I squished across the soggy front lawn in my pumps. It was past midnight, only a sliver of a moon flickering through the clouds, and my gun was inside Zoloski's house. My big overweight leather bag threatened to dislocate my shoulder. Or take off Mac's head. Keep that thought.

After several unladylike grunts, I managed to drag the gate open. Its hinges squealed. My nerves twitched. I followed the cement walk around the house to the barbecue, found the key taped to the underside of the handle, and breathed easier.

Greasy key in hand, I retraced my steps, heaved the gate closed, then crossed the awful wet grass—heels sinking—all the while hoping Zoloski wouldn't wake up, mistake me for a burglar and shoot me.

The key turned without a sound. As I stepped inside, I breathed in the warm air and locked the door. "Zoloski?"

It was too still. But he was a heavy sleeper. I chased the phantoms from my mind and moved quietly toward the bedroom. From the doorway the tiny beam from my penlight caught a gleam of steel. "Stephanos?"

The bedside lamp snapped on, revealing a hairy-chested Zoloski, gun in hand. "Shit, you nearly gave me a heart attack!" He put the gun on the dresser.

I shoved the light into my purse. "I told you I'd be here around midnight."

Zoloski brushed his tangled hair off his forehead. He looked better than great. Part of me wanted to leap onto the bed, smother him with kisses, the other part recognized the stamp of irritation in the line of his lips. But he sounded relieved as he slipped from bed, "I'll make coffee." He grabbed a pair of jeans and pulled them on.

He looked even sexier.

I smiled. "Forget the coffee."

"You missed one hell of a good dinner, Sweetheart," he drawled as he came toward me. "What about some compensation?" He took my shoulders, drew me close, the heat of his palms spreading magic. His kiss ignited a chain reaction in my brain, a nuclear experiment gone crazy. I inhaled the smell of soap and him, a smell I suddenly realized I loved.

"I missed you," I whispered, my hands playing lightly over his bare back.

"Yeow!" He flinched. "You're freezing." He pulled away, disappearing into the bathroom. Water ran. He poked his head out the door. "How about a hot, steaming, sensual bubble bath? Together?"

"What happened to the talk?" I teased.

His eyebrows wiggled Groucho Marx style. "All in good time."

My insides warmed.

With Zoloski's fuzzy chest as a backrest, I snuggled down into bubbly hot water, and sighed. The sight of his knees sticking out of the water next to mine made me chuckle. His kiss on my neck made me wish the tub were two feet longer.

Much later, wrapped in his "extra" bathrobe, a tan silk number that smelled new, I watched as he fixed coffee. The domesticity boggled my mind. It was two a.m., and though I knew I'd suffer later from lack of sleep, I was hungry and wide-awake.

"French toast or scrambled eggs?"

"Coffee, then French toast."

Zoloski poured us both a mug and sat down. The man made a mean cup of coffee. His lips settled into a firm line as we stared at each other. "Anytime you want to tell me why you went to LA and didn't bother to call me, I'm waiting."

I thought of Barry's eyes, a mere shadow of Zoloski's jade perfection, but right now, the green looked very determined. "My cell phone was dead. I didn't get to a phone until I was on the plane. I left a message at your office." The truth sounded flaky, even to me.

His eyes flashed. "I called Wright and he said you left the

same time as Sunny's ex-husband."

Uh-oh. "I'm sorry if I worried you." I meant it. I explained about the two boxes of photos Nathan had given me. "I needed names to go with the photos, and Barry offered to look at them on the plane."

Zoloski remained silent.

Worse than uh oh. "He was very helpful, identified practically everyone."

"From what Wright said, Mr. Barry Michelson wanted to help you into bed."

I smiled. "Barry's mistake."

Zoloski's gaze measured me. Shades of his ex-wife? Then his mouth twitched and his quirky smile appeared.

Here was a man whose ex had cheated on him and hurt him, but he was trying. He also knew how to laugh. And cry? Probably. Not the typical cop, I realized. The epitome of men? Maybe. I was falling hard.

He broke into my romantic ruminations. "Next time talk to me before you go running off, okay?"

I read concern in his gaze, but the edge in his voice made me feel like a kid. I bridled, then told myself to grow up, and swallowed a sarcastic retort—all in one breath. "Okay," I promised.

"I'm not your jailer, Blaize. You do what you need to do—just keep me informed. Worry sparks insanity in my family."

"And you inherited it?"

He grinned. "Must have."

I love you, almost popped out. I took a long sip of sobering coffee. "So, what have you been up to since I left?"

He sighed. "Found three cases, four or five years apart, that look like Mac's handiwork. Talked to the detectives involved." He paused. "I want you to have around-the-clock protection."

Somehow my fear of Mac had grown dim after a few hours in Zoloski's arms. Now it blossomed with autopsy pictures flashing through my brain. "Forget the French toast," I murmured. "Protection for how long?"

His gaze nailed mine. "Until we catch him."

What if Mac waited? How long could the police budget survive the expense? "Tell me what the detectives said."

"The consensus is all three cases were done by the same guy—no semen was present, but they were all carved up in the upper torso after they were dead. No suspects."

"Four or five years apart," I thought aloud. "Then two at once, both raped. Something changed his MO." I took another sip of coffee and tried to come up with an idea.

Zoloski stared out the window. "Yeah, or there's other cases we haven't turned up."

"Maybe Mac recognized Sunny, sent her the letters, planned to kill her, then Connie got in the way."

Zoloski lowered his gaze to the table. "He's after you, Blaize, and we don't have shit!"

My stomach tightened. I wanted to say, "Let's look at the bright side," but what was it? I still considered Whitman a good bet. Zoloski kept saying someone would have spotted the guy. That and his alibi made the timetable damn near impossible.

"You can't guard me forever," I said.

Zoloski didn't have an answer.

"Did the other three women get threatening letters?"

Zoloski shook his head. "If they did, they were never found. But their bodies were arranged in the same way, arms crossed, chests carved up. All were brunettes. The rest, zip."

I could see he was studying my hair. It would take one hell of a leap to call it brunette. Dirty blond, yeah—light brown, maybe. Did that make the connection a fluke? Or had Mac picked me because I was with Sunny all those years ago. Or was it something else?

A sick feeling crept into my stomach. I sipped my coffee, avoiding Zoloski's gaze, hoping it would pass. Then I thought of the victim's arms crossed; the image of Sleeping Beauty holding the rose came back. My subconscious wanted to tell me something, but I wasn't getting it. Frustration.

"VICAP's sent a psychological profile of the killer—based on what we've got. This guy is smart. He enjoys the game, the hunt. Power. Control. Killing." He paused, reached over and took my hand. "Move in with me for awhile."

An entirely different panic hit. "Shouldn't we wait for the magic to wear off?"

Zoloski's mouth tightened. "You end up dead and I'll never

forgive you."

"You think I'll forgive myself?" I joked.

"I think you'd rather jump off a cliff than commit to anything beyond one night. Isn't that what your nickname is all about. Running when things get serious?"

The words, so matter-of-fact, struck hard. Tears filled my eyes and I blinked them back. The sexual afterglow had been replaced with fear. "I'll think about it."

Zoloski stood, pulled his shoulder holster off the back of the chair and strapped it on. He moved to the counter top, picked up a file and tossed it on the table. "Maybe you'd better look at those pictures again." His tone was harsh.

I held back a sarcastic retort about how cops didn't prevent crimes, they cleaned up the mess. I had a better chance of protecting myself than depending on someone else.

Zoloski sat down, tapped his foot for a moment and studied the table. "Move in with me."

I studied the table, too. When I looked up, our gazes locked. "I don't think your boss would approve."

"My boss, or you?" His tone was irritatingly neutral. A good sign or bad sign? We didn't have the history for me to know.

I shook my head and headed into the bedroom. He followed. "I'm not ready to live with someone, Stephanos." I threw on a long dress, jammed my feet in a pair of boots and headed for the door. "I've got to get to work."

He trailed me outside, his tone angry. "Damn it, Blaize! I'm trying to keep you alive!"

I yanked open the car door and froze. On the seat, right where I park my derriere, was a white envelope. This couldn't be happening!

Zoloski took one look at the envelope, and pushed me toward the house.

I resisted. "The pictures are in the trunk!" At least I hoped they were. Mac had opened my car door without trouble.

Zoloski let go.

I glanced around the quiet neighborhood. Too quiet. There was no one on the street except a paperboy. "The note wasn't there last night," I said calmly.

Zoloski slipped his arm around my waist.

"He could be watching right now," I added, my tone shakier.

Zoloski tightened his hold, kissed the top of my head. "I'll assign someone."

"What?"

"I'm assigning one of our guys to tail you." He squeezed my shoulders. "Don't try to talk me out of it."

"I won't," I said as I thought of the note on the seat of my rental car. Rental car! How did Mac know it was mine? My mind raced. He had to have followed me.

"Get inside," Zoloski ordered.

"I'll call your buddies at the station," I said, remembering the drill from last time.

"Thanks." He headed to the neighboring houses.

I went into the kitchen, made the call, then remembered the pictures and swore. Going back out, my neck prickled as I walked down the sidewalk. Like when I'd stood over my father's grave, the winter chill nipping at my skin, making me feel as though I belonged in the black hole too. That's how I felt now. That black hole was waiting to swallow me.

I popped open the trunk, saw the two boxes and slammed the trunk closed, the sound too loud. I was getting jumpy, I thought. I had to do something. Now.

First, I canceled all my counseling appointments for the next two weeks, then I set the boxes of photos on the floor. I still had the feeling Sunny had left me the pictures for a reason. She'd met Whitman. Had she realized he was Mac the Knife? Fifteen years was a long time. I wished now I'd studied the legislator more closely during our confrontation. But Sunny was still alive then and I hadn't dreamed he could be Mac. I tried to visualize Mac's face, but all I could recall were pale blue eyes. I'd hardly noticed him before the rape, and I'd spent fifteen years blotting that memory from my mind. If he was Whitman, I'd talked to him face-to-face. I shuddered.

Zoloski's voice sounded from the doorway. "You okay?"

How long had he been standing there? I shoved to my feet, and stepped across the room to meet him. "I'll move in," I whispered. How much crazier could life get?

He gathered me in his arms. I clung to him. If this was crazy, I liked it.

THAT AFTERNOON, seeing the mauve and gray gingerbread Victorian and stepping inside my flat, conjured up second thoughts. Move in with Zoloski—commit? I must have been crazy. Yeah, give yourself a seventy-five on the GAF and wise-up. Seventy-five on the Global Assessment of Functioning Scale indicated a slight impairment in social functioning due to psychosocial stressors. How about Psycho stressor? I thought of Mac's second note: *See you soon. Mac.* I glanced through the window at the street. Sitting in an unmarked sedan was a middle-aged cop Zoloski had introduced as "A buddy and a great cop, Murphy." Seeing him gave me the momentum to push worries about Mac away.

The place smelled stuffy, looked neglected. The landlord had slid my mail under the door. I left it on the floor. My phone-mate blinked like a red police beacon. I hit the "play" button and sat at the kitchen table, pen in hand. The first message was welcome.

My brother, Ian. "Your car's finished, Andy. Your insurance is picking up the tab. Keep the two hundred deductible."

That surprised me; Ian was not the type to give money away. At least the brother I remembered from childhood didn't. Nearly forty, maybe he was changing in his old age.

The next message. My brother again. "Got a weird phone call. Thought you ought to know. Call me."

Uh-oh. Nothing rattled Ian. I looked up his number as the phone rang. I picked up the receiver.

"Blaize?" Zoloski's voice warmed me.

"Miss me already?" I figured he'd been at work all of a half hour.

"Grab what you need. Take it to my place. Stay there." His tone was hard.

A metallic taste crept into my mouth. "What is it?"

"Another murder." Voices in the background. "Gotta go. Call you later." He hung up before I could ask more.

I settled the receiver back in slow motion. It took three tries to punch my brother's number.

His hearty voice helped ease the tightness in my chest while I tried not to think of knives, butchered meat, and Mac's calling card.

"I have a customer, Blaize. Tons of work. Why don't I meet you at the rental place? Five o'clock? You can drop me home after." His tone held a note of impatience.

Reluctantly, I agreed. I glanced around my apartment, mentally assessing what I wanted to take, and what I really needed. I moved into my bedroom and stopped. My underclothes were strewn across the floor. Dresses shredded, the blanket and bed attacked. Broken shards from the bedside lamp and the wall mirror lay like jagged jigsaw pieces on the floor. Red lipstick writing on the far wall filled my gaze: *Roses are red, violets are blue...it's got to be you....*

I backed out, ran to the phone and called Zoloski, my breath caught in my rib cage.

I managed to force out a description of my bedroom, my gaze sweeping over the kitchen, dining area, and living room. Nothing appeared changed.

"Jesus," he said. "Murph's outside. I'll call him on the radio. Have him come up. Don't touch anything."

"Too late," I murmured, thinking I'd touched the answering machine, the furniture, the doorjamb into the bedroom. Gun in hand, I packed my notes regarding Connie and Sunny's cases, took some underwear and clothes from the laundry basket in the living room corner where I'd left it the week before, stuffed everything into my suitcase of a purse, then perched on the edge of the couch.

Murphy called his name through the door; two guys, probably fingerprint technicians were behind. They showed me their shields, then got to work. I answered questions, let them print me, then followed Murphy down the stairs, drifting along like I was floating through fog.

The street looked like always, yet somehow different, malevolent. Murphy checked my car. No notes, no bombs. I threw my stuff into the back seat, climbed in, locked my door, and drove like hell to Zoloski's.

Murphy met me there and checked the Z-man's house.

I sank into a dining room chair, still feeling dazed, but mustering a smile for Murphy. He had a likeable face and non-threatening teddy-bear physique that made me grateful for his presence. "I'd offer to cook an early dinner," I said, "but it might taste like road kill." The thought of eating made me queasy, even though my stomach was hollow.

"How about a stiff drink? I'm not allowed, but you sure are." He went straight to the booze cabinet.

"How about coffee and brandy?" I said, shoving to my feet, thinking I'd rather be doing something. "You can have the coffee and I'll have both."

He chuckled. "Wife says I drink too much coffee, but she must go through three pots a day to keep up with our two boys. Between soccer, baseball, and basketball practice, she deserves a chauffeur's license." The pride in his voice touched me.

"How old are they?" I asked after grinding fresh beans and pouring the water.

"Twelve and fourteen. Thank god they're both into sports. Keeps 'em out of trouble."

Over the hiss and bubble of the Braun, he related a few anecdotes on how he'd met his wife—a blind date.

"So there she is telling her girlfriend she's bailing with a headache if she doesn't like me, her back toward the door. I'm behind her, hearing every word while her friend's gesticulating like a wild Italian. Totally oblivious, my wife's going, 'What's wrong with your hands?'"

He moved on to stories about him and Zoloski at the Academy. "You should have seen the way the women flocked around him in uniform—he couldn't wait to get into plain clothes..."

By the time we finished our drinks, I'd laughed myself silly.

At a knock on the door he was all cop again, moving along the wall, checking the peephole, then pulling the door open. Another cop, I thought, as the two men conversed in low voices.

He closed the door, crossed to where I sat and handed me an envelope. "One of the techs brought this for you. From Zoloski." He glanced toward the street. "Guess I'd better return to my station outside."

"I'm glad you're there," I said as he cracked open the door.

He touched his hand to his forehead in a "take care" salute and left. When this was all over I wanted to invite him and his family over for dinner. I went to the window, pulled back a curtain, saw him climb in his car. The car remained parked. I let the soft, tweedy fabric slip through my fingers, turned away, and opened the envelope.

"Blaize, If I'm lucky I'll see you around midnight. There's a casserole of macaroni and cheese in the fridge. Help yourself! Take a bath and relax. If that doesn't work, try the Chablis. H & K, Z."

I smiled thinking of his hugs and kisses. Then I thought of the snapshots. I'd gone to my flat to retrieve some clothes, and left the boxes stacked against Zoloski's living room wall. Coffee in hand, I knelt down, ready to tackle the contents.

One picture caught my eye as it fluttered to the carpet. A snap of one of the male leads conjured up a memory about Mac. He'd been part of the production crew—he'd also been a back-up performer for one of the singers in the final show Sunny and I did together. Funny, I couldn't remember his voice, except the whispery version that remained fixed in my subconscious.

Was Mac in the picture? One pair of eyes held mine, danced a waltz of intrigue. But I could make out little of his face. Were the eyes blue? Or brown? Was it him? He had short, dark hair. A rather long, thin face. Why did he look familiar?

I opened the box of two- and three-year-old photographs Barry had identified, pulled the one that had sparked my interest and stared at it. The blurred couple behind the "old goat" and Amanda Stretman didn't change. I compared photos. Two blurry male faces. Sunny had never been very good with a camera. Inspiration failed to strike.

Had I made a useless trip to LA?

I went through half the pictures. There had to be hundreds crammed into the "Musicals" box. Barry had gotten off lucky. My lower back protested my hunched position. It was after three and I'd been sitting for hours.

The phone rang. I jumped at the sound, then groaned as pain radiated up my spine. Zoloski's voice answered before I could pick it up. "This is me. Leave a message at the beep and I'll get back to you." Beep. "Blaize, pick up the phone. It's me, Stephanos."

I grabbed the receiver. "What's up?"

"You okay?" He sounded relieved.

"A-okay." I glanced at the mountain of pictures, started to tell him what I hadn't found when he interrupted.

"I gotta run. I just wanted to make sure you got settled in. I'll call later. On my dinner break."

Someone yelled in the background, "A dinner what?" Laughter followed.

"Just come home," I said softly as he hung up. Then I remembered my brother, the rental car, my Saturn. I called Zoloski's work number, got his voice mail and left a message. Gathering up the photos, I crammed them back in their respective boxes, except the two I'd singled out. Those I took with me, to a one-hour photo lab, Murphy tailing me all the way. I asked for blow-ups and then called my friend, Pat. I wanted Whitman's home address and I figured she could get it. I got her voice mail too. I tried Lon. No one home. With my frustration brimming over, I tried Maria. She had the address and after a stilted conversation, gave it to me.

I stared at the numbers I'd written. Whitman lived off Fair Oaks Boulevard. Probably near Eastern in the upper crust House and Garden neighborhood.

The rental place was on Fulton, near Fair Oaks. I snagged a cup of Bavarian coffee from La Bou and snaked down Fair Oaks. Whitman lived in a fenced estate, heavily shaded by two-hundred-year oaks, protected by wrought iron and electronics. I'd need an invitation to get past.

I climbed back in the car, telling myself to forget it—for now—and raced back to the photo lab. The sign in the window said *Closed*, but I rattled the door anyway. No response. Swearing under my breath, I realized I was going to be late to the rental car place too. *Double damn.*

Ian was later. Still wondering how Mac had known the rental car was mine when he left the note, I questioned the help. No luck.

When Ian drove into the parking lot with my pride and joy sparkling like new, I forgot Mac for a second. The crimson paint glowed over curves of perfection.

"It's beautiful!" I hugged him, excited to have my own wheels back.

He pulled away. "You okay?"

I nodded. "Now I am!"

His gaze remained serious. "Some guy called. I didn't want to talk about it with a customer waiting."

Niagara Falls roared. I placed a steadying hand on Ian's shoulder, tried to clear my throat.

"He asked me to give you a message." Ian pulled a piece of paper from his pocket. He unfolded it and handed it to me, his falcon eyes asking what the hell I'd gotten myself into.

My hand shook.

Roses are red, violets are blue, sit tight, I'll come for you.
Tell Andy not to leave town again.

I glanced at Ian.

His eyes were watchful, tense, his voice tight. "He sounded furious."

I looked around, feeling overexposed in the rental car agency's parking lot, as though he were there behind one of the cars, watching, laughing at my fear, plotting. What was it Zoloski had said, the killer was into power and control, into the game and the killing. I crushed the note in my hand. I'd rather be dead than be victimized again. I was not going to freeze, or run. I would be ready.

I climbed into the driver's seat of my car, and waited for Ian to get in. As I drove him back to his garage, I explained in brief, clinical terms what was going on.

Ian listened without interrupting.

I gave him Zoloski's number so he could reach me, told him not to worry, but asked him to watch for strangers around his shop.

His eyebrows drew together, his mouth a worried line.

We listened to the blues the rest of the way to his shop. He climbed out, leaned into the open doorway, shook his head in parental fashion, then offered a weak grin. "This guy Zoloski must be okay. You haven't said one mean thing about him or men in general today."

I snorted. "Give me time."

A somber look crossed his face. "Be careful, Sis. I love you." He closed the door and disappeared into his shop before I could muster a ditto.

Emotions choked me on the drive home. Those words were the nicest Ian had ever spoken to me. Was the family of Lone Rangers finally showing a few vulnerable cracks?

Mac's call had obviously shaken him. Hell, it had me rattling in my boots. I'd gotten so caught up in the photos I'd almost forgotten about Mac being inside my apartment, going through *my* snapshots, case notes, and address book. Everything. Why had I assumed he'd touched only the stuff in my bedroom? The realization my friends and family were in danger was more than I wanted on my plate.

Chapter 15

I SAT ON Zoloski's couch missing him and feeling like I'd wandered into no-man's-land. I saw the dead woman's picture flash on the TV screen. Another brunette. I was blond. Why was Mac after me?

I didn't know the woman. Was Mac crazy enough to kill someone else just because I wasn't around? Wasn't shredding my clothes and trashing my place enough? Had my trip to LA cost the woman her life? How perverted could Mac get? But I knew the answer to that.

The TV commentator speculated the three killings might be related, that a serial killer could be at large. The Chief of Police looked harried as journalists shot bullet-like questions at him. He dodged like an expert.

Eleven-forty p.m. I switched off the TV. The house felt creepy as a mausoleum. I dug through the rest of the photos. Nothing. I pulled out a torn and yellowed flyer from the bottom of the box and stared at it: *Kingston Productions Presents: A Music and Dance Review.* Kingston was the director, and the guy who'd thrown the cast party.

A key turned in the door. I lunged for my gun, kicking a half-eaten bowl of popcorn off the coffee table in a snowy white flurry.

"It's me!" Zoloski opened the door.

I set down the .32 and righted the bowl. By the time I got my heart back in its cage and looked up, Zoloski was standing over me, staring. Memorizing the moment? Blaize, the little woman, waiting at home, gun at hand? Sorry, hadn't cooked or cleaned. Mean thoughts. I was hurting, I wanted to lash out and he looked available. Damn poor reason.

He knelt and helped me scoop popcorn. In the last couple of days a few new lines had appeared under his eyes, yet he radiated energy. Caffeine high? Dead body fumes? What?

With me it was pure and simple fear, and I resented his energy. I clamped my lips shut, afraid I'd start a fight. As though sensing my mood, he stood and took the popcorn bowl into the kitchen. The refrigerator opened and dishes rattled. I stifled my curiosity and waited.

The microwave hummed. The smell of cheese wafted into the room. He came out with a large plate of macaroni and cheese and a glass of fruit juice. Setting his dinner on the coffee table, he threw his tweed jacket and navy tie over the back of a chair, pulled off his gun and placed it near his foot. No tie, shirt unbuttoned at the neck, he looked good.

He ate like a Great Dane. Wolfing down half the macaroni and cheese in seconds, he came up for air, took a swig of cran-grape juice and grinned. "Glad you're awake."

"Just be glad I didn't shoot you," I snapped. Shit.

"Hey, don't shoot the sheriff! I'm the good guy, Sweetheart."

A piece of cheese stuck to his chin. I leaned over and wiped it off, a smile pushing at my lips. "What I'd really like to do is shoot Mac. Any idea where I can find him?"

Zoloski ignored the question and responded to the real issue. "I can handle a little anger. Long as I know where it's coming from."

I wiped my hands on a napkin trying to contain my pent up hostility—i.e. Fear. "I'm lousy at this." I was scared and I didn't want to depend on anyone.

Zoloski set down the plate. "The question is: Do you want to talk or just stuff it?"

Had he read my mind? "I'm good at stuffing."

"Talk to me."

What to say? I listened to clients, nudged them toward insights I hoped would lead to change, but I didn't talk much.

He shook his head at my silence. "You're a counselor. What would you tell yourself, Blaize? If you were someone else?"

I cracked a smile. "I'd say hang onto this guy, he's one in a million. Communicate. Do your best."

Zoloski grinned. "Good advice. You gonna take it?"

I grinned back. "Maybe."

Zoloski finished the last of the juice and pushed away the glass. "I just talked to the ME. The new homicide—it's not Mac's handiwork. Someone jumped to conclusions."

Was my mouth hanging open? "But Mac left a message with Ian—my brother! He said—"

Exasperation flared in Zoloski's eyes. "*Now* you tell me? When did he call?"

"Yesterday evening. Ian told me about it today, when I got my car."

"Got your car? Damn it! Don't you ever stay put?"

I straightened. "Murphy was tailing me."

Zoloski's gaze challenged mine.

I pulled the folded note from my jeans pocket. "This was the message."

Zoloski unfolded the note. "'Roses are red, violets are blue, sit tight, I'll come for you. Tell Andy not to leave town again.'" He crumpled it. "The ME could be wrong." His tone said he didn't think so. He stood. "I'll have a tap placed on your brother's phone." He did his police stuff, then returned to the couch. "First thing in the morning."

"He's out there. He knows about you." I swallowed. "Probably knows I'm here."

Zoloski's green eyes were patient, calm, watchful. "Probably does. And when he comes, we'll be waiting."

I shook my head, wanting reassurance, yet realizing no amount would make me feel safe. Except for the nights I'd spent in Zoloski's arms, I'd never felt secure, even with my baseball bat. Here, I kept a taser under my pillow, but missed my bat.

I pushed my fears down, irritated at myself. "I still don't understand why Mac's after me. I don't fit the pattern."

"The pattern's all in his mind, Blaize. Don't try to figure it out. It'll drive you crazy."

"But I'm a psychologist," I protested. "Figuring out people is my job." That's why I liked it.

Zoloski rolled his eyes.

So much for whining. "What about this latest victim? Why doesn't she fit?"

Zoloski shrugged, his thoughts hidden behind a noncommittal expression. "The PM isn't done. Let's wait and see."

And what if the post mortem showed the latest corpse wasn't

one of Mac's victim? His phone call to Ian might refer to the trashing of my bedroom. I thought about all the people I knew, their addresses and phone numbers in my directory, Mac thumbing through the list. I had a mental image of Ian taken by surprise, knifed to death. I told Zoloski.

He ruminated, picked up the dishes and walked into the kitchen. Water ran. Stopped. "We can't assign protection to everyone you know." He sounded as frustrated as I felt.

I skipped to the next item. "I found a couple of pictures. They might be important. I'm having them blown-up. I'll pick them up tomorrow."

His eyebrows rose. "Busy woman. You get a death threat, the guy breaks into your apartment, and it doesn't slow you down."

I didn't appreciate the sarcasm. "What am I supposed to do? Hide? Wait for him to knock on the door? I don't even remember what he looks like!" I was yelling, standing, wanting to pulverize something.

Zoloski's face turned red. "Yeah, well driving around, making yourself a target won't help!"

"I'd rather be a moving target than a prisoner waiting for my execution!" I took a deep breath, counted to three, let it out and sat down. "I remembered something, Stephanos."

The red of his face slowly receded. "What?"

"Mac was back-up for the lead vocalist in the production Sunny and I were in." I snagged the old flyer from the floor and handed it to him. He turned it over. Scrawled across the back were at least ten signatures—one of them was mine. She'd had the cast sign it! How had I forgotten that? I snatched the paper and held it under the light. My voice rose with excitement. "Someone might remember Mac, know his real name." I paused. "Has Whitman ever used an alias? Performed on stage?"

Zoloski flashed me an are-you-kidding expression "He's a politician." He shook his head. "There's no record of an alias."

I studied the scrawls. Two names leaped out: Sherry Davidson, the female lead singer and a former Miss Sacramento; and the producer-director, *Stuart* Kingston. They were the only legible names besides my own. I grabbed the phone book and found Sherry's number. There were four S. Kingstons.

"First thing in the morning, we talk to the guy." His energy was catching. I felt like Zoloski was quarterback, I was his wide receiver. A team.

THE RINGING IN my head wouldn't stop. I kept hearing the explosion of a gun next to my ear, then more of the high-pitched whine. Mac was nearby, breathing, whispering, but I couldn't make out the words because of the repetitive peal.

"Shit!" Zoloski's voice cut through the fog in my brain as he half-rolled, half-climbed over me to get to the phone. I groaned. Now what? Who would call at this time of night? Only an asshole. Or his work.

Except for the VCR clock—God, three-fifty—the living room was pitch-black. As I strained my eyes the kitchen light clicked on. I squinted.

Zoloski swore under his breath, grabbed the receiver and half-yawned his name while brushing his hair back from his forehead. His expression went from half-asleep to red-alert.

A ripple of cold shot into the pit of my stomach.

Zoloski said nothing, even after he pushed down the button to disconnect. He immediately dialed, listened, spoke. "He just called. Get over here. Now. I want all my calls monitored."

Roses are red, violets are blue. Had Mac whispered it into Zoloski's ear? Coming out of sleep, the nagging mystery of Sleeping Beauty, the victims arms crossed and their carved chests came together. Sleeping Beauty had her arms crossed and held a rose in all the Disney picture books. I knew why Mac carved up his victims' chests.

As Zoloski listened, I stumbled into his office, pulled out photographs of his victims as they were found. Dried blood made it hard to see a pattern, but it was there. Excited, I took the bunch into the kitchen, set them on the table and impatiently shifted from foot to foot. The Z-man gestured at me to sit down.

I slipped past him to the sink, ran water, and started the coffeemaker.

"So it's conclusive. Different knife pattern." Zoloski drew back a dining chair and sat, the phone resting between his ear and shoulder, scratching down notes on a small pad, studiously avoiding my eyes. "Yeah?" he said into the mouthpiece.

Yeah what? I wanted to rip the phone from his hand and ask my own questions. "Knife pattern?" I asked as he hung up.

Zoloski frowned, then relented. "This stays in your head."

I nodded.

"Mac made a shallow pattern of cuts on his victims' chests. This latest murder, there's overkill, but the shallow pattern isn't there."

"I think he's drawing," I said. "Roses are red..." I didn't like the picture in my mind. "Carving a rose in their chest, then crossing their arms so they can hold it."

Zoloski's face reflected interest. "Is this intuition or something else?"

"Intuition." I sipped my coffee. "But why is he doing it?"

"Sweetheart, when I know that I'll be dancing at his trial."

I shivered. I'd be dancing when he was dead.

AT FOUR A.M. the phone guys appeared at Zoloski's front door wearing plumber outfits. I glanced outside. They even had a truck. They were in and out quickly.

Zoloski and I shared a four-thirty pancake breakfast, making plans. We decided I would call Sherry until she answered, then, with Murphy following, drive over to talk to her, woman to woman. Zoloski would pick up the photos on his way to work. We'd meet for lunch. At which time, I planned to talk him into letting me tag along on his second round of interviews of Sunny's neighbors. One of them might recognize the blurred face in the picture.

Damn if that thought didn't make me want a cigarette.

Chapter 16

THAT MORNING, the former Miss Sacramento was home and willing to talk. Yee-haw, lucky for a change! I told her I'd see her within a couple of hours.

I tried the listings for S. Kingston's. The first three were Sam, Sid, and Steve. My heart pounding, I jabbed in the fourth number and got a busy signal. If it was Stuart, he was home. I called Zoloski to ask him to meet me there, but he was interrogating a suspect in another homicide. I left a message: I'd see him at lunch.

Passing Murphy, slouched in his tan Ford, I waved.

SHERRY DAVIDSON had a well-kept duplex near Carmichael Park, a partial match to the woman who answered the door. Mid-forties, good make-up job, straight hair dyed black and fastened back from her face with filigree gold barrettes.

I thanked her for seeing me and followed her into a warm, clean, but cluttered living room. She moved slow, her five-six frame that must have been a knockout once, now carrying an extra sixty pounds. Miss Sacramento had died long ago.

The coffee table and end tables were covered with candy wrappers, unopened candy, and half-eaten candy bars. A massive television screen occupied the corner.

"A projection TV," Sherry said with pride as she followed my gaze. She flashed me a fifty-tooth smile, reminding me of a car salesperson and I noticed her lipstick had peeled off. Her strong chin eroded into a jowl, which shook as she talked. "I could watch movies all day." Her voice sounded wistful as she sank into a permanent indentation in the couch and looked at me expectantly. Despite the cheerful countenance, she had worry lines permanently imbedded between her eyebrows and around her mouth.

I opened my file folder, took out the flyer for the show and handed it over. There was plenty of room on Sherry's lap. Her spread reminded me I hadn't worked out in days. If I survived Mac, I'd better get my butt into the gym.

She chuckled as she read it. "Long time ago."

"Do you remember the guy you sang with? Some duet about—" My mouth went dry as I croaked, "flowers." Not just any flowers. Roses. *Roses are red* ran through my mind. Where had I dredged up that memory?

Sherry had a far-away glow in her eyes. Then they narrowed. "I can still sing it." A note of challenge hung in the air.

"You had a nice voice," I lied. "Do you remember the lead singer?"

She smiled. "Marty Sherman."

I prodded, feeling like a English Pointer on hunt. "Do you remember his stand-in?" You didn't call him Mac the Knife by any chance?

She shrugged. "No. Wouldn't remember Marty except we did several shows together. He *talked* me into this one." Her tone implied he'd talked her into other things as well.

"It was a pretty small show," I persisted.

Her expression changed. "You were in it, weren't you? One of the dancers!" She sounded happily surprised. "And now you're a private investigator?"

Yeah, funny what rape, and a few bad relationships can lead to. I gave her an impatient, "Yes," not willing to explain I was a psychologist investigating Sunny's murder, not a PI.

"It must be exciting!"

"Most of the time it's pretty low-key," I glanced at the book. "What happened to Marty Sherman? Is he still around?"

"I have no idea, dear. I met my husband not long after the show ended. Quit seeing Marty." The wistful tone was back. "If you find him, maybe—" Embarrassment flickered in her eyes as she handed back the flyer.

"People change." Gravity pulls everybody down. But if you have fun, who gives a damn? "Do you remember anyone named Mac?"

She pursed her lips, then slowly shook her head. "No." Her gaze asked if it was important.

Only to his victims. I asked to use her phone.

I tried Kingston's number. Still busy. A glance at my watch told me I had twelve minutes to get to his place, ten to talk, and ten more to make it downtown. If I hit all green lights I'd make it.

Back in my Saturn, I shifted into first and shot down Fair Oaks, my thoughts racing ahead. In my rearview mirror I caught Murphy's tan Ford still dogging my trail. I felt excited. I had another name to follow: Marty Sherman. If this Kingston was the producer, Stuart Kingston, and he remembered Mac, I might not need it.

I nailed green all the way to Kingston's. He answered on my third ring, a mobile phone glued to his ear. A navy blue jogging jacket covered his beer belly, the matching baggy pants thin at the knees. "Just a minute," he barked into the receiver. "What?" he asked in an irritated tone.

Now I remembered him vividly. He hadn't changed much, except for the belly. The lines over the forehead and around the eyes had deepened into furrows. It gave him a grim-reaper look. Long, limp strands of dark hair surrounded a large bald spot. A first class asshole.

"I'm a private investigator, Mr. Kingston." The lie slid from my tongue. "I'd like a few minutes of your time." Nine to be exact.

"What?" he spoke into the mouthpiece and looked away, started to shut the door as though I didn't exist. "Now listen to me you little shit!" He noticed I wasn't about to leave. "Ah, crap. I'll call you back." He slammed the antennae down and bent it in half. A vibrant string of curses reminiscent of my stepfather followed. "Lady, whatever you want I ain't got!" He glared at me.

First class all the way. I stepped into the doorway and smiled. "You have a brain don't you?"

The semi-joke registered. He stared at me, eye to eye. "What's my brain got to do with you?" he sounded vexed, like he wasn't sure what to do with an assertive female.

I threw down the challenge, hoping his male ego would pick it up. "If it's still functioning, I'd like it to process some information—see if the memory bank still works."

He grinned. "What the hell. It's been a crappy day, might as well keep the ball rolling. Come in." He gestured me inside and closed the door.

Compared to Sherry Davidson, Stuart Kingston was slob gone crazy. Ashtrays overflowed on every available surface, two with smoldering cigarettes. And the place stunk. A few days without a cancer stick and the smoke was already burning my eyes. Still, a small, niggling part of me missed the joy of poisoning myself.

Two once-beige recliners and a matching sofa, all yellowish, matched the tobacco colored walls. He dropped into one of the recliners. I took the sofa and watched as he picked up a burning cigarette, inhaled, exhaled, smiled. I mentally promised myself to make a dental appointment.

"So, who are you and whaddaya want?" he asked, curiosity badly hidden behind his belligerent tone.

"My name is Blaize McCue. I'm a private investigator and would like some information." I showed him the show flyer.

He looked puzzled. "What about it? The show was for charity. Big pain in the ass. Never did another one."

"I just talked to Sherry Davidson. She mentioned Marty Sherman. But I'm interested in his stand-in."

"Sherry and Marty..." He gave a lewd grin.

"No, Marty's stand-in. The guy who filled in, in case of illness, disease, death?" I glanced at my watch. Two minutes to countdown.

"Yeah. So?"

"Who was he?"

"After fifteen years!" King shrugged. "How the hell would I know!" He took a drag on his cigarette.

"You remember anyone named Mac?" I asked as he stood and handed me the flyer.

"Who?"

Were we rehearsing Bud Abbott and Lou Costello? "Never mind."

As I climbed into my car, I told myself I still had several leads: Marty Sherman, Gordon Whitman, and Sunny's neighbors. If Sherman didn't remember his own stand-in, then what?

How long would Whitman be on vacation? As I shifted into fourth and zoomed through a yellow, I told myself that jail for breaking into Whitman's house was preferable to the morgue.

I CAUGHT ONE red light, was only sixty seconds late, and found a parking space near The Firehouse. In a few weeks, the Dixieland Jazz Festival would strike, filling Old Sacramento like a bucket of water overflowing a teacup, and I'd be lucky to find parking two miles away. Today I had to walk only a couple of blocks. I assumed Murphy was watching, but didn't spot him.

On the brick patio, under the shade of plantered olive trees, Zoloski sat at a table far from the clatter of kitchen noise. He had dressed in a smooth gray silk jacket, a light green Oxford button-down shirt, and a black silk tie with a thin emerald stripe. His slacks matched the jacket, the crease on each leg leading to black polished shoes. Spiffy! I beamed as he stood and pulled out a chair.

"You look pensive," he said.

A smile pulled at my mouth. "You look better than lunch."

"Ah." He smirked. "If I had more time I'd take you home for lunch."

"Promises, promises."

The waiter interrupted. We ordered and turned to business. Zoloski pulled out an eight-by-ten envelope. "Got the pictures." I opened it. They were worse than before. What did I expect when multiplying a blurred face by ten?

"I dropped the snaps at the lab. Asked them to see if they could get a sharper picture, enhance the background subjects. They're gonna work on it tomorrow morning and call when they're through."

I swallowed my disappointment, shoved the worthless photos back into the envelope, stuffed it into my overflowing purse, then told him about the interview with Sherry and Kingston.

"I appreciate you talking with them without me. I'll run a check on Kingston and Sherman," Zoloski promised.

Our sandwiches came. We ate like people on the run.

The waiter poured coffee and took our plates. "Where you headed?" I asked Zoloski, thinking about Sunny's neighbors and the fact that he was going to interview them again. Although a part of me wanted to put this off, one way or another I was going.

He gave me a wary, sidelong look. "You know where." Then he smiled. "All right. You can come. But *I* ask the questions." He touched my ear with a finger. "You listen."

After a meal I used to indulge myself with a cigarette, but

thinking of Stuart Kingston's yellow teeth and foul breath, I stifled the urge. The first thirty days of any kind of abstinence were the worst. I was halfway down the plank.

"How long since you quit smoking?" Zoloski asked as he left the tip.

"Almost three weeks."

He gave me the evil eye.

"Except for two brief spells of madness."

He draped his arm across my shoulders and gave me a squeeze. "This is how we'll play it. We're interrupting these people's lives. They're gracious to give us their time. We're grateful. Polite. Expedient."

"Not Arnold Schwarzenegger, huh?"

Zoloski growled in true Terminator fashion, "I'll be back." He opened the passenger door to his Z. "Only that part."

"No shoot 'em ups?"

He grinned.

THE FIRST NEIGHBOR on our list was a very nice, haired-haired grandma who usually worked at home as a computer programmer, lived in the condo above Sunny's. Today she was at the Lincoln Center downtown in a ritzy office surrounded by brick and an arboretum I'd have liked to transplant around my flat. A very knowledgeable woman, she was absolutely no help.

Zoloski looked glum. "I was hoping she might remember something more."

I strapped on my seat belt, wishing she had. "Didn't hear a thing until the police sirens." It was a good try.

Zoloski pulled into traffic. "With Mussorgsky's *Night on Bald Mountain* blasting over her stereo, I'm surprised she heard anything."

Damn it, I needed a suspect. "Caldwell found Sunny's body?"

"Yeah."

I rummaged through Zoloski's cassette tapes for some jazz, found a George Winston tape and stuck it in the deck, rummaged through my purse for a stick of gum and after a few chomps threw it away. "Are we talking to him next?"

Zoloski shrugged. "Couldn't reach him by phone. We'll drop

by his place, see if we can catch him."

Soft strains of piano lilted from the speakers. "What's Caldwell do?"

Zoloski glanced sideways, his expression wary. "Sells boats."

"Why the funny look?"

"He's Whitman's relative. A great uncle, third cousin, or something."

My heart skipped a beat. A connection to Whitman. A wild coincidence? "When did you learn this? Why aren't you leaning on him or something?"

"Because if you go back far enough everybody's related. Caldwell hasn't seen Whitman in years. Didn't even vote for him. They're not close. I interrupted Whitman's vacation long enough to ask about Caldwell. He said the same thing. Caldwell's sister concurs. Also, Caldwell's sister was visiting him at the time Sunny was killed. According to her, Sunny's screams woke them up. Caldwell went into the hall, saw the open door and went in."

"I'd like to talk to the sister."

"She lives in LA." He parked, glanced at me and shook his head. "You're not going there again."

"You could come with me," I offered.

Zoloski got out and slammed the door. "For once, take things slow," he said with a hint of exasperation.

I joined him on the sidewalk, thoughts flashing through my mind like a fast-forward movie. Take things slow? With a knife-wielding maniac on the loose? "I'll *call* the sister," I said in a compromising tone. "But I want to meet Caldwell."

Zoloski gestured down the sidewalk. "Let's see if he's home."

If he was, he wasn't answering the door.

As we walked past Sunny's door, sealed with yellow tape, I hesitated. "I'd like to see."

Zoloski held up a key. "Thought you might."

"Do you always think this far ahead?"

A wry smile tugged at his lips. "Only since I met you. But you better not breathe one word of this to anyone."

I had a vision of obedience school for potential mates, and said, "My lips are sealed."

Zoloski opened the door, and like Alice Through the Looking

Glass, I stepped into another world. The cemetery stillness wrapped me in a gauze of hyper-awareness. She'd let her killer in. Had he worn a disguise? Or had she not recognized him after all these years? In two steps we went from tile entry to living room light-brown carpet. Chalk marks near the far wall outlined where they found Sunny's body. Dark, unmistakable bloodstains lay inside and outside the lines. She'd obviously tried to crawl to the phone. The outlet was only a few feet away.

I suddenly found myself in the kitchen, the tap running, splashing water on my face as I gulped air. I dried my face with my tapestry vest and looked up to find Zoloski in the doorway.

"You okay?"

I nodded, took a deep breath, and exhaled slowly. "Anything else to see here?"

"Furniture was moved a couple of days ago," Zoloski said. "There was blood on the coffee table and phone. Nothing to suggest Sunny or her attacker went anywhere else."

I realized all the sarcasm and jokes in the world couldn't erase the stark reality here. I felt Mac's presence much more keenly. The apartment was smothering. I race-walked for the hallway and breathed deep. "Who's next?"

Zoloski stepped to the next door, his knuckles poised. "You up to it?"

"I'm fine," I lied.

The sharp sound of heels on tile responded to Zoloski's rap before the door opened a crack. "Ms. Findley, I'm Detective Zoloski. I called this morning."

The door opened grudgingly. The woman cast a sharp glance at me. I glimpsed a pointed nose, ferret eyes, and thin, disapproving lips. No unnecessary words passed through there. "This is Blaize McCue, my associate."

I liked the sound of that. Close associate. I mustered a smile.

She seemed flustered at my presence, pushing her platinum-dyed hair back behind her ears as we entered. She had the kind of hair nobody wanted, limp, wispy, blunt cut at the shoulder, black roots at the part. She wore no earrings, no make-up.

I followed Zoloski inside. The layout was the same as Sunny's, living room to the right, kitchen to the left, hallway, bathroom and bedroom straight ahead. Same color carpet. A pleasing scent of pine air freshener greeted me as she ushered us into the living room.

Although the cushions had begun to flatten from use, the sofa and matching love seat were wrapped in heavy plastic. Evidently, Margaret Findley liked to avoid cleaning costs. Was there a CA, Cleanaholics Anonymous, group I could recommend? I stifled the thought as Zoloski and I sat. Snap, crackle, pop.

A soap opera played from the corner TV, a couple in a clinch of passion. Findley's gaze followed mine, her face reddened and she reached for the remote. The picture blinked off.

Zoloski apologized for intruding and asked to go over her experience the night Sunny died "one more time." The woman's expression became irritated. "I've gone over this. I don't remember anything else."

"Sometimes when relating a memory things come back," Zoloski said.

"Sunny's killer is still out there," I added. "Anything you remember will help us."

After a sigh of resistance, she described hearing yelling around midnight. "I cracked my door, wondering if I ought to knock on Sunny's door. A tall guy, your size I guess, came out, Sunny behind him, yelling at him."

Anderson, the bodyguard.

"He had a cell phone in his hand and was telling her to calm down." Her nose wrinkled. "I shut my door and turned up the TV. The yelling continued a few minutes more." She sniffed. "I started to call 911, but it stopped before I could."

Zoloski jotted something in his notebook. Looked up. "Then what?"

Findley brushed back a few strands of limp hair. Hesitated. Glanced at me.

I smiled reassuringly and leaned slightly forward, woman-to-woman. "It's important you tell us everything you can remember."

She swallowed. "Ten or fifteen minutes passed because another commercial came on. I always put the TV on mute during commercials. When I did, I heard her scream again." She shuddered. "It was different."

"How?" I asked softly, my tone encouraging.

From Zoloski's posture and his expression, I knew Findley hadn't told him this before. The flicker of his gaze in my direction said I'd earned my keep.

The line of Margaret Findley's mouth softened. "I have a six-month-old niece I baby-sit occasionally. When she cries for food, her voice hits a certain pitch. When I put her down for a nap, her cries sound different." She looked from me to Zoloski, back to me, as though my being a woman automatically made me an expert on babies. Wrong.

In my counselor's voice, I asked, "How were Sunny's screams different?"

"She'd been angry before. This time she sounded scared."

I caught the look from Zoloski that said I was in charge now. "How long did the screaming last?"

"Oh, she just screamed the once. Then I heard a thud, like something hit the wall." She pointed toward her kitchen. "I went in there and listened. It was quiet."

"What happened next?"

"My show came back on. But I kept the mute on, thinking if I heard anything else I'd call the police."

"Did you think of going across the hall, or calling Sunny?"

Findley shook her head. "We only said hello to each other on occasion. I wasn't sure—I mean I couldn't believe I'd heard what I heard, you know?"

I nodded. Her gaze went from me to Zoloski. He nodded sympathetically.

She glanced at the blank TV screen. "I picked up the remote to turn the sound on when I heard a whimper. Like a dog in pain." She rubbed her arms. I felt the chill too. Her voice dropped, made me strain to catch it. "Only it wasn't a dog. I knew it. That's when I called the police." Her tone held remorse, guilt.

Zoloski flipped the page on his notebook. "When I talked to you last time, you said you thought maybe fifteen minutes separated the angry screams and when you dialed nine-one-one. Now, you say you heard another scream and a whimpering sound in between. How much time elapsed between the last scream and the whimper?"

She hesitated and I nodded encouragingly. She addressed Zoloski again. "Maybe five minutes. It could have been less, but it seemed a long time."

Long enough for a killer to clean up and get away.

Zoloski reviewed her timetable again, then asked, "Is there anything else you can tell us about that evening? Did you open your door again? See anyone else?"

She took a deep breath. "I opened the door when I heard the sirens, the police arriving. Mr. Caldwell was in the hallway, like I told you before." She paused.

I felt as though I was holding my breath.

"He looked strange. I suppose he would, finding a dead body like that." She didn't sound convinced.

"But it was more than that?" I queried, reading the "yes" in her expression.

She stood and went to the door, opened it. We followed. She pointed to the door one down and across the hall. "He lives there, but he was outside Sunny's door. It was open. His sister was behind him in the hallway. When I came out, well, the impression I got was that he hadn't gone into her apartment at all. That he'd just come into the hall."

Her brows drew together. "But then, he said he'd gone in, and found her." She shrugged and forced an uncertain smile. "I'm not the best judge of situations," she shook her head sadly. "Or I would have called the police sooner."

Yet she felt strong enough about what she'd seen to mention it. Zoloski's expression confirmed this was another new piece of information.

Margaret Findley was still remembering. "His sister was standing behind him. She said, 'They're coming, Matthew. Pull yourself together.'" Margaret Findley met my gaze. "I grabbed a coat, and went outside."

I remembered the scene, neighbors on the grass, the police, the bodyguard. Zoloski leaving me outside, then handing me off, Joe Montana style, to a patrolman.

"Thanks for talking with us," I said, while considering what she'd told us, and wondering about Caldwell. Had he found Sunny as he claimed? Suddenly I felt desperate to see his picture.

In the hall, admiration in his tone, Zoloski said, "You should be wearing a badge."

I did the "Aw Shucks" routine, but not too well.

"I did everything short of standing on my head to put Findley at ease when I talked to her the first time. You waltz in and she opens up." Zoloski's praise warmed me.

I asked, "You have a picture of Caldwell?"

Zoloski shook his head, his gaze thoughtful. Still thinking about the interview? "Margaret Findley has a history of schizophrenia, is on medication. A terrible witness. Even if the impression she got is correct."

"Too bad Caldwell's not home. You think he could have done it?" A shot in the dark.

Zoloski pulled out his keys. "No one else heard anything, or saw anything suspicious. Caldwell's clean. His sister was staying with him for Christ's sake. Findley is questionable. Maybe she's bored and decided to jazz up her life. Impress you."

"Maybe she was afraid a big hulk like you would chalk her story up to mental illness. A lot of men doubt what women say."

Zoloski climbed into the car, and unlocked my door, his face unreadable.

"Any other neighbors to interview until we get a hold of Caldwell?"

"No. The lady on the other side of Sunny's place was gone for the weekend. No one else heard, or saw anything."

I dropped my massive purse between my feet. It landed with a fifty pound THUNK. "What now, Sherlock?"

His eyebrows rose. "I want you to meet Caldwell. He works out on the river, off Garden Highway sometimes. We'll cruise by. Then we'll look up Marty Sherman."

There was a lot of hammering and sawing going on near the river. *New office buildings* a sign read. I smelled sawdust and fish, water and sycamores as we walked along a small marina. Caldwell, and Whitman? More wild thoughts followed. I waited impatiently while Zoloski questioned boat owners: Caldwell hadn't been on the river for a few days.

Zoloski drove me back to my car. "I'm putting you back in Murphy's capable hands. When I find Caldwell, I'll call you."

"I want to talk to Marty Sherman. Then Caldwell's sister."

Zoloski reached for the radio. "Let's see what I can get on

Sherman." By the time we reached my car, I knew Marty Sherman was not living in Sacramento, and my hot streak had ended one short of results. I felt like Mac was slipping through my fingers. Caldwell seemed too sudden and easy a suspect—and an unlikely one if his sister was with him. That left Whitman.

Zoloski glanced at me. "DMV will fax me Caldwell's picture, and Sherman's. I'll bring it home. You can spend tomorrow tracking Sherman down. We'll talk to Caldwell together."

"But don't leave the house alone?"

Zoloski grunted.

"Promises, promises," I teased. "If I keep mine, you better keep yours."

"I haven't made any. Besides, don't I always deliver when it counts?"

I grinned. "So far." I thought about the resolution I'd made after meeting our former Miss Sacramento. "I don't suppose you'll be home in time to escort me to my health club?"

Zoloski perked up. "Racquetball?"

The idea was gaining momentum. "And the Stairmaster."

"Weights?"

"You don't have to show your pecs to me, big guy."

Zoloski laughed. "Pending half a dozen felony assaults or homicides, I'll be home by eight."

At eight-fifteen I decided to go without him, picked up my gym bag and headed for the car.

Murphy met me at the curb. "He's a block away. I was just coming to tell you."

Zoloski zipped up right on cue. I dumped my stuff behind the seat and climbed in. "What about your gear?" I asked.

Zoloski pulled a U-turn. "In the back. Lots of nights I work out on the way home."

"Dinner?"

He shifted. "Fast food. You?"

"Your macaroni and cheese. Good stuff."

"Polished it off, did you?"

"I was lucky there wasn't much left or I'd be at the club all night. You should have been a chef. 'Course then you'd probably weigh two hundred fifty pounds."

Zoloski didn't laugh, his gaze fixed on the rear view mirror. "I think we have company."

The macaroni and cheese felt like a lead ball in the pit of my stomach. I glanced behind. Two glaring spots amidst the darkness. We passed the next intersection, hopped on the freeway, exited at Madison and headed for Manzanita. The headlights stayed with us. The worst tail in the world or he wanted us to know. Which didn't make sense. Mac? Was he getting too sure of himself? I said as much to Zoloski.

"Hell if I know, but I'm going to find out." He pulled into a gas station and parked the car.

Our tail slowed. Zoloski ran toward the street trying to see into the car. Whoever was driving evidently thought better of a confrontation and picked up speed. I dug the binoculars from my purse and focused. For a woman who carries everything, I had a heck of a time finding something to write the license number on. I repeated numbers and letters under my breath until I'd scrounged a gum wrapper.

Zoloski climbed back in the car, a disgusted look on his face. His gaze flickered from the binoculars to the gum wrapper in my hand. I grinned, pleased with myself. "I missed the first letter."

Zoloski stared, then chuckled. "Maybe I ought to carry a purse."

"Earrings and I'm out of here."

He laughed and called the number into DMV, argued with someone, talked to another someone, waited, talked, waited, then described the sedan as dark blue or black, foreign make. I fidgeted on the seat. We didn't have to wait long. There were over twenty possibilities. The night was young, but I didn't feel up to checking cars.

"It's probably not Mac anyway," Zoloski said as he revved the engine. "Probably some jerk I busted who wants to get even."

I hoped he was right. I didn't want to think of Mac getting any closer than the phone. "Let's go work out."

BY THE TIME we finished two sweat-drenching, neck 'n neck games of racquetball, I felt copper-topped energized. Twenty minutes on the Stairmaster and a circuit of weights mellowed me out. I headed for the shower.

Later, we met in the lobby, and I badgered him to call Caldwell. Zoloski told me in no uncertain terms that he knew how to do his job. But he dialed. And Caldwell answered. "Five tomorrow?" Zoloski said. "That'll be fine."

My stomach tightened in anticipation. I needed to keep my mind occupied. Zoloski must have had the same thought. He kept me occupied all night.

Chapter 17

SKIP TRACING was an art Ross had taught me years before. From the comfort of Zoloski's living room, I made up a tale of inheritance and after a series of phone calls discovered Marty Sherman had moved to LA. I left a message on his recorder, my thoughts already jumping to Caldwell's sister, Lillian. All signs pointed south.

I glanced around the living room. Would Mac dare break into a cop's house? No, I decided, he'd lure me somewhere else. When? How? God, what had I gotten myself into?

Zoloski called to say the car that had tailed us belonged to someone just released from prison. "He's pissed 'cause I put him there. He's all bluster. I put the fear of God into him."

"What a relief," I quipped. "How come I don't feel better?"

Zoloski's tone grew hard. "The only guy you have to worry about is Mac." A pause. "He'll have to get past me to get you, Blaize."

I wanted to say, "I love you," but it seemed too soon, or was it that other cops might be listening in?

Zoloski murmured, "See you at four-thirty."

I hung up, warmed by his tone, but disgruntled that the plate number hadn't led to Mac. I dug through the refrigerator for something non-fat, struggling with my practical, workaholic self. I'd promised to stay home. I punched my buddy Lon's home number and left a message. I was still interested in Gordon Whitman and whatever a little rummaging through his house might tell me about him, or his distant cousin, Caldwell. Were they best buddies? Golf partners? What?

By four I'd skipped rope twenty minutes, showered, washed and dried my clothes and put them back on. If I had to spend another day inside I'd go nuts. I called Maria to ask about my mail. It'd been a week. We were both too polite. I didn't like it, but wasn't sure I wanted to change it.

She asked if I'd learned any more about Connie's murderer. I heard resentment and stifled the urge to remind her I'd quit her employ, that I was doing this for myself. "I have some ideas," I said. "Nothing concrete."

A long pause.

I asked about my mail.

"There's a handwritten envelope here," she said.

Mac? My stomach knotted.

"The return address says Belinda Bowers."

Connie's friend. She'd promised to mail me her notes about her conversation with Connie. Relieved, I said, "I'll pick it up," then thought of my promise to Zoloski. "Tomorrow." The conversation dragged into silence. I said goodbye.

The phone rang. Zoloski, I thought. "Hello?"

"Roses are red," Mac whispered, his tone smooth, no hint of a real voice, "I'm so blue. Soon, I'll be happy, seeing you." The line clicked in my ear.

Frozen, I held the receiver, unable to think. The dial tone buzzed like wasps in my ear. A minute passed before I could breathe. I dragged in a chest full of oxygen and fumbled with the phone buttons as I punched in Zoloski's number. Some damn woman patched me through to someone else, who finally patched me through to him. The delay almost killed me. "He just called," I blurted.

"I know. It's okay." Zoloski sounded calm, but I pictured him pacing. "I just talked to the guys. He wasn't on long enough for a trace. Murphy's still outside, across the street. You're covered." His tone softened, yet held a determined steely quality, "I won't let the son-of-a-bitch hurt you."

My heart continued to thump, a loud bass drum in my ears.

"I'm on my way, Blaize. Hang in there." A pause as he talked to someone else.

How did he know I needed him?

He came back on the line. "You up to meeting Caldwell?"

I'd forgotten. "Sure." My hand tightened around the receiver, "I feel like a turkey the day before Thanksgiving."

Zoloski faked a laugh.

I paced the kitchen. "I found out Marty Sherman is in LA. I

left a message on his machine."

Zoloski didn't speak for a moment. I could almost see him shake his head as he said, "Stay put."

"Stephanos, be reasonable!"

"Stay!" he growled. The line went dead.

"I am not a dog!" I shouted at the fridge. It paid no attention. Twenty minutes later, Zoloski picked me up. I sat stubbornly on my side of the car.

He gave me a sidelong glance. "You mad?"

No, I wear this expression all the time. "Yes." I was proud of my monosyllable reply. It was progress over stone-dead silence.

"Is this going to be a chronic condition?" he teased.

Why did he bring out the best in me? "I think this is called testing the relationship." I studied Zoloski's profile. "Damn it, do you think I like being Mac bait? I want to get on with my life!"

Zoloski reached over and pulled me against his shoulder, kissed my brow.

I straightened up, feeling better.

His gaze held a question. "Caldwell's meeting us at his condo. While we're there I want you to think up some excuse—"

"Excuse for what?"

If you'd let me finish, Zoloski's expression said. "An excuse to look around."

"Like using the toilet?"

"Yeah. Check for photographs, anything that rings a bell."

"Shouldn't I have a warrant?"

"I wish. The guy's clean, but he did find the body."

"You think there's a chance he's really Mac?" My tone should have blown his hair back. It didn't.

Zoloski frowned.

"You really think Caldwell would call me on the phone a half hour before we're supposed to meet?"

Zoloski shrugged. "Maybe. Whoever Mac is, he's gotten away with years of careful murders. We don't know shit. That's bound to make him cocky."

I wished it wasn't so, but Mac was winning. He'd written the rules to the game.

We fell into silence. My stomach curdled as Zoloski parked in front of the condominiums where Sunny had died. I wiped my sweaty palms down the sides of my navy slacks. Wished I'd worn a blouse instead of the matching short-sleeved sweater.

Zoloski didn't move. "I got the pictures back from the lab." He pulled a file from the back seat, handed it to me.

Inside were two sheets of paper, filled with one and one-half-inch squares. First page, variations of a man's face. Second page, variations on a woman's profile. Who-dun-it checkerboards.

"They're computer enhanced from the snapshots. Best they could do."

"Like twenty versions of reality?" My gaze fell to the bottom row where a light pencil line circled a picture. "Caldwell?" I pointed.

Zoloski shrugged. "I circled it as the most like him."

"Sunny's ex, Barry Michelson, said the guy's name was Harper, or something close to that."

"Time to meet the man," Zoloski said, glancing at the dash and staring out the windshield, his thoughts ticking to some inner clock I couldn't read.

I closed the file.

CALDWELL OPENED the door on Zoloski's first knock. Medium length brown-brown hair, furrows on his forehead and around the eyes placed his age at an old forty-five, an average fifty-ish, or young sixty. The right age, but he looked too small and his face sparked no memory. His eyes were a deep blue, not the watery cornflower I had locked in my brain. As soon as our eyes met, his gaze shifted to Zoloski. I felt uneasy.

He was drying his hands on a towel and didn't offer to shake. His nails were lined with grease. "Been working on a boat engine for a friend. Come in." He wore new blue jeans and a worn blue work shirt, sleeves rolled up.

We followed him into the kitchen—neater than June Cleaver's television home—he paused to throw the paper towel into the garbage, then led us into the living room. I scanned the walls, bookshelves, and end tables for personal photos. None. From where we sat I could see down the hallway, two doors to the right, one to the left. Two bedrooms and a bath? Probably.

Caldwell sat down. "We went over everything twice. Why again?" He sounded curious, not upset.

Still, no bells. He was smallish, five-eight or so, slender, his movements economical. Wiry strength, I thought. Not the Mac I remembered. He glanced at me, his gaze unreadable. Nothing hinted that he knew me. If he had any antisocial disorder, he was masking it effectively. I expected Mac to have a long history of acting out with violence, sex, whatever; some kind of arrest record. But then some psychopaths were extremely bright, I reminded myself, capable of duping almost anyone. Including me.

In between Zoloski's questions, I asked about the bathroom.

Caldwell answered in the same unconcerned tone he used to respond to Zoloski. "Down the hall, first door on the left."

I doubted he kept any guilty secrets in the toilet, if he had any, but I actually did have to pee. Afterwards, I stuck my head out, saw Caldwell's head turned toward Zoloski and tiptoed across the hall into the master bedroom. How would I explain my wandering if the need arose? Duh, I got lost?

The five o'clock sun shone through the window above a mirrored headboard, giving me plenty of light. Black lacquered furniture flanked a king-size waterbed. On the bedside table stood a small, pewter-framed photograph of Caldwell and a woman. Caldwell was smiling at her. She was smiling at the camera. The photograph looked recent. So much for old pictures. The walls were empty.

Zoloski's voice rose and I realized I'd overstayed. My heart thumped as I snuck a look into the hall. Caldwell started to turn his head!

Something fell with a heavy thunk. Caldwell's gaze snapped back toward Zoloski. I jumped into the bathroom, flushed the toilet, and heard Zoloski apologize for dropping his glass as I wiped the sweat from my forehead, my heart still beating like castanets.

"Would you like something to drink?" Caldwell asked as I took my seat.

I shook my head.

He turned to Zoloski, his manner calm. Too calm. "You had another question?"

Zoloski threw me a quick look. I shook my head the tiniest bit.

He leaned forward. "You said Sunny Wright's door was ajar when you stepped into the hall?"

"Yes." Caldwell swallowed a long draught of water. Was he upset? Stalling? "My sister and I weren't sure what to do. Finally, I went in."

I cleared my throat to draw his attention. His dark blue eyes were inquisitive. I forced a smile. His answering one might have been a smirk, but was gone before I could tell. I felt another twinge of uneasiness. "Did you see anyone in the hall?"

He shook his head. "No." A pause. "Oh, yes I did." His words startled me, Zoloski too. "My neighbor, Margaret Findley." His tone cast aspersion on Findley. Did he know about her schizophrenia? Findley had thrown doubt on Caldwell too. Great.

Five minutes later we were out of there.

"Thanks for spilling your drink," I said as we crossed the manicured lawn. "For a moment I thought I was a goner."

Zoloski's lips curled. "All in the line of duty." His smile disappeared. "So, did he spark anything?"

"He *seems* like Joe Average." I considered my feelings as Zoloski started the car. "Something about him makes me uneasy. But it could be disappointment—because I don't think it's him. I saw a picture of him with a woman. Looked like his sister. Neither looked like Charles Manson."

Zoloski threw a sideways glance at me. "What bothered you about him?"

I closed my eyes, tried to will something to the surface of my brain. I shook my head.

Zoloski looked thoughtful. After a long pause, he said, "Let's talk to Sherman."

"LA?"

"I want to talk to Sunny's ex about these pictures. Show him a photo of Caldwell and his sister. Maybe he's mistaken about the name Harper."

Good old LAX Hollywood-stud Michelson mistaken? Naw. "Maybe we're stretching our leads."

"I also want Sherman to look at the pictures." Turning onto the freeway, Zoloski added, "Those pictures made you feel something. Caldwell made you feel something. You said so. Don't discount it."

"Discount is my middle name," I retorted, "but I'm working on it."

Zoloski's lips formed the ghost of a smile. "All I ask."

WE STOPPED BY my flat on the way to Zoloski's. As I stared at the living room's dust on dust, I felt a sense of not belonging. Everything was a mess. I felt Mac's presence like an ocean undertow.

"I'll just be a minute." I went into the bedroom, pulled my suitcase and baseball bat from under the bed, ignoring the red lipstick smear on the wall and pulled several pairs of leggings and tunics from hangers. I threw in underwear and socks: herbs for the clothes soufflé.

"You have some messages," Zoloski called from the other room.

I went rigid. One caller was Lon, inviting me out to dinner. Pat had called too, asking how the Z-man and I were getting along, and saying she had some good news, to call her. Zoloski and I smiled at each other.

The last was from my mother. Long explanations were not on my agenda at that moment, nor the emotional shit that went with family. Suitcase in one hand, bat under my arm, I surveyed my apartment, swallowed, grabbed my Bell Jar painting, slung my leather coat over my arm and towed Zoloski out the door.

Zoloski caught the bat as it slipped from my overfull grip. "What's this for? Thinking about joining the major's?"

I gave him a look that I hope said *You're hopeless*. "Protection. You can smash a guy's skull in with this."

"Yeah?" He stepped back eyeing the bat playfully. "Ever used it?"

"Not recently."

At the bottom stair he asked, "Who's Lon?"

No one you need to worry about. "A friend."

He paused at the car. "He sounded—chummy."

I smiled. "He's a great guy, a good friend, and not interested in women."

"Oh."

I kissed him passionately. "What now?"

Zoloski took a deep breath, "Well—I'm curious about the painting...why you painted it. It doesn't look like something you'd create."

I swallowed. "I've changed."

A teasing tone crept into his voice. "So, any other hidden talents?"

I chuckled, thinking of sensual delights. "Why don't you find out?"

He stowed my things in the back. "I'm afraid Murphy gets to enjoy your company." He sounded regretful. "I go back to work."

Disappointment lodged in my throat. I consoled myself with thoughts of the phone calls I could make to Matthew Caldwell's sister, Lillian; Barry Michelson; and Marty Sherman; maybe I'd catch them home and avoid LAX. "Okay." I clicked my heels. "There's no place like home."

Zoloski's tone registered surprise. "Great. I'll see you around eight or nine, then."

Did he expect an argument? "If I can't reach Caldwell, Michelson and Sherman, I'm leaving them a message: see you tomorrow."

Zoloski promised to get their addresses and accompany me to the depraved land of face-lifts and money. "But only if necessary."

"Okey-dokey, Smokey."

Zoloski chuckled. What more could a woman want?

THE LAND OF plastic surgeons and green it was going to be. Between Zoloski's job, Murphy's shadowing, and my zooming by the office to pick up mail, my nerves and Zoloski's were a bit tight when we finally settled into our economy seats. Zoloski's knees supported the chair in front. I felt cozy relief. No Mac here.

In the air, we reviewed Connie and Sunny's case files, mine and his, with me jotting questions.

1. Did Mac know both Connie and Sunny? Acquaintance?

2. Caldwell's background? Z's job.

3. Michelson wrong about the name Harper? Connection to Caldwell? Z & I will meet/ask.

4. Would Lillian Caldwell lie to protect her brother?

5. Does Sherman know either Caldwell? We'll see.

Zoloski pointed at number one. "What's that say?"

I crossed my feet and shoved the paper in my purse. "Just a note to myself." I asked Zoloski what had been on my mind since early morning, but because of the rush, I'd forgotten. "Why don't you test Caldwell's DNA? Steal a hair or something."

Zoloski stretched his legs into the aisle. "You've watched too many movies."

What did he mean?! I was the next slated victim! A little legal irregularity seemed reasonable to me. I kept the thought to myself.

"If we get the right answers, we'll have enough for a search warrant. Get samples from Caldwell, or write him off."

I munched a peanut and washed it down with diet soda. "I always thought the finder of the body was guilty eighty percent of the time." I smiled. "That's the movies too, I suppose."

Zoloski leaned back and closed his eyes, his voice filled with cynicism, "Unless you can sell it to a judge."

I closed my eyes too, tried to turn off the brain. Useless. I glanced around. Zoloski was snoozing or doing a good imitation. I opened the envelope from Belinda Bowers, Connie's chum, and skimmed the three hand-written pages. Zoloski opened his eyes and stretched as the seat belt warning chimed. I told him about the letter. "Looks like recap of what she said before." I stuffed the pages in my purse.

As Zoloski pulled down our bags, I steeled myself for another round at LAX. If we could get out of the place without being mugged, we'd be talking to Marty Sherman by ten.

No mugging—thank you Zoloski—and we were.

Chapter 18

MARTY SHERMAN, once lead singer in the show that changed
my life, now worked as an insurance agent in a downtown high rise.
Zoloski and I slid into the two available chairs in front of his desk.
My glance skimmed from the tight fit of Sherman's three-piece suit
to the dirty window. The sun was lost somewhere beyond the haze.

With a voice as smooth as his bald pate, Sherman said hello,
offering no apology for ignoring my phone messages. His
expression suggested more important pursuits, like insuring
Hollywood's finest talent against the loss thereof. When I asked
about insurance for murder victims his mouth drooped.

I continued before he regained control, "You were in a show
about fifteen years ago. Produced by Stuart Kingston. Sherry
Davidson was your *co-star*."

He frowned. "Fifteen years!" He smiled. "Sherry..." His
expression stuck between gloating and arrogant. "Sure, I remember
her. How is she?"

Fat. Sorry Sherry. "She's okay." I leaned forward, demanding
his attention with my gaze. "What we're interested in is the name of
the man who was your backup. He might have been called Mac, but
that wasn't his real name."

Sherman shrugged, his expression blank. "Just some guy on
the production crew who had a good voice."

Disappointment lodged in my solar plexus like a nail. Was the
guy that nondescript?

Zoloski slid the two photographs across the desk. "Is he in
either of these pictures?"

Sherman pulled out a pair of hip black-framed glasses, put
them on, peered at the snapshots, the more recent photo first. He
pointed to the guy Michelson called Harper, then to a blurred face
behind himself in the picture Sunny had taken fifteen years before.
"This could be him." He handed the pictures back to Zoloski. Mac,

huh?" He swiveled in his chair, stared out the window. "Sherry said it was a joke. I don't remember why."

I sat still and straight, clenching the armrests, afraid any movement might make him lose his train of thought. "His name was a joke?"

He cleared his throat. "Ask Sherry. She talked to the cast more than me—knew everybody."

I hesitated. That wasn't the impression she'd given me.

Zoloski spoke up. "What about you? You must have known your own backup." He leaned forward, his posture intimidating.

A sheen of sweat had appeared on Sherman's forehead.

I leaned forward too, painting a sympathetic expression on my face. "Think about it—I'm sure you'll remember him."

"But I don't!" Sherman removed his glasses. His hand shook slightly. "All I cared about was, uh, Sherry."

I sat back a little. "So what was the joke?"

Sherman shook his head. "I don't remember. Christ! It's been fifteen years!" If he'd had hair it would have been sweat-plastered to his head.

Frustrated, I strangled the armrests.

Zoloski handed him the computer printout of Mac possibilities. He also handed him a picture of Caldwell. "Do you recognize this man or any of the men on the print-out?"

Sherman took his time and I poured him a glass of water from the pitcher on the credenza. The contents disappeared in one long gulp. His eyes flashed with gratitude. He studied the pictures some more.

I poured myself a glass. It was clear and cold. Tasted thirst-quenching great, but didn't last.

"Don't know any of these guys," Sherman said at last.

I beat Zoloski to the next line. "You're sure?"

Sherman nodded. "It's been a long time. I just don't remember. I'm sorry."

I stood and thanked him.

"You think Sherry Davidson doesn't remember?" I asked when Zoloski and I reached the car, "or is she lying?"

Zoloski shrugged. "We'll check on that when we get back."

I fastened my seat belt and gazed through the windshield. May was just around the corner but it felt like December. "She's the one who told me about Marty Sherman," I thought aloud. "Why would she lie? Face it. Mac didn't make much of an impression on anyone." I stared glumly at the dash.

Zoloski started the car. "Let's see if Lillian Caldwell is home."

"What about Michelson?" I asked, trying to keep my voice casual.

Zoloski gunned the engine and the tires squealed as he pulled out of the parking lot. "Leave him for last." A dangerous smile pulled at his lips, then settled into a firm, straight line.

I eyed Zoloski as he drove, liking that he wore one of his nicest suits, a light blue silk tweed with dark blue chalk lines, a white button-down shirt, and navy tie. With his lizard skin boots adding to his six-two frame, he'd tower over Michelson. I fed my imagination on the two of them in a face-off.

We got off the freeway and wound through the mountains to Woodland Hills. LA traffic made me long for Sacramento. I put Michelson from my mind, and spouted directions to Zoloski.

Lillian Caldwell lived in a first-floor condo. Decorative bars covered the windows, a heavy, metal screen barred the entrance. I leaned on the doorbell, smoothed the wrinkles from my tan slacks, retucked my blue blouse and hoped my print jacket wasn't too wild for police work.

The woman who answered appeared to be in her mid-fifties, dark hair swept back and held in place by a mother-of-pearl barrette. Zoloski introduced himself, referring to me once again as his associate. I liked the way he said it.

Lillian unlocked the screen door.

I stepped inside first, smiled and shook her hand. It was cool and dry. Pencil thin eyebrows and false eyelashes, the kind that appeared individually attached to each natural lash, sable eyeliner, and blue shadow, enhanced her pale blue eyes. We studied each other for a moment that felt longer.

She gestured toward an arched doorway. A smattering of knickknacks trailed from the entry to the sunken formal living room. My feet sank in the muted gray carpet. Like her brother's place, the neatness rivaled television's finest families. "Would you like some iced tea? It's quite warm today."

Her manner suggested Southern hospitality and genteel manners. The smoothness of her neck suggested plastic surgery. Large gold medallion earrings graced her ears. They, no doubt, were real, but I wasn't sure about the rest of her.

I answered, "Yes," to the offer, hoping it would curb my hunger-pangs.

Zoloski added, "That would hit the spot, thanks."

Her dark brown silk palazzo pants made a swishing sound as she stepped toward the kitchen. Gold jeweled sandals flashed and I could hear the heels click once on kitchen tile. It looked like she spent thousands to look casual.

I glanced at the walls, skimming past framed floral prints, eyeing the eight-by-ten black and white wedding picture balanced on a bookcase. As soon as she was out of the room, I went over and picked it up. The frame was heavy, solid silver. It gleamed. Lillian looked like a mature twenty or young thirty. The man was much older, fifty, fifty-five. It was a grainy picture, like a bad copy. Strange.

Zoloski studied the books. Making a psychological profile based on reading taste? I put down the picture as she returned, a full silver tray balanced between her hands.

"Nice wedding photo," I lied.

She smiled, showing even white teeth as she handed me a glass of tea. "Thank you."

"You read all of these?" Zoloski asked in a voice that hinted of admiration.

She sat down. "Yes, I enjoy reading." Handing him a glass, her smile became seductive, reminding me of Sunny.

I drank half my tea in one long gulp, then nearly gagged—she must have used half a box of sugar. Passive aggressiveness, or did she like it this way?

Zoloski grimaced. At least Lillian hadn't played favorites.

She twisted the wedding ring on her right hand, a three-carat rock I'd be embarrassed to sport. Zoloski sat to one side, I took the other. Did she feel hemmed in? I hoped so. Her gaze went from me to Zoloski.

He put down his glass. "I'd like to ask you a couple more questions about the night Sunny Wright was murdered."

She settled her hands in her lap, her face calm. "I answered all your questions before. Signed a statement." Her tone was controlled, yet contained the hint of challenge.

Zoloski's eyebrows rose. "I'm looking for a murderer, Ms. Caldwell. Possibly a serial killer."

"Oh?" Politely inquisitive as though he'd said the weather might change. Much like her brother.

Zoloski leaned forward, holding her gaze, his voice low, but forceful. "I have an eyewitness account that doesn't match yours. I'd like you to recount the events of that night again." The words cut sharp and fine.

Lillian's back straightened, but her ice-cave blue eyes didn't waver. "What if I refuse?"

"Then I'd have to wonder why."

No one said a word. The tension thickened.

Zoloski's cool green eyes stared back at her. "If I have to haul you in for questioning, I will."

The lines of Lillian Caldwell's face hardened. Her lips compressed.

Zoloski didn't move. "If you're protecting your brother, lying for him, that makes you an accomplice. It'll make quite a show for the neighbors—me hauling you outside in handcuffs."

"The press might be interested, too," I said. "With a few phone calls, reporters will be camped on your doorstep."

Her gaze narrowed. It flickered from me to Zoloski. "All right," she snapped. "All right!"

Her capitulation surprised me. I hadn't expected her to cave. Zoloski flashed me a look of gratitude.

It was strange to watch Zoloski fire questions at this seemingly "dainty" middle-aged woman whose clothes, hair and manner projected softness, but whose voice was tough and brittle. When he got to why she'd awakened, she said, "I heard a woman screaming. She'd been doing it on and off for what seemed like most of the night. I was glad when she finally shut up." She slid one of her diamond rings up and down her finger.

I jotted notes.

She lowered her gaze to the floor. "Not very Christian of me, but I was tired from traveling the day before, and Matt and I had quarreled earlier."

"Quarreled?" Zoloski asked.

"A stupid sibling argument." She flapped her hand in the air as though waving away smoke. "I heard Matthew open his bedroom door, and that's when I got up."

I scribbled down her words.

"I dressed. When I came out his door was ajar." She paused, took a sip of iced tea. "He wasn't there."

Was this where the rubber met the road?

Zoloski leaned forward, his tone sympathetic, urging her to continue. "Where was he?"

She took a deep breath, exhaled. "The front door was open. He was in the hallway. Another neighbor was standing in her doorway, staring at Matthew, and I realized from her expression what the police would think."

Lillian Caldwell's earlier statement—which Zoloski had let me read—had said she'd met her brother in the hallway outside his bedroom, that she went with him to Sunny's apartment. He'd called the police. This new statement supported Findley.

Zoloski's neck muscles were tight as steel bands. "Was there blood on your brother's clothes?"

Lillian Caldwell seemed to study the carpet. She looked up and stared Zoloski square in the eyes. "No, Detective. His clothes were clean."

"What did your brother say?"

A glimmer of secrecy shone in her eyes. Did Zoloski see it?

"He said the woman in the apartment was dead. He wanted to go outside, get some air."

According to her new story, if Matthew killed Sunny, he'd had fifteen minutes to wash, change his clothes and destroy the evidence. Long enough. The man had just moved to the top of my suspect list.

Zoloski asked a few more questions, made some notes, then paused.

I jumped in. "Does the name Mac or Harper mean anything to you?"

She looked surprised. "Harper is my stage name. I haven't used it in years."

Bingo. The blurred faces in the three-year-old picture Barry Michelson had identified as "Harper and her brother" fell into place like a puzzle piece. But I felt resistant to follow where it led. When I'd been inside Matthew Caldwell's place, talking to him, I hadn't felt anything alarming. He hadn't seemed threatening the way I imagined Mac would. I glanced from Zoloski to Lillian. "What about the name Mac?"

She shook her head.

Zoloski pulled out the snapshot Barry Michelson had identified. "Is this you and your brother in the background?"

Lillian looked grim. "Yes. At a party. I was hoping to talk to the producer about a part." She shrugged. "As you can see, he preferred younger women."

I fired in the dark. "Did the party have anything to do with Gordon Whitman's campaign?"

A small degree of puzzlement entered her eyes, as though she'd anticipated where the conversation would go and this wasn't it. "Yes, the party was a fundraiser for Gordon."

Zoloski stuck the snapshot back in his file. "Why was your brother there?"

Yeah, if he and Whitman never saw each other?

"Matthew came to see me." War was being waged; it showed in her hesitation and the drop of her gaze. "I'd been avoiding my brother." When she looked up again, her voice came out low and rough. "He wanted money."

Blackmail? A loan? "Did you give him any?"

Lillian's eyebrows rose as a humorless smile flashed. "Oh, yes. He was blackmailing me."

I don't think I hid my surprise as well as Zoloski.

She stood and paced the room as though on stage. "I won't tell you what for." She paused. Waiting for a protest? When we didn't, she continued, "That's the reason I was in Sacramento three weeks ago. To pay him—again." She wrung her hands. "As always, for the last time."

Zoloski stood too, his gaze intent. We were on the same wavelength. "So you offered your brother an alibi in return for an end to the squeeze?"

She flashed a cool smile. "It seemed so—perfect."

I asked what she'd done that was worth blackmail.

She shrugged, obviously wasn't going to answer.

Zoloski looked down at her. "Why are you telling us this now?"

"Because it's his fault you're here," she said, her tone vindictive. "I'm sick and tired of him...you should be bothering him, not me."

For a second I saw her as a young girl, the kind of sister that might enjoy shutting her little brother in a dark closet and leaving him there, or washing his mouth out with soap.

I threw her another question, trying to get her talking again, hoping to circle back to her brother. "How long have you been paying your brother off?"

Her eyes narrowed. "Figure it out." She gestured toward the door.

Damn.

"Just one more question, please." Zoloski's green eyes would have melted the buttons off my jacket. "Do you have any old snapshots of your brother? Ten or fifteen years ago?"

Lillian Caldwell registered surprise. "No. My husband died in a fire nearly five years ago. Everything was burned." A note of triumph or something I couldn't get a fix on strayed into her voice.

I opened the screen door, glad to be breathing fresh air. Well, LA air. I felt her eyes, like darts, follow us to the car. One vindictive woman.

I FIGURED IT was no longer necessary to talk to Barry Michelson. Zoloski disagreed. We stopped at a fast food joint and stuffed our faces with greasy hamburgers and French fries while Zoloski related what he knew about Caldwell. Matthew and Lillian had grown up in California, moved every year or two with military parents, and had lived in every big California city and a few small ones. Their parents died before the kids finished high school. Matthew and Lillian lived in a foster home until they turned eighteen. Matthew went to work in a machine shop, attending college at night. He'd graduated with a degree in business. Lillian had moved to LA where she met and married her movie producer.

As we got in the car I voiced opposition to visiting Barry.

"What can he tell us that someone else can't?"

"Mr. Money Bags makes me curious," Zoloski admitted with a mischievous twinkle in his eyes. "I've never met a *big* Hollywood producer who lives in Beverly Hills. I don't want to pass up such a wonderful opportunity. Humor me."

I'd humor him all right. I slapped him playfully on the arm.

Zoloski groaned emphatically. "Watch those snappy hands!"

"They're not snappy!" I said with mock defensiveness. "They're sending you a message, Morse Code style. Let's go home."

He shook his head. "Sorry, Ma, never learned Morse."

Feeling frisky after our big score with Lillian, I leaned over and ran my fingers down one shoulder and across his chest. "How about Braille?" My fingers trailed lower.

Zoloski gave me a husky: "Hey, wait til we're parked."

I moved back to my side of the seat.

He pulled off the freeway and for a moment I thought he was serious, until he stopped next to a phone booth. "I'm gonna call the office," he said.

I almost offered him my cellular, but figured he didn't want me eavesdropping or he would have asked for it. So much for roadside fun.

He talked into the phone, his expression wary as he glanced in my direction. I shifted in the seat, uncomfortable, wishing I could listen in and wondering how much he would tell me.

When he climbed back in the car, his expression was unhappy. "We had Caldwell's condo staked out, but our guys lost him downtown."

Tension twisted its familiar path across my shoulders and into my neck. "You think he's Mac? And you didn't tell me?"

Zoloski's lips tightened. He turned the ignition. "Maybe. I sure as hell would like to find some evidence."

I played with the corner of my too-bright jacket, which suddenly felt like a target. "Do you think we shook him up enough yesterday to make him run?"

Zoloski shrugged. "He didn't act it. There's tons of people downtown right now for the free Children's Festival in Old Sac. He disappeared in the crowd."

Was he Mac? What about Whitman? I voiced my questions aloud, Zoloski listening, offering no answers, then I added, "Caldwell has at least one connection to Whitman."

"Remote," Zoloski reminded me. "It's Lillian that bothers me," he said a moment later. "Did you check out her eyes? Like her brother's, cold as death. Seemed to want to implicate her brother in Sunny's murder, but only to a point."

"Playing with us?"

"Maybe."

"Lillian admitted she and Matthew attended a fundraiser for Whitman, too."

Zoloski was unimpressed. "So did thousands of others."

"Including Sunny," I reminded him.

He shrugged.

"Whitman is up for re-election. He can't afford to be linked to a serial killer, no matter how distantly related."

Zoloski shot me a warning look. "That's a helluva jump you just made. You think if Caldwell's a murderer, then Whitman knows it?"

"Why else would he deny ever seeing him?"

"Because it's true!"

"I know Whitman was behind my car wreck," I shot back. "My questions about Connie shook him up."

Zoloski turned onto Sepulveda Pass, leaving one set of hills for another. "An illegitimate daughter he didn't want anyone to know about. Understandable."

"Understandable?" I repeated, angry at the way he had tossed off the word. Like if he had an illegitimate daughter he wouldn't want anyone to know either.

"From Whitman's point of view. Not mine."

I took a deep breath. "Oh."

"Besides," Zoloski added, "Sunny was still alive when you visited Whitman. He couldn't have been worried about Caldwell—" His hands tightened on the wheel. "Unless he knew Caldwell murdered Connie."

I sat back in my seat, feeling vindicated. "Sounds like you ought to talk with Whitman." And I planned to be there.

Zoloski's gaze narrowed. "Maybe so."

I turned on the radio, found a golden oldies station and let my thoughts sift facts until I felt like the computer on an old Star Trek rerun, *Insufficient data* flashing in my brain.

As we approached Beverly Hills and wound our way past walled estates and iron gates, Zoloski adopted a reassuring tone. "Most likely Caldwell will go home and we'll pick him up again."

He pulled into a tree-lined driveway and stopped at an electronically-controlled fence. "If he's Mac, he won't return. I wouldn't anyway."

Zoloski hit the intercom button. An unfamiliar voice answered and we were buzzed through. We rolled over the cobblestone drive at a snail's pace.

"We can still run his DNA," I suggested, thinking it'd take at least two weeks to get results. Would Mac wait that long?

"Provided we find something to run it from."

I picked up my purse. "What if you get a sample and it doesn't match?"

"Then we widen our net." Zoloski turned off the ignition. "What if the DNA matches Caldwell and you can't positively identify him as the man you and Sunny called Mac?"

Bad news. I got out of the car. "If the DNA matches, my testimony won't matter."

Zoloski looked at me over the top of the car, his mouth a line of skepticism. "Tell *that* to a jury."

My stomach clenched at the thought of Mac going free.

We climbed two palatial stairs to a wide, double-paneled oak door. The two-story, all-white mansion had an onion-domed turret, a Southern plantation whose roots had been transplanted, first to the Middle East, then here. An architectural nightmare, if you asked me.

I hit the doorbell. The afternoon sun was brutal and I could feel a trickle of sweat drip between my breasts. In two more months, Sacramento would feel the same way. If I were alive. My lunch filled my stomach like a lump of lead, the energy from the coffee long gone. It was nearly two o'clock.

Barry answered his own door. Amazing. He looked debonair in tan slacks, a dark blue silk shirt open at the neck, and a multi-colored linen jacket. A blue handkerchief—it matched his shirt—

peeked out from his pocket. He smiled, exposing his Dracula eyeteeth.

Zoloski smiled too. Breathtaking, or maybe intimidating, since he stood a head taller than Barry. "I'm Detective Zoloski. I talked to you on the phone."

News to me.

Zoloski gestured toward me. "You know Blaize."

"I do." Barry extended his hand, appearing calm, not the least intimidated by a six-foot-three detective. The two shook hands.

I thought I was ready for "impressive" opulence. One look at the inside of the house told me I wasn't. A marble entryway bigger than my whole flat led to a sunken living area. Pale beige Berber wool covered the floor, a massive crystal chandelier hung from the ceiling. I wondered if Barry had ever shot a movie in the place—it looked so perfect. I glanced around for some sign of the blonde.

"I was reading over some movie scripts." Barry led the way into a dining area adjacent to a smoke-colored tiled kitchen the Galloping Gourmet would have swooned over. Every cooking utensil imaginable sparkled from ceiling racks over a central butcher-block unit that outsized my entire kitchen. The smell of fresh brewed coffee permeated the room. The house more than made up for Barry's five-foot-eight inches.

At a polished mahogany table big enough for twenty, amidst a scramble of scripts, each in its own pile, sat a dark blue mug that matched his shirt. Talk about color coordinated! Barry gestured for us to take a seat. "Would you like some coffee?"

What, no maid? "Sure."

Zoloski's face was unreadable. "Sure," he echoed.

Barry brought over two steaming mugs that matched his own.

When we were all seated, a moment of silence lingered. Barry's gaze went from me to Zoloski. "You must be the boyfriend Blaize told me about."

My face grew warm.

Zoloski put down his coffee. "And you must be the movie producer she told me about."

Barry smiled tightly, perhaps considering what I might have said. "So, you wanted me to look at some pictures?"

Zoloski opened his file and handed over the two snapshots.

Barry glanced at them. "Derek Jones and Amanda Stretman—at some political or charity gig. Three, maybe four years ago."

"And the couple behind them?"

Barry frowned as he studied the picture. "Harper somebody." He paused, his tone thoughtful. "Lillian Harper."

Zoloski's voice was quiet. "Her escort?"

Barry shrugged. "Just some guy. Her brother—I think."

"What can you tell me about Lillian Harper?"

Barry tapped his foot. "Small-time actress. Her husband was a producer, had money, got her a few small parts. He died four or five years back." He shook his head. "That's all I know."

But Zoloski didn't quit. "Does the name Caldwell mean anything?"

"No."

I took a sip of coffee, burned my tongue and went back to inhaling the fragrance.

"Did you know Lillian Harper's husband?" Zoloski asked.

Barry shook his head. "Not personally. Once in a while we talked business. That's it."

Zoloski beat me to the next question. "Is there anyone you could recommend that could tell us more?"

Barry lifted his gaze from the table, studied Zoloski for a moment, then looked at me. "Why don't you give Lillian a call? This picture's only a few years old. She probably still lives here."

Zoloski answered. "We did."

Barry seemed to digest the information. "Oh, well—then you might try the *Los Angeles Times*. When her husband died, the paper ran a big story about them. The way the paper wrote it, Harper died in a fire, although there was a nasty crack on his skull. It could have happened when the roof collapsed, but..." He shrugged.

"Did the cops check it out?" I asked.

"She had an alibi. Nothing was ever proved." Barry stood. "I've got to run." He walked us to the door. I breathed a sigh of relief.

"We're not going home yet," Zoloski said as he gunned the motor. "Check the map and find the nearest library, okay?"

I did. "We have to get back on the freeway," I moaned. How could people live in this city?

The library confirmed Barry's story. The house had burned down, fire started by a cigarette. Husband had a crack on the head.

Lillian had been at a movie. With her brother!

The story gave me the creeps and I laced my arm through Zoloski's, wondering: Did murder run in the family?

Chapter 19

HOME LOOKED good, even though it wasn't really mine. I liked the thought though. Zoloski dropped me off, Murphy playing watchdog, and went back to work.

I spent the early evening returning phone messages. Lon was "unavailable." Mother her usual self. Negative. Pat shocked the hell out of me with news of a June wedding in the works. This from the woman who had stayed single past the age of thirty-three and swore she needed a man like a hole in the head. Who was I to talk?

Zoloski called at six p.m.: he was on his way home; Caldwell remained unaccounted for. I forgot to tell him about Pat, then figured it was probably old news at the office.

Over a cup of decaf, I pulled Belinda's three-page letter from my purse for something to occupy my mind.

The front door opened and I jumped. The Z-man had the case files on Connie Donovan and the other victims. I studied the two-inch thick heavy black binder a moment, then held up Belinda's letter. I read the last few lines ending with: *"My father has a boat. Maybe I'll go there."*

"Does Whitman have a boat?" Goosebumps rippled up my arms.

Zoloski picked up the phone, and after a moment hung-up. "Busy."

I spilled some more thoughts aloud, "Caldwell sells boats, repairs them, and according to a neighbor, spends lots of time on the river. Had Connie tried to find her father and run into Mac instead? My head spun with possibilities.

Zoloski got on the phone. He talked, sighed and talked some more. A half-hour later, he was on the phone again, swearing under his breath one second, overly nice the next. "Bloody red tape," he slammed down the phone and grabbed his coat. "Whitman owns a cabin cruiser docked near Old Sac, Miller Park."

I was a step behind Zoloski as he started for the 240Z. "It may just be a wild goose chase," he tossed back at me. "You're safer here with Murphy."

Safer? Try again. I jumped in the Z and snapped on my seat belt.

Zoloski revved the engine, his face a mask of irritation. "I could order you out."

"And I could drive myself."

His jaw tightened, but he backed out, tires squealing, rubber burning.

Sorry Z-man, I had to see this through. I had to know whatever the boat might tell us. My gut said we'd find something there. Trophies? Some killers kept body parts, some kept underwear, movie videos of the murders, whatever they needed to get off on the fantasy again. Kick the cycle into high gear. And kill again.

I TOOK DEEP breaths, trying to relax while Zoloski drove and information squawked over the radio. Every now and then he picked it up and talked. Other patrol cars would meet us there.

We turned down Broadway, lined with restaurants and decrepit buildings that looked worse at night. A few people were on the street, their occupations questionable. Zoloski slowed, bumped across railroad tracks, and turned into the marina.

The crescent moon glimmered off the water like tarnished silver. We parked—no sirens—everything quiet. Two uniformed cops stepped to the car. The pier was well-lit, two long metal ramps leading down to a cement pier and a hundred or more boats and yachts moored in long rows like a parking garage. Some were under a tin roof awning—sheltered parking, some were uncovered. Several patrol cars were parked near the entrance.

Zoloski eyed me. "I'll handcuff you to the car if you so much as crack the door." He got out, pointed me out to a young cop. "Make sure she stays put."

I smiled, my jailer didn't respond. I rolled down the window and tried small talk. He glared, as though it was my fault he had to miss the fun.

Zoloski returned within thirty minutes. His frustrated expression told me no one was there. I got out, cursing myself for not reading the entire letter earlier.

"Can I see the boat?"

Zoloski hesitated. "You might not want to. He kept souvenirs."

My throat tightened. "I have to," I croaked. God, was this it? Was Caldwell Mac? It's Whitman's boat, my mind whispered.

"Okay." Zoloski's expression reflected unhappiness, but he didn't argue.

A breeze cut across the water chilling me to the bone as I followed through the unlocked door and down the ramp. My tennis shoes slapped lightly against the metal planking. My flashlight skimmed across the side of the 40-foot boat. *Bayliner Motoryacht*, I read. *The Merry King* titled its back. Not for much longer. I swallowed and stepped on board. It tilted and I bent my knees to steady myself, keeping my hands, and fingerprints, at my side. The knot in my stomach tightened with each step.

We used our flashlights to descend into the cabin. "Don't touch anything," Zoloski warned as I ducked beneath the yellow police tape, and stuck my free hand in my jacket pocket.

My beam fell across teak paneling, upholstered seats, an unmade bunk. The cabin was about the size of my bedroom, big for a boat, small for living space. I smelled beer, accidentally kicked an empty Miller can with my foot, the sound abrupt. I tore my gaze from the can. Everything else was scrupulously clean. June Cleaver again. A cat's yowl cut through the stillness. I imagined Mac not far off, watching, waiting. A stab of tension drove between my shoulder blades.

Zoloski motioned with his light toward a wall closet. I lowered the beam to the floor. Not Dante's hell, but bad enough as I stared at the dried blood, moved the light over a shirt, pants and the toe of a pink, turquoise and white running shoe. An image of Connie, dressed in these clothes, flashed in my mind. "Connie Donovan wore this when Maria brought her to see me." Fresh guilt struck. Somehow I had let her slip between my fingers—into Mac's.

I felt sick, found it hard to breathe. "Is that the bathroom?" I stepped toward the tiny opening. Zoloski moved aside. A small mirror hung above a polished sink, magazine pictures of mutilated bodies, and sexually explicit pictures jammed in the edge of the wood frame. The beginnings of his fantasy? Sickening thoughts skidded through my mind. I closed my eyes, shutting them off.

The tiny bathroom walls closed in when I blinked. I backed out, my hand automatically touching my purse, seeking the reassurance of my gun. "Let's get out of here." Did my voice tremble or was it the rest of me?

Zoloski walked me to the car. "I've got to stay. Officer Vallerie will take you home. Murphy's there."

Vallerie looked slender, young and innocent. I wanted Mr. Universe. Out of breath from the climb back up the long ramps, and physically nauseous, I didn't have the strength to argue.

Zoloski gave me a hug, and I inhaled the smell of him. I love you. "Be careful," I whispered.

Zoloski mustered a warm smile. "I'm always careful, Sweetheart."

I FIDGETED ALL the way home, trying to blot out the horrible image of Connie fighting for her life, and losing. I tried to imagine the rose garden at the Capitol. Anything but gore. Nothing worked.

My mother and brother were sitting on Zoloski's doorstep. I wanted to stay in the patrol car—I loved them both—but this wasn't the time for family.

When my mother saw me, her smile flashed, despite worried eyes, the proverbial jar of homemade chicken soup in her hands. Some unknown Jewish heritage, no doubt.

Despite his size, Ian fidgeted like a little boy. He'd undoubtedly told mother about Mac. Just what I needed. S-mothering. In the yellow porch light, Mother looked closer to fifty than sixty. Ian, on the downhill slide toward forty, with his red hair and smooth face, looked twenty-five. We shared the same genes, yet at thirty-one, I looked it. Dorian Gray reflecting the family peccadilloes? A sad thought. I gave mother a hug and she clung to me. Who would she focus on and offer unending advice, if I were dead? I felt like a child again in Ian's embrace, then an adult as I unlocked the door to my lover's house.

"I'll put this in the fridge," Mother said, holding the soup up. A moment later, her heels clicked over the tile.

Ian broke away. "I'm gonna have a cigarette. Join me?"

I shook my head, thinking of all the times we'd shared a

smoke. "I quit."

He rolled his eyes as if to say "sure." "Tell Mom I'm in the car."

Still the middleperson. "I'll tell her."

The door closed. I could hear water running in the kitchen. Now what?

Mom gestured toward the cupboards, her movements bird-like. "I hope you don't mind. I thought you might like some tea. Or are you hungry?"

"I've eaten." I thought of Whitman's cabin cruiser, Connie's bloody clothes and my stomach roiled. I wanted to lie down, not talk, yet something compelled me to sit. Every time I was around my mother I seemed to regress into my family role—the lost child. It made me mad. "Tea sounds nice," I mustered.

We sat, nursing our orange spice, my mother reassuring herself I was okay. I wondered if I'd see her again. Premonition or just negative thoughts?

She stood. "Well—"

I walked her to the door, ignoring the dampness in her eyes. My thoughts felt scattered and an emptiness blew through me that made my throat ache. "Bye, Mom," I managed.

She hugged me and I squeezed back, feeling her frailness as I stooped.

Ian was leaning against the car, cigarette butts littering the curb, one between his fingers.

Mother paused at the edge of the cement step. "Take care, okay?" Love shone in her eyes.

"I'll call." When it's over. "Soon." I hoped.

I closed the door, locked it, and poured myself another cup of tea. Ruminations about my past made me wonder how I'd do with Zoloski long term. He'd asked me to stay until Mac was captured. But I had bills to pay, no money coming in, and hadn't been to my office in days. I had a cushion in my savings account, could go awhile, could refer my clients to another therapist for a few more weeks, but not indefinitely.

Tired and lonely, I played with the TV remote, skipping through channels.

I pulled back the blinds to check on Murphy. Still there. I

looked in the fridge a couple of hundred times. Nothing good to stuff my feelings with. I gave up the wait and went to bed with Jay Leno, longing for the sexy Z-man.

I awoke in an icy sweat, the frigid claws of a nightmare clutching at my throat. I held my breath. Soft breathing in the room, not mine. I blinked, saw a vague shape looming over me in the darkness. My heart slammed against my ribs. It wasn't a nightmare. It was steel. Cold steel—against my neck.

I tensed, my mind shifting into overdrive, my thoughts tripping over themselves. Where the hell was Murphy? Was it Mac or the parolee out for revenge? How'd he get in?

The smooth, whispery voice cut through the darkness, and my hopes died. "Wake up." The whisper curdled my insides. Mac.

I lay on my back, one hand buried beneath the pillow, the other across my waist. Did he know I was awake? I slowly burrowed my hand further under the pillow, searching for my taser, peering up under my lashes. As my eyes adjusted to the dark, I could see his outline, face covered by a stocking mask.

"Don't move," he whispered.

The blade pressed into my skin, the chill of it seeping into my bones.

Where was the taser? "I won't," I lied with all the sincerity I could muster, the metallic taste of fear in my mouth.

His arm relaxed, but not enough. He leaned closer like a black shadow, the smell of his leather gloves in my nose.

The phone rang and he flinched, the blade nicking my throat. I drove my fist into his stomach and slid sideways. The knife hit my jawbone. I screamed, grappling with his arm to keep the knife away, feeling the warm wetness on my neck as I kicked the covers back. The knife sank in the pillow beside my head as I kicked at his groin. Missed. The phone's shrill ring continued.

I lashed out with my leg again, hit his knee and felt him stiffen. Scrambling off the bed, I reached for my purse. He stabbed, everything in slow motion as the blade burrowed into my flesh. A strange ache pulsed through my shoulder.

I lurched backwards, dodged around the end of the bed, and threw my purse. It hit him square in the chest. He staggered backwards a step.

Dropping to my knees, a lipstick rolled between my feet as my fingers closed around the solid wood of my baseball bat.

Mac lunged. It was the bottom of the ninth—tie score, full count, fast ball coming in—and I swung for the fences. CRACK. Home run, right to his forearm. Surprise.

He screamed, the sound high and shrill.

My next swing hit the window, shattering it, and I swung again, screaming in rage, obliterating the lamp. The phone toppled to the floor, Zoloski's faint voice calling my name: "Blaize! Blaize!"

Mac backed into the hallway, hugging his arm, his eyes burning through the eyeholes of the mask like glowing pieces of blue steel.

Sirens rang in the distance as our eyes locked. Then he turned and ran. My muscles began to spasm as his dark shirt blended into the night.

Blood pounded against my temples, drowning thought. I touched my neck. My fingers came away wet and sticky, my arm dripping blood. I felt no pain, part of me wondering if it was all a nightmare. The neatly cut hole in the sliding glass door whispered "no."

Weakness flooded over me, my legs feeling like over-cooked spaghetti. Where was Murphy? I reached for the phone, it seemed miles away, then slippery in my hand. My fingers felt too clumsy to punch the buttons, my arm too heavy to get them there. In a woozy voice, I said "help" and sank to the floor, my body leaden, my thoughts floating: "Sunny, yesterday my life was filled with pain..." the song whispered eerily through my mind. Zoloski's voice drifted into the words, his face became part of a hazy dream, the touch of his hand almost real.

WHEN I CAME TO, I felt groggy and brain dead, the smell of disinfectant lining my nostrils. Footsteps echoed far away, heavy, cavernous. I felt uneasy about the unidentifiable sounds. Dim light filtered through my half-closed lids as I struggled to force them open. I squinted, fighting the drugged sensations that pulled at my eyelids. My throat felt like steel wool inside, porcupine prickly outside.

Someone held my hand. I tried to turn my head, felt the skin stretch across my jawline as pain shot into my ear. Then I remembered. "Mac—" I croaked, the sound frog-like.

Zoloski leaned over me, his face coming into focus. "You're safe, Blaize. It's okay."

I felt my lips curl at the corners. "You look like shit," I rasped. That brought a look of relief, a brief grin. I cleared my throat. "How long—"

"Twenty-four hours."

"How long have you been here?"

He hesitated. "Twenty-four hours."

My heart swelled with love. Tears pricked my eyes as I noted the dark circles under his. "Get some rest, big guy." I was glad he was there and glad when he didn't move.

He smiled, pressed his palm against my forehead, brushed my hair back. It felt wonderful. "Your brother was here." A pause. "And your mother."

Great. He'd met the whole family. "Mac?"

Zoloski frowned. "Got away."

"Water."

Zoloski helped me sit, bolstered my pillows, then held a glass with a straw to my lips. After several sips I felt almost human. "I broke his arm—with the bat."

Zoloski grinned, but the tired circles under his eyes remained. "Did you see who it was?"

"He wore a ski mask. He was small, slight, wiry. Had on a heavy black shirt, black jeans." I recalled the smell of leather. "New gloves."

"Caldwell?"

I shivered. "He didn't say much. Just a whisper. It sounded like Mac." Something bothered me about that whisper, but I couldn't tag it. "Everything happened so fast."

Zoloski squeezed my hand. He stroked my forehead, his fingertips warm and soothing.

I sank down into the pillows. My eyes closed as he said, "Whitman's on vacation. Another good alibi. Caldwell's surfaced. Says he was at an all night poker game. We're checking it out." His tone was worried and I wanted to murmur something encouraging, but darkness swirled behind my eyes, like an inviting warm pool. "Take it easy," he said. "There's a guard outside. You're safe."

"Murphy?" I felt sleepy under his caresses.

Zoloski's voice sounded weary. "We'll talk later."

I knew something was wrong, but the warm pool slipped up over my scalp, drawing me down into a sweet oblivion I couldn't resist.

Chapter 20

I WOKE UP with the sheet pressed against my nose, the smell of Zoloski in my nostrils, an empty space beside me. Vaguely, I remembered Zoloski rolling me in a wheelchair to his car and driving me home, then tucking me into bed.

I rolled over and stiffened as pain shot through my shoulder. Damn! Another twinge twanged its way to my ear. Not only was life a pain in the neck, it was an Excedrin headache too. Squinting against the morning sunlight, I sat up carefully and slid from bed. Too bad I wasn't Arnold Schwarzenegger; he could take a licking and keep on kicking.

I gingerly touched the bandage along my jawbone. God, the Bride of Frankenstein! The thought of how close I'd come to having my throat slit turned my stomach.

Zoloski's voice drifted from the other end of the house like a pleasant breeze, easing my grumpiness. Judging from his tone, he was on the phone. I tied my robe, slid my feet into a soft pair of slippers—his—and padded toward the smell of French roast.

Zoloski was at the table, soft blues playing on the radio, a pad of paper in front of him, phone plastered to his ear. Case notes were spread all over, files on the floor. I checked the sliding glass door which had been replaced and had several new locks. Big deal. I peeked through the front blinds, squinting past the early morning sun to a car parked across the way. Not Murphy's.

Zoloski hung up and joined me at the window. "What are you doing up?" he asked, his arm slipping around my waist and drawing me close.

"Where's Murphy?"

Zoloski's gaze skidded away. "Dead," he said softly. "The bastard killed him."

I sagged, shocked.

Zoloski wrapped an arm around my shoulders. "I tried to call you. When I didn't get an answer I called Murphy. When he didn't answer I drove like hell."

My mouth felt drier than a wad of paper towels. I should have smashed Mac's head in with the bat. "I'm sorry," I said, feeling inadequate.

"We graduated from the academy together," Zoloski said in the same soft voice, pain laced in every word and every silence between. He gripped my shoulders in his large hands and looked into my eyes. "You really should be in bed. It's barely seven o'clock."

I eyed the lines of fatigue around his eyes. "So should you." I glanced toward the window. "Who's outside?"

"Vallerie and Owens." Zoloski's gaze strayed to the files and piles of papers.

"Leave it, Stephanos." I pulled him down the hall.

We cuddled like spoons while he talked about Murphy. Somewhere amidst words and silence his breathing deepened. I held him close for awhile, loving him with all my thoughts, then got up and made a new pot of coffee.

I was on my second cup when he came in, looking refreshed in a clean shirt and slacks. Our gazes met. "You going to work?"

He poured himself a cup of my magic brew and sat down. "I took a few days off. Murphy's funeral is tomorrow." A significant pause. "Thanks for listening." So much pain lay hidden behind those words.

I felt uneasy. So much promise too. I needed to feel useful. Right now I felt small, tired. My hand kept straying to my neck.

"Looks worse than it is," he said, patting my hand. "You lost more blood from your shoulder. They put forty stitches below your jaw. Eight in your shoulder. Doctor said the redness will fade given time and the scars hardly show."

"Thanks." I lost myself in the sea of his eyes. A part of me reveled in the intimate connection, another part balked, wanted to run like hell.

"You're welcome."

The moment lingered a second more, then Zoloski took a sip of coffee and said, "I talked to Sherry Davidson. She remembered the name Mac. One of the kids in the show had a speech problem.

Mac was really Matt."

Matt? Matthew? Suddenly my headache wasn't so bad. We were making progress.

Zoloski stood up. "Problem is, he has six guys who'll swear he was playing poker when you were attacked. And his arm is fine—no bruises—no nothing. I'm gonna haul him in anyway, but it doesn't look good. I'm also going to have Sherry Davidson look at his picture. Maybe we'll get a break there."

"I thought you were taking a few days off?"

"From the rest of my job, not this case."

"You leaving now?" I took a quick gulp of coffee and scalded my tongue. Yeow!

His expression softened. "I was going to leave before you woke up." He stood up and slipped on his coat, a worn tweed number that looked great on him. "There's two guys on the patio, two out front." He kissed my neck—the good side. "I'll be home for dinner."

This was one time I just couldn't muster the energy to protest. Every muscle in my body twinged or ached. I felt like a damn pincushion.

I walked him to the door and watched as he climbed into the Z. Locking the door, I felt like a kid that had just been thrown in the water and told to swim. I wanted to cling, wanted to hide away, yet knew I needed to take control of my life. I headed back to bed, telling myself Mac would be caught, I would live to see Pat married in June.

But wedding bells didn't pursue me into sleep, Mac did.

THE NEXT MORNING, after a shower and leg shave, I donned a dark turtleneck tunic, which didn't quite hide the neck bandage but came close. The stitches pulled like gum stuck to the bottom of my shoe. My black leggings drew glances from Zoloski and the bodyguards, the coffee brought polite "thank yous."

The newspaper blasted Legislator Whitman about Connie Donovan. Whitman's back was caught by the news camera. He deserved the bad press.

Caldwell's alibi held up. Sherry Davidson had not been able to ID any of the pictures Zoloski had shown her. Were Matthew

Caldwell and Mac the same man?

I'd spent my time calling hospitals and local clinics asking about broken arms, with no results. I questioned whether I'd heard that bone-cracking sound. Replayed the moment a thousand times, hearing the high-pitched scream of pain. That arm *had* to be broken. So who the hell had I hit?

I switched off the TV, angry that Murphy was getting less press than Whitman or Caldwell. Journalistic justice.

Murphy's funeral was at the Church of the Blessed Sacrament, a beautiful old greystone church with lots of stained glass. Zoloski and I stepped down the aisle, searched for a seat, and finally squeezed in near the front.

A lump stuck in my throat at the sight of Murphy's widow and two boys, their straight backs, rigid and unmoving in the front pew. It's not your fault, I told myself, but little comfort came in the face of their grief.

After a traditional offering by the priest, several police officers spoke, all bigwigs dressed in spit-and-polish, class-A uniforms. Zoloski, like the other detectives, had worn a dark suit. He squeezed my hand every time tears appeared at the corners of his eyes. He swiped them away with a handkerchief when he took his turn at the pulpit.

Sorrow clouded his eyes, his mouth a grim line. Emotions swirled around me like heavy incense as he talked about a man I'd barely known.

By the time he finished, I was emotionally strung out. "I'm not up to the cemetery," I whispered.

He nodded, a hint of relief in his eyes. His gaze strayed toward a group of men and women near the back and I knew he needed to talk to his buddies about Murphy. I told him not to rush home, I was going to bed. He flashed a grateful smile and Vallerie drove me home. As I crawled into bed, I wondered if the next funeral would be mine.

THIRTEEN DAYS passed, to the end of May. Matthew Caldwell had dropped out of sight. Connie and Sunny's cases remained open, so did the assault on me. Although Zoloski tried to assure me Mac had most likely gotten out of the country, I knew better. He had tried once—he'd try again.

My outside guards had been pulled, but Vallerie was still around, though I thought not for much longer. Long-term protection wasn't in the city budget.

Alone in the bathroom, I gently touched my jaw, the ridge of stitched skin. The thread had been removed, but the skin still looked red and puffy. Zoloski said my shoulder scar looked sexy—a purely male response—but appreciated.

Over breakfast he stared at my neck. "Looks like a giant hickey." He winked.

"Thanks." I'd rather have one. "Any leads?"

He shrugged. "The trail's cold. The police are keeping tabs on Matthew's condo and Lillian's place—in case we turn up new evidence. She won't even answer the door, has her groceries delivered, turned into a recluse."

Zoloski grabbed his jacket, leaned over and kissed me goodbye. I planned a good aerobic session, then work. I'd been to the office twice during the week—Officer Vallerie in tow—seen a couple of clients and talked briefly to Maria. She looked like a ghost and I'd recommended she talk to a psychologist who dealt with grief issues.

"I am," she assured me, but I saw the lie in her dark eyes. She wanted to sink, maybe felt it fair punishment.

After the workout, I spent the afternoon staring at computer printouts; oh the joys of statistics. The numbers kept running together. I walked around the suite to get my blood pumping again. Maria wasn't around and the place seemed too quiet. Finally, at 5:30 I allowed myself to whistle retreat.

When I got home, Zoloski had left a message: "I'll be home late. Don't wait up. Vallerie's being pulled tomorrow." His tone said he disapproved, but couldn't change it.

I wondered when Mac would surface. Would I stay with Zoloski after the "storm" passed, or move back to my flat? I missed my own space.

When the phone rang I was unprepared for Maria's quivering voice. "Blaize?" A ragged pause. "Are you alone?"

My stomach clenched at the desperation in her voice. "Yes." I thought of Vallerie.

"Is Zoloski there?"

"No."

"Is the line tapped?"

The bad feeling wound its way up my spine. "No." Actually I didn't know.

"*He's* here. He says—" Her words died in a soft gurgle.

My heart lurched, jammed in my throat as I croaked, "Maria!"

"Oh God, Blaize—" her voice was a moan. "Please..."

Her voice faded away. I couldn't swallow, couldn't talk.

Mac's whispery laugh sounded in my ear. Caldwell? Whitman? Then who had the broken arm? "No more rehearsals, Andy. Time to finish the game."

Game?

"You do exactly as I say, your friend lives. Otherwise..."

THROUGH THE CAR window I could see a yellow half-moon glimmer off Folsom Lake. I thought of Folsom Prison, wishing Mac trapped inside, this all a bad dream. As a kid, on such nights, werewolves terrified me until dawn. Right now I was scared spitless, yet knew I had no choice but to do this alone. Mac the Knife— funny how I still thought of him that way—had given explicit instructions: no police, no company. Only me.

I didn't have silver bullets, but I did have a Glock 17 semiautomatic pistol loaded with eighteen .9mm full-metal-jacket hollow-point rounds on the seat beside me. Courtesy of Zoloski. When he got my message he'd be pissed, but that's what he got for not being available in an emergency, and I wasn't about to trust Vallerie or anyone else. I'd told Vallerie I was going to bed, then snuck out through the garage.

In addition to the Z-man's contributions, I'd emptied my purse and stashed the weaponry beneath my black sweatshirt and dark cotton pants. I felt like an armory, my faithful .32 in an ankle holster, tear gas at my waist, binoculars around my neck, and night vision goggles on my head. If the California Highway Patrol stopped me now I'd be in thrown in the clink. That didn't sound half-bad.

As I neared Maria's my hands trembled, sweat making the palms slippery. I felt as tight as catgut stretched over a fine-tuned violin. The cut beneath my jaw twinged, reminding me of my mortality.

Why had Mac picked Maria? Because of me? The newspaper gossip about her and Whitman and Connie? Was Maria even alive? The questions tied my brain in a knot of horrible images. I wished I'd never stepped foot on Whitman's damned boat or seen the gruesome photographs.

I slowed as I approached the hill where Maria lived and cut my lights. Knowing the long walkway to her house would brighten automatically by movement-sensor beams, I parked several houses away, then gathered my thoughts. The breeze off the lake felt cold and ominous, not at all like Memorial Day weekend. More like October—Halloween.

I stifled a shiver. This is where the heroine triumphs, I assured myself as I carefully closed the door and crossed the asphalt. Crouching beneath a massive oak, I checked the Glock, my .32, extra ammunition, the tear gas at the back of my waist, the Swiss knife in my pocket, binoculars around my neck, then pulled down the night vision goggles. Everything appeared a luminescent green. I felt like I'd dropped onto another planet.

Maria's house was downhill two hundred yards, maybe more, with plenty of ivy, ferns, and other vegetation I couldn't identify. The curtains were closed. That could work to my advantage, unless Mac was outside, anticipating my moves.

I crossed the lawn, the smell of new-cut grass heavy in my nostrils along with honeysuckle and camellias. The hem of my pants flopped with dampness as I treaded through the wild tangle of underbrush surrounding the house. A mosquito whined past my ear. I ignored it, focusing my attention on the terrain. It was hilly, the vines and ivy like a wall of thorns. I stepped carefully into a pocket of ivy, hoping I wouldn't crunch a snail, immediately feeling ludicrous—I was about to face my fifteen-year-old nightmare.

I heard something move in the brush to my right and hit the ground, the binoculars thumping against my chest. A cat skittered out of the dense undergrowth and disappeared into the darkness. My heart skipped erratically. I took a second to regroup and checked my watch. Eleven-thirty.

Had Zoloski listened to his voice-mail yet? Was he on his

way?

I got to my feet, knees and hands wet, water seeping into my aerobic shoes. The soles squished as I circled the house perimeter. Three sets of sliding glass doors showed in the expanse of stucco. All locked. I'd brought everything but a glass cutter. That was Mac's specialty. I crept behind the garage to a side-door where I hoped to use my old lock-picking skills. Thank you very much, Ross. My nerves screamed: *take cover* as I inserted the picks and moved, prodded, and pushed. *Snap*.

I turned the knob, suddenly needing to pee again, though I had done it four times before leaving Zoloski's. The Glock in my right hand, I took a deep breath and slid into the black-black darkness. Maria's car filled half the garage, no cover in the other half as I crouched and eyed the door leading into the house.

Go back! He was watching! Paranoid thoughts, I told myself, but that didn't mean they weren't real. I discarded the binoculars, and crept across the concrete to the door. Turning the knob, I slipped inside and quietly shut it behind.

Underfoot lay tile.

Phfft. A match flared from the next room.

I hunkered down and duck-walked across the kitchen. Kneeling, I risked a glance around the doorjamb. A candle flickered on the sideboard, casting shadows. One slid across Mac's face, his ghoulish smile like a Halloween Jack-o-lantern. Mac. Matt. Matthew Caldwell. His eyes burned into mine, straight on: intense, hungry, deadly. Not the eyes of the man Zoloski and I had talked to only a few weeks before. Nothing was masked now. He wore black slacks and a white short-sleeve shirt. I could see dark blotches on his clothes, like shadowy tie-dye. Blood? I should shoot, knew it, but couldn't. Maria first.

He laughed, the low, sinister sound snapping my neurotransmitters into overdrive, my senses into hyper-vigilance. In a hoarse baritone he said, "It has to be you."

My finger tightened on the trigger. "Where's Maria?" The words came out a strangled whisper. "Where is she?" I repeated, this time with more strength.

"You broke the rules, Andy." His voice was frighteningly calm.

I aimed for his leg.

He blew out the candle, blanketing me in darkness. Damn! I jerked the night-vision goggles over my eyes, saw a glimmer of sleeve disappear into the hall. Did he want me to follow? What choice did I have?

"Maria!" No answer. I worked my way through the maze of furniture, goggles on, the Glock out front. How many rooms were in the back of the house? Three? Four? I paused, listening.

I heard what Sunny's neighbor had described as an animal-like whimper, but couldn't tell where the sound came from. Was Maria still alive, or was Mac leading me on? Then I had the horrible notion that Caldwell hadn't come alone—that whoever had the broken arm was here, too.

Every hair on end, every muscle tensed, I made my way down the long, dark hallway, feeling along the wall with my free hand. One door at a time, I dropped to my left knee, the gun gripped in my right hand while I scanned the room, everything cast in green. Sweat poured down my back, underarms and chest as my heart pounded in my ears. Two doors to go. One right, one left.

I swallowed, paused in the doorway of bedroom number three and listened. Something brushed my ankle. I jumped and almost shot one of Maria's cats as it bolted down the hall. Where was the other one?

The door to the left was ajar: the bathroom. I couldn't see in, but a picture of the bathroom mirror on the boat briefly filled my mind. The final doorway, on my side would be the master bedroom. Right or left?

Had Mac led me this way to trap me or to show me more of his handiwork before he moved in for the kill?

I stood frozen, every muscle motionless until my legs screamed for activity. Still, I remained inert, listening to the sounds of the night. The wind rustled, distant sirens howled like banshees. Had Zoloski found my note? I prayed he was on his way.

I imagined Mac watching from the master bedroom as I moved into the bathroom, found whatever he had left for me. I adjusted the glasses, stepped toward the bedroom, slid my back silently along the wall and rolled inside. I whirled at the sharp intake of breath behind me, saw the masked face and casted arm, the flash of a gun barrel. I squeezed the Glock's trigger.

The figure slammed into the wall and dropped like a marionette cut from its strings. I ripped off the glasses. I shot a cautious glance toward the doorway, then stepped close, reached out and yanked off the ski mask. Lillian!

Jesus. Had she attacked me before to give her brother an alibi? Or were they a murdering team? I pressed my fingers to her neck, couldn't find a pulse, felt shaky as I straightened. Jesus, I thought again.

I heard the bathroom door click shut. Was he inside?

I thought of Maria, knew I needed to take Matthew alive—to find out what he'd done with her. By millimeters I turned the knob and pushed the door open. Back pressed against the wall, I put the goggles back on, adjusted the focus and slid inside. My shoulders touched a towel rack and I moved forward a half step. Beyond the sink and toilet, the glass shower doors were partly open. Goosebumps ran up my arms as I saw the long smear of blood across the tile and into the tub. The outline of a man crouched beyond the shower door. My stomach tightened into a knot as I pulled the goggles off and felt for the light switch.

As I flipped it up, a mass of bloody fur hit me in the face. I fired wildly, screaming, wiping it off. My foot slipped and I grabbed for the sink, wrenching my shoulder as I swung off balance to my knees. My knuckles hit the porcelain. The Glock skidded across the floor. I dove for it.

Mac snatched it first.

I got up slowly, half-expecting a gunshot blast, to feel the impact launch me backwards.

Grinning, madness in his eyes, he pressed the barrel against my sternum, the grip in his right hand. A bloody switchblade glistened from the other. A lefty, I thought. My attacker at Zoloski's had been right-handed. Lillian was right-handed, and an actress. I felt stupid.

Mac's shirt and pants were blotched with blood. Behind him, dark crimson smears glimmered over the tub. Death shrieked in the silence.

"Time to pay," Mac said with a smirk.

Without a distraction I'd never reach the gas canister hidden beneath my sweatshirt. Even if I did, I wouldn't have time to use it.

"What about Lillian?"

"What about her?" A short quiet pause. "Hands up—up!"

I complied, remembering the feel of Lillian's knife as it sliced open my jaw, punctured my shoulder. Mac would be stronger. Don't panic. He wouldn't kill me yet. He'd tease first. I tried to imagine Zoloski's voice guiding me along—getting me out of this. Shit, I was the shrink, not the Z-man.

"Back up, bitch. Into the hall. Move!"

I did.

"Keep going. Faster!" He switched on the hall light.

A sharp prod to my ribs drove me back toward the living room. I stumbled, my hands momentarily dropping.

His knife flashed, a glint of silver that came away wet. Pain burned across my forearm. Slice and dice. Pictures of Sunny's corpse shot through my mind. Keep your head, Blaize. But even my inner voice trembled.

I waited. What next? Would he tie me up? I smelled flowers and gun oil. Wait for a distraction, I thought. Or create one. Do something! my inner voice snapped. I gauged the distance to the .32 at my ankle.

"Lillian?" Mac called.

I sank slowly to the edge of the couch.

He scowled, then yelled like an irritated master of a dog, "Lillian!"

When she didn't come, his blue eyes narrowed on me. "You shot her?"

Unsure how he'd take the news, I asked, "Why was she helping you?" My voice was surprisingly calm.

He grinned, his silver-gray hair slightly mussed, perfect for a shampoo commercial. "I helped her get rid of her husband, and kept proof. She gripes about helping me, but she likes it, too. Except when you busted her arm." The grin vanished. "Lillian!"

"Why Connie?"

"Bad timing." Said so simply. "Whitman let me use his boat. It was quiet on the water. I liked that. The kid showed up looking for Dad."

I felt like a blob of jelly, my synapses working overtime, rolling out the scene between Connie and Caldwell, and making me queasy.

I had a knack for talking my way out of bad situations. But how could I reason with insanity? What would set him off? I felt like dry cheerios lined my throat. "What happened on the boat?" I managed, dropping my arms slowly to my knees, waiting for the knife to move. Blood ran down my fingers and dripped on the carpet.

"I heard the gunshot." He cocked his head. "Lillian's not answering." His voice dropped to the gravelly whisper I remembered, "Must mean it's just me and you. We can talk all night. It won't change the outcome." His gaze flickered away, then came back. "The kid tried to talk too."

Death's ghostly scythe cut down my spine, like a blade of ice, spreading gelid tentacles.

Another grin. "I was pretty juiced."

Like now? The dull taste of fear turned me rigid as he described in detail what he'd done to Maria's daughter. I wanted to yell "stop," but had to keep him talking.

"Lillian liked my idea of leaving a mark."

"The rose?" Knifework by a maniac.

A smile blazed. "I knew you were smart."

How much time did I have? "Was Whitman involved?"

"That chicken shit! He didn't want to know what I was up to. Only let me use the boat because I had something on him, too." Mac's eyes glittered with condescension.

He slapped the flat of the blade against his thigh.

I swallowed. "Why bring me out here?"

An eerie smile. "A warning to Whitman to keep his mouth shut—unless he wants his wife and kids to end up the same way."

My breath felt trapped in my lungs. Where was Maria? I was afraid to ask, afraid the rage in his face would explode into action. But I had to try. "Where's Maria?" I used my counselor's voice: reasonable, calm.

The nasty smile returned. He licked his lips. "She's around."

No! My heart skidded to a stop.

His gaze veered for a second toward the entry hall.

I slid my hand toward my calf, my fingers inching toward the ankle holster.

The tiny movement brought his gaze back, alert, ready, waiting.

I froze, searching for more distracting words. What are you feeling right now? popped into my head along with additional psycho-babble.

I feel like blowing your head off, he'd say and that would be it.

Despite lock-jaw, I forced out, "Is Maria dead?"

Mac didn't answer. Some of the tension left his face. His blue eyes fixed on me with an unpleasant gleam.

Spinning a fantasy with me as the star? Or remembering what he'd done with Maria? I wanted to panic, scream, shout, fall apart. I stared at the Glock's black hole, prayed for a chance to reach my gun. "Did Lillian like to watch?"

A glimmer of impatience. "Sometimes." He scratched his cheek with his knife, the Glock still leveled at my chest. "The bitch had a mean streak."

I was amazed at how calmly we were talking. The night had a surreal quality, like the yellow half-moon and cool breeze that whispered Sleepy Hollow, not Folsom Lake. But the ache in my forearm was real enough. I floundered for conversation. "You're the one who rear-ended my car."

His expression glowed with malevolent pride.

"Did you see Sunny's picture in the paper. Is that why you sent her the notes?"

He nodded. "She played the game real well. Led me to you, too."

I was batting a thousand. "Did your sister tell you I called?"

A flicker I couldn't read. His knuckles grew white around the knife. "Yeah. Told me to stop the game. Wait until things cooled down. Stupid cunt!" The flat side of the knife brushed across his pants in a slow back-and-forth rhythm.

Was the Q and A over?

The knife rhythm increased to 3/4 time against his thigh. *Brush, brush, brush.*

My pulse jumped into high speed.

He grinned. Savoring my fear?

I slid my right hand lower.

"Hands on your knees!" he snapped.

The knife whipped past my arm as I slid forward off the couch, onto my left arm and left leg, kicking with my right. I missed his knee and caught his shin with my tennis shoe. The knife edge shaved my arm, felt like road burn. I scrambled to my feet.

The Glock fired, shattered my eardrums, hit me in the chest and knocked me onto my back. I wheezed, my eyes tearing. Pain radiating outward from the center of my torso. Mac dropped to his knees beside me and yanked on my shirt. His gaze fixed on the burnt spot on my bulletproof vest. Then his eyes narrowed in rage.

I rolled away, pulled the gas canister from my waistband and hit the button. The spray hit his face. He screamed and slashed blindly. I scrambled backwards like a three-legged crab. He crawled after me, tears streaming down his cheeks, his hair plastered to his forehead.

I lifted the canister again but his knife gouged my wrist. The canister dropped to the floor and rolled under the recliner. I kicked him in the stomach and resumed the three-legged crawl. The blow barely slowed him.

I slid sideways between the recliner and couch, brought my leg up and grabbed the .32.

He caught my ankle and slashed. Screaming, I yanked free before the blade struck. A horrible grin stretched across his face, one eye now a pale blue marble, the other contact-lens dark.

I shoved the safety off.

He lunged.

I squeezed the trigger.

The knife fell. A bloody hole appeared in the palm of his hand, blossomed like a starburst. He stared, disbelief written across face. "It has to be you," he whispered and lunged at me again.

I forgot why I needed him alive, fired again, hitting him in the chest.

He lurched back, his mouth agape, amazement in his eyes. The hunter had been shot. I kept squeezing the trigger. The last round caught him square in the pale marble. Bull's eye.

Chapter 21

I WHEEZED like an emphysema victim as I staggered to the phone. No buzz. No life-line. Dead.

I stared at Mac's inert body, a macabre contrast to the tasteful Native American decor, and stumbled down the hall, my nerves feeling frappéd. In the bathroom, I grabbed a towel and pressed it against my arm. Lightheaded, I felt as though I'd stayed up all night and overdosed on caffeine.

Zoloski, where are you? Could I make it to the neighbors? In my condition they might not let me in. And what about Maria?

Indecisive as a cat on a fence between two dogs, I leaned against the sink for support, my gaze fixed on the bloody tub. I half expected Anthony Perkins to jump at me as I moved toward the spattered beige enamel. I wasn't sure if the blood smelled sweet or the potpourri basket over the toilet.

I sucked air, held my breath, leaned forward and looked inside. Matted fur. Entrails. Whiskers. One of Maria's cats! Oh God. Now I knew what had hit me in the face. Vomit spewed up my throat like hot acid, adding to the mess. Wiping my mouth on a soft pink towel, I wheeled from the bathroom.

"Maria!" I called reeling down the hall. "Maria!" I felt disoriented, knew I should sit down, but had to find her.

Ping. A strange sound drew me toward the kitchen. *Ping*. It repeated like a metal spoon on a tin can. Mac?

No, no, he was dead.

Moments felt like hours. My arms and legs were numb. Drowsy, I forced myself to move, a rag doll ready to drop. A quick glance at Mac's inert body reassured me. All my hyper-vigilance sank into a quagmire of fatigue. I felt like I was running through syrup, managing only small steps with great effort. Beyond the formal dining room, the kitchen gleamed.

Ping. Louder. From the pantry? I remembered it: a large one, well-stocked the night I attended a party here. I remembered thinking I could live in that much space.

The doorknob was smudged with blood. I thought about destroying evidence, thought about Maria and turned the knob. Locked. Where was the key?

Fighting mental sluggishness as well as physical, I scanned the kitchen for a key hook. Blackness fringed the edges of my vision. I rifled through drawers haphazardly. I had this vision of lying down. Sweat stung my eyes. The floor looked comfortable. I steadied myself with a hand on the counter.

I could shoot the lock. But what if I shot Maria—if she was inside? Odds were, she was dead. Odds were, she was inside. Odds were, I would faint any minute.

I staggered into the living room, found the Glock and reeled back to the kitchen. The only nasty thing about having a really nasty gun is having someone take it away. Even with the vest, the bullet's impact had hurt. Each breath still did. I stood there, my brain felt fuzzy. *Wham*!

My breath caught. I struggled to make sense of the explosive noise. For a moment I thought I'd fired the gun or Mac had rigged a bomb, blown me to smithereens. Jelly Beans, my mind rhymed as I realized I was still alive. A hand came down on my shoulder. I shrieked, bringing up the Glock.

"It's okay." Zoloski.

I could hear myself sounding like an overgrown mouse as he took the gun. He looked me over and yelled for help.

"She's inside. Door's locked," I croaked into his shoulder.

"We'll handle it," Zoloski said, tightening his hold on me. Other cops pushed past. A few seconds later I heard wood splintering. I turned to see the door being pulled off. Light from the kitchen flowed into the shadows like an ocean tide, revealing the toe of a woman's shoe. Paramedics moved in. Put Maria on a stretcher. Then me. I murmured, "I'm okay."

Zoloski swore, "Damn it, Blaize, you are not *okay*!"

I tried to talk as they carried me from the house, but my tongue felt thick, my lips paper dry.

Zoloski shushed me with a gentle touch to my lips. "We'll talk later." His furrowed brow and the sharp glint in his eyes said it wouldn't be all hugs and kisses.

I'd pissed him off. Again. Out in another Blaize of Glory? Undone by my independence? I closed my eyes. Life was joy.

MY SECOND hospital stint was longer than the first. After a transfusion and lots of stitches—across my bicep, down my forearm, across my wrist, and down my calf, I awoke to daylight and pain. Jeez, Louise, only half the cuts had registered during the fight. I felt a real kinship to Frankenstein.

Zoloski looked like he'd spent the night in the chair beside my bed, slumped, and rumpled, shaggy-haired, a slight snore sounding on occasion.

I tried to sit up and groaned.

In a second he was on his feet. "You're awake."

"Unfortunately," I mumbled.

He kissed my forehead, his lips warm, the smell of him comforting, reassuring.

"Maria?"

Zoloski smiled. "She's going to be okay."

"Lillian?"

"Dead."

I figured I should feel something about having killed her and her brother, but nothing came. I gingerly worked at pulling the covers back. Freed one leg before Zoloski piped up.

"You're staying here." He sat on the edge of the bed and took my hand. "No arguments."

And then what? Back to my upstairs flat? Loneliness crept into my soul. "I hate hospitals."

A mischievous glimmer shone in his eyes. "I'll take you home in the morning."

"Home?"

He brought my hand to his lips, kissed it topside.

Frisky hormones erupted. I scooted over on the bed, gritting my teeth as I twinged in all the wrong places, determined to have company while I put in my time in antiseptic heaven.

He stretched out beside me and draped his arm gently across my waist, his breath mingling with mine. I lifted my leg and put it over his. He rubbed my bare calf. "Nice."

"My best asset at the moment," I murmured, thinking about sex and sutures.

"Oh, yeah?" Zoloski rasped. He ran a finger along the curve of my jaw and the ridge of my scar. "I think that's your best asset. Gives you character."

I shifted my arm. "I could do with a little less character right now."

He gave me a long look. I read exotic carnal thoughts in his green, green eyes. Warmth rushed down to my toes. Did hospital doors have locks?

Then I felt a tremor of misgiving. I'd questioned his statement about going home. He'd side-stepped.

Did I want the answer now or later? "Do you want me to move out?"

He kissed me, the moment tender, poignant, full of wanting, waiting, loving. Then he sat up half-way, leaning on one arm. "I want you to stay." The briefest glimmer of anxiety showed in his gaze.

The Z-man strikes again. In some untapped part of my mind I knew I wanted to stay indefinitely. "How about a six-month trial?" I asked as I slid my hand up his chest to his shoulder.

He traced a line around my lips. "I'd like that, Sweetheart."

"I don't do maid service," I murmured as he kissed my neck. "Or cook."

"So I noticed." His mouth slid to my ear. "I don't wash panties and bras."

Neither did I if I could help it. "I like a varied routine."

He chuckled. "I live one." He got up, jammed the chair under the doorknob, kicked off his boots and jeans, then rejoined me on the bed. He slid his arms around me. "No more bedtime with Letterman or Leno." His lips grazed mine. "I want you all to myself."

"Mmm." I pulled the covers up and he gave me lots of tender loving. And care.

~ The End ~

Louise Crawford

Award winning author Louise Crawford lives in Sacramento with her husband and daughter. She is a member of RWA, MWA, and holds an MA in Psychology.

Louise is published in contemporary romance, short science fiction, fantasy romance, and mystery genres. Louise is happy to hear from readers by email: lcrawford@pobox.com

Don't miss the second Blaize/Zoloski mystery, *Hat Trick*, also available from Hard Shell Word Factory

Watch for the third mystery:

12 Jagged Steps

coming in October 2001!